THE TRAIN

GOD CARES FOR HIS CHILDREN

JOYCE CRAWFORD

Publisher's Name: Joyce Crawford

ISBN: 978-1-968442-45-3

"By day, the Lord went ahead of them in a pillar of cloud to guide them on their way and by night in a pillar of fire to give them light, so that they could travel by day or night."

Exodus 13:21-22

"God, who at sundry times and in divers manners spake in time past unto the fathers by the prophets …"

Hebrews 1:1

"I will say of the Lord, He is my refuge and my fortress; My God, in Him I will trust."

Psalm 91:2

All scripture quoted are King James Version

Victor Burton, U.S. Army Medical Corp:

My Hero and Inspiration

"You have always heard it said that you never hear the one that hits you. Well, I didn't," said Victor Burton.

In 1941, the United States Armed Forces drafted Victor Burton into the Army when he was twenty-seven years old. One of the first things the draftees learned in an abbreviated boot camp was to duck when anyone detected incoming mail—military slang for enemy artillery.

After training, Burton earned his Staff Sargent stripes, and his unit shipped out to the European theater in August of 1944. Once in Europe, the GIs marched in two columns through France toward Belgium. They reached the front lines in early November. Burton pulled up the rear as Allied and enemy artillery flew above their heads.

As the troops marched, five men fell, two behind him and three ahead of him. Following orders, the uninjured troops had to keep moving forward, so Burton went to the rear of the line to help the two injured men. He never made it to the first one. While trying to reach the fallen men, Burton failed to detect the incoming mail.

Around four o'clock in the afternoon, flying shrapnel covered his body, wounding his right leg severely. Shortly after being hit, Sgt. Burton realized that he couldn't see, a sign of shock caused from the wound. Burton spoke of this as his most vivid memory, not only because of his wounds but because he believes it was the hand of God that allowed him to survive.

As this young soldier called out for help, a young gentleman whom he had never seen before and would never again see came to his aid. After bandaging Burton's leg and helping him inject himself with morphine for pain, the man said he had more soldiers to care for. Morphine has a sedative effect on most people, and Burton soon began to worry that if he fell asleep an ambulance crew would think he was dead and pass him, leaving him to freeze to death.

Burton furiously fought sleep there on the ground. He didn't know how long it would take or if he would be able to stay awake until help arrived. However, just ten minutes later, an ambulance arrived in front of a very grateful man. Miraculously, the ambulance had only one slot remaining before it would have to turn back. Aa a strong believer, Mr. Burton says it was God's hand that provided a perfect stranger to come to his aid, an ambulance only ten minutes away, and exactly one spot left before turning back. Call it God or call it fate, but to both believers and nonbelievers alike, it is a truly amazing story.

By nine o' clock p.m., the ambulance carrying Burton was well on its way to the town of Nancy, in eastern France. There, a hospital had been set up in an old hotel, with the basement serving as an operating room. At about three-thirty o' clock a.m., the hospital staff checked Burton in and gave him a bed, which was just a canvas cot, not a real bed at all. However, Burton made good use of that cot and said the next thing he knew it was the 13th of November. He awoke with a glucose bag on one arm and a pint of blood on the other. He had been unconscious for nearly five days.

As Burton recalled, a caring doctor explained that his leg was badly wounded, and the Army would need to transport him back to England for surgery. Burton's only request was that he get back to the US as soon as possible. From France, a transport plane took him to England, and once in Liverpool, the medics loaded injured soldiers aboard a ship on its return voyage to America. The ship set sail on Christmas morning of 1944. When word came that the ship was entering New York harbor, Burton was determined to see the Statue of Liberty, so he shimmied himself up the ladder to the deck. He shared that The Lady was a beautiful sight. What a wonderful Christmas gift!

Burton stayed in a hospital in New York where doctors performed multiple surgeries to stitch up the remaining portion of his leg and helped him recover. He now had to face the fact that he would have to live the rest of his life with a disability. However, unlike so many others, at least he had a life. This young man remained strong and determined, making sure his injury never got him down.

This brave medic, Victor Burton, was my Daddy.

Growing up, I witnessed how Daddy suffered from phantom pain, but I also witnessed how he always had time to visit people in the hospital who faced surgeries such as his. He was a good provider for our family, a wise investor, and a giant prayer warrior who talked with God.

Daddy returned to Florida and married Vivien, the lady he loved, the woman who waited, cried, and prayed for him.

When asked what the most important lesson was that he learned from his war experience, he thought long and hard. His answer? "Gratitude." That's how he lived his life.

After Daddy's discharge, his brother, my Uncle John, served in World War II. He survived the Battle of Hürtgen Forest but suffered from severe frost bite and begged the doctors not to take his feet. In another miracle, the medical staff was able to save his feet with extensive treatment and care. Remarkably, Uncle John retired after a long career in the Army.

Daddy's final words of advice were, "Don't ever forget your heritage."

TABLE OF CONTENTS

PREFACE

The angels—Faith, Hope, Serenity, Courage, and little Curiosity—played in the dewy morning of the Garden. Flashes of colored lights, energy, and giggles helped rejuvenate their powers as they played among soft grasses, bubbling ponds, and sweet flower bouquets. Soon the angels would tire of playing games and rest.

The angel, Peace, sat beside the diamond-bedecked pond. Her cushion was a generous growth of cool, moist sphagnum moss, while her footstool was ginger lilies adorned in pastel colors. However, Peace was not entirely at rest, for inside her grew a desire. This desire was so strong that she had to share it with her sister angels.

Peace called to her friend. *"Faith, will you come sit with me?"*

Of course, Faith was more than happy to accompany Peace, but she was not alone. Soon, the other angels gathered on the bank of the pond to take in the beauty of The Creator's Garden.

"Is something on your mind, Peace, dear?" asked Faith.

"I was just thinking," began Peace, *"we have been resting quite a while now."*

"Are you tired of resting?" asked Serenity. *"I do so enjoy our quiet time."*

"Yes, I enjoy our quiet time, too, but I have this funny feeling inside, right here," Peace said, pointing to her heart. *"Will you all sit with me and see if you feel it, too?"*

"Let's all sit with Peace and see if we can feel what she is feeling," suggested Faith.

So, as a good friend would do, Faith sat beside Peace. Serenity and Hope sat on rocks and dangled their tiny feet in the cool water. Curiosity stretched out on a bed of cool moss. A breeze blew through the Garden, rustling the leaves on the trees. Willowy branches of leaves dressed in shades of green bent over the pond and played their thanksgiving music to The Creator. Goldfish in assorted colors of yellows, golds, or white with dark patches chased each other through the flowing watergrass. Purple dragonflies with their iridescent wings flew and hovered above the sparkling water, hoping to catch a glimpse of their reflected beauty.

Indeed, it did not take long before the angels shared the same feeling as Peace. *"We need to speak to Wisdom,"* advised Hope, and in a flash, they darted off to speak with the senior angel.

As the angels approached Wisdom in the place of the Elders, the experienced angel looked up in greeting.

"You went to Sir once before, didn't you?" asked Wisdom. *"What did he say to your proposal?"*

"He laughed," sighed Curiosity.

"Not exactly," replied Hope. *"It was more like a kind chuckle. He did offer us an alternative, and we were able to help Him."*

"Well," continued Wisdom, *"I suggest you go back to God and tell Him what's on your heart. See what He offers this time."*

With renewed excitement, the angels left Wisdom at the place of the elders and went to speak with God.

"Courage!" shrieked Hope. *"Where is Courage?"*

"Don't fret, Hope," replied Serenity. *"Courage and Curiosity have already gone ahead. Courage said they would meet us in the Garden."*

When the angels arrived back at the Garden, they found Courage and Curiosity waiting.

"Do you know what you are going to tell Him, Peace?" asked Faith.

"Not exactly," murmured Peace. *"However, He always seems to know even before I ask."*

Serenity and Hope nodded their angel heads in agreement.

"Shhh," whispered Faith. *"He's coming."*

As was His custom, The Creator walked through His Garden, visiting with His creations. Flowers and insects smiled up at their gentle Master, and birds flew down to His shoulders to nestle His cheek through His beard.

"Sir?"

"Yes? Who needs Me?" the kind and omniscient Creator called.

"It's me, Sir. It's Peace," the angel whispered.

"Well, hello, My dear. Where are your friends?" asked God the Father.

"Here we are," Courage squealed as she flew from her hiding place. She stopped just in time before bumping into Peace, causing a rupture of giggles.

"Ah. I see." God greeted the other angels. *"Now, what's on your pretty minds today?"*

"Sir," Peace began, *"we have this funny feeling in here."* The other angels nodded in agreement and pointed to their hearts. *"We don't know what it is, and we are hoping You could explain."*

"Very well," said God the Father softly as He took a seat on a stone. *"You angels are very intuitive, and I think you are sensing that someone needs help. Am I right?"* asked God.

The angels were wide-eyed in amazement that God always knew how they were feeling.

"What should we do?" asked Serenity.

Curiosity and Courage tensed in anticipation, waiting to hear what God would ask of them.

"Will you go to the earth again? Watch and listen. You will soon hear a cry for help. It could very well be a silent cry, but a cry, nonetheless."

The angels shook their heads in enthusiasm, for they enjoyed going to the earth. Curiosity knew it meant children with whom to play. Serenity remembered all the animals and looked forward to seeing them again.

As the angels fluttered in the air, God the Father stopped them and said, *"Remember, My dears, you must not interfere but protect children and the aging. Then report your findings back to Me."*

Although God did not need reports from the angels, He enjoyed their excitement of adventure and being helpful.

Chapter 1

The Lord is my Shepherd ... Psalm 23

August 29 turned out to be one of the hottest days in New York City in 1945. On a typical day, the capacity of Grand Central Station was 15,000 souls. On this day, however, Grand Central Station's sides appeared to bulge when the human capacity doubled. Yet no one complained, for the extra bodies were American troops coming home from World War II.

The thermometer mounted on the wall of the train station registered ninety degrees, and telltale sweat stained military blouses of Army brown and Air Force blue. There were many American GIs coming home severely wounded in both mind and body, and doctors and nurses had no time to wipe sweat from their eyes as they tended these wounded. And they really didn't care. The war was over! The boys were home, and patriotic songs such as, "Hurray For the Red, White, and Blue," still rang in their ears.

As fast as a train engineer could engage his packed locomotive and coax her out of the terminal, another engineer pulled his empty machine into a waiting pattern. Each train pulled a firebox loaded with coal, two restaurant cars, no fewer than thirty-six coaches, each accommodating at least thirty-six GIs, baggage cars, and a few Pullman cars for officers. America required massive rail power and personnel to bring her troops home, but that was a small price to pay for freedom for which the soldiers sacrificed so much.

Amid the hissing locomotives, pushing bodies, and baggage trucks, four tiny angels darted through the crowds, trying to keep their minds centered. Hope, Courage, Serenity, and Curiosity flitted among the masses as if evaluating the expanse of humanity.

Near exhaustion, Serenity and Curiosity escaped the throngs of pressing bodies inside the terminal building for a shady place outside to rest.

"Hope! Courage! Over here," Serenity called to her friends.

Grateful for the invitation, Hope and Courage flew over the commotion to join Serenity and Curiosity nestled among the leaves of a small tree.

"Have you ever seen so many people?" exhaled Courage.

"How are we to find someone more needy than the next in this crowd?" asked Hope.

"Let's just let God lead us. He always knows what we should do," replied Serenity as she snuggled back on her bed of leaves.

The angels rested in the cool tree until Curiosity abruptly announced, *"We need to go!"*

"Go where?" asked Courage.

"I don't know. We just need to go," Curiosity replied.

"All aboard!" The conductor sang out. After completing a 24-hour circuit, the weary conductor waved his signal lantern a little slower, and he had to force his voice from his now raspy throat. Still, he found himself caught up in the celebration of GIs going home, for he, too, had two sons coming home.

"There!" Curiosity stated with certainty, pointing to a train. *"We have to go there."*

So, the four angels from the Garden flew off in a blur of gemstone colors and silk organza to board the troop train bound for Kentucky by way of Cincinnati. Their mission, to search out those men and women who needed God's help the most. Apparently, that would not be an easy task since everyone here was in need one way or another.

Thousands of American GIs searched and jostled as they boarded the train. The contagious excitement spread among the GIs when each one realized he was going home.

Hank, the fireman, stoked countless shovelfuls of coal into the engine's greedy firebox. With each feeding, showers of red and orange hot embers blasted through the heavy cast iron door. These red-hot embers swirled and glowed through the night air as they blazed a path over the length of the train. The frigid wind cooled the cinders slightly. Still, when hot ashes blew into an open window, the sting gave an unsuspecting GI a jolt. However, truth-be-told, the warm embers were a welcome relief for the GIs just returning from winter in Germany.

I am one of the last to board the troop train in New York City. My name is Lieutenant Sam Burkett, serial number 14-593-682, 82nd Airborne Division, U.S. Army.

We GIs returning from WWII had no idea what lay ahead of us. My parents died when I was overseas, and I am coming home a disfigured shell of who I used to be.

However, my story is not all gloom and doom, for the Lord chose a unique way to speak to me and direct my path. Through a train's whistle, He encouraged me, reminded me of His love and presence, and even warned me of danger. Most important of all, He sent me a special friend. This is our story of heartache, faith, friendship, and love.

There was standing room only on the train. I stowed my duffle in an overhead compartment, then picked my way through the crowd of exhausted GIs, many lying in fetal positions on the crowded compartment floor. But I stood, fighting sleep, willing my red sleep-deprived eyes not to close. I stood and rocked back and forth as the steam locomotive *clickity-clacked* over iron rails.

I must have resembled the walking-dead I once saw at the

moving pictures. In a self-imposed sleepless vigil, I was afraid to sleep, for sleep meant dreams, and dreams meant another tour through hell.

The smallest catalyst would set off unrelenting nightmares. First, it was a headache. It felt like a jackhammer, pounding, and drilling into my brain. Then flashing lights behind my eyelids intensified the pain. Each time those lights flashed, my muscles tightened, and I winced.

When we first embarked for the European Theater, we were young and eager, ready to save the world and our beloved America. We were of one mind and our patriotic blood ran hot and in unity.

Upon arriving in England, the 82nd Airborne Division trained at the Berkshire before our first real combat in Normandy on D-Day. After our initial jump, life for me and my fellow paratroopers was a series of battles behind enemy lines, digging into frozen ground and sleeping in muddy foxholes with the smell of fear, blood, body parts, and burning flesh as constant companions.

Across the enemy line, German cannons fired 1,500 rounds of ammunition per minute. At that rate, red flames and tongues of white fire never stopped. Shells exploded upon impact, blasting craters into the ground and sending clouds of dirt and deadly shards of hot metal into the air, obliterating soldiers' bodies, and often soldiers' minds.

Panzer tanks pounded the Allies with 75-millimeter shells in their "lightning war." Airbursts exploded above the soldiers, showering Allied forces with deadly shrapnel.

Waiting for orders from command, I could only watch dead-eyed, as scared GIs from other units, armed with only rifles, screamed as they charged the German lines. Rifles blazed. Enemy shells exploded. Allied helmets blew into the air. One moment GIs were there, running, screaming, charging. The next moment, they were gone. Only a shower of dirt and blood and charred flesh strewn over the land and hedges remained. Everywhere I look lay devastation and misery brought on by German cannons. However, as leader of my unit, I had to suck it up and lead my frightened troops into the fray and, more than likely, death.

These nightmares seemed to continue for hours, playing and replaying in my mind. When at last they ended, I was quaking, terrified, and sweaty. REM sleep followed this night terror. However, this level of sleep was no less cruel, no less relentless than the flashing lights. Dreams of battles did not come in succession but switched from day to night and back again, from ground attacks to paratrooper jumps. In quick succession, these dreams magnified my fear and confusion.

In deep, fitful sleep, I relived every campaign of the 82nd Airborne Division, remembering how when we jumped, fear gripped my gut when the red light in the fuselage turned green, and someone yelled, "Go! Go! Go!"

As I jumped into the thick black night, thousands of exploding bombs in the air and on the ground looked no bigger than a match light.

Equally wicked were Holland, Belgium, and Germany. But it was the Battle of Hürtgen Forest in Germany, followed closely by another campaign known as the Battle of the Bulge, that gave me the most potent taste of hell.

When the 82nd dug into the Hürtgen Forest, we were ill-prepared for the freezing weather and snowdrifts piled thigh-high. We GIs had no coats, no change of socks, no blankets. Our government-issue boots, now worn through, exposed feet and toes to burning frostbite. However, we did have chocolate.

After a battle, medics put their lives in further danger to evacuate the injured to the medical field hospitals, where the medical staff fought their own battles, trying to save lives. However, some GIs endured yet another dehumanizing torture. Compassionate surgeons amputated limbs mangled by artillery. The weary surgeons also amputated countless feet, toes, or other exposed body parts blackened from frostbite.

Only because I refused the pain-killing morphine could I argue and plead with the surgeons not to take both my feet.

Because I was more concerned about losing my feet, I lost track of the burning pain in my fingers, ears, and even places on my face. Though the pain from my frostbitten feet was excruciating, I did not want my body parts amputated and disfigured.

"Doc, what will I do without my feet? How can I work!? How can I have a family!? What am I to do!?"

"I'm sorry, soldier," replied the war-wearied doctor just before he placed the ether over my burning mouth and nose. "I will do the best I can for you. We will just have to trust God."

The last thing I saw was a white lab coat blackened by dirt and stained red with blood. As it turned out, I lost only one foot—my left foot—and three toes on my right foot. A seemingly small thing, but as I later found out, losing a foot and three toes were life-impacting. However, that was not the last of my sacrifices; I also lost parts of my ears and nose, and enough of my face to create a gruesome countenance.

Upon waking from anesthesia, I found my right hand and entire head bandaged. My whole body burned and trembled with excruciating pain. The stained bandages, the result of oozing bloody fluid, needed constant attention. Strong medications and a mild form of blood poisoning caused my body to wrench in fits of vomiting, but tired army nurses and orderlies faithfully bathed me and changed my linen. For six days, I went in and out of consciousness. That was a blessed relief from some of my pain and gave my body time to heal itself.

When at last the blood poisoning, pain, and fever abated, I received yet another shock. The morning the doctors removed my bandages, a nurse handed me a mirror. After several attempts, I finally managed to hold that mirror between my thumb and the stumps of my amputated fingers. I recoiled in horror when the doctor removed the head bandage.

"How much more, Doc? How much more am I expected to give?" Seeing my reflection in a mirror, I winced and cried.

In the frozen Hürtgen Forest, when all my buddies and I were freezing, I never imagined frostbite would ravage a body like this. How could I not have known? Simple, I guess. We Allied soldiers did not have time to think about it. We just fired and ducked, trying to evade the wicked enemy artillery.

When I saw my reflection in the mirror, shock overwhelmed my mind. The doctors had removed most of my ears, several large spots on my face, and a good portion of my nose. My face and ears looked like a victim of third degree burns whose skin burned away.

Deep depression followed.

When I returned to the states, the Veteran's Affairs and Hospital in New York provided mental counseling, therapy, compassion, orthopedic equipment, and training.

To be sure, I put in the time relearning to balance and walk. The orthopedic foot and custom-made shoe required several fittings, and with each fitting, I fought to conquer my fear, pain, and mobility. I spent months at the military hospital to strengthen my muscles. Eventually, I was able to lift myself from a seated position with just one hand and the stump. With just that effort, my muscles quaked, and sweat exploded over my face. The stench of medicine-laced sweat ran down my back and drenched my shirt and pajama bottoms.

After a few weeks of bodybuilding, games began, and I excelled in a rope climbing event and won accolades from buddies and doctors alike. This exercise was strenuous, but the exertion and accomplishment were euphoric. The event began with six GIs seated on the gymnasium floor. We extended our legs—or parts of them. When an orderly blew his whistle, the gym erupted with cheers and whistles while we injured GIs climbed the thick ropes attached to the ceiling beam. The winner was the first to lift his entire weight, legs or parts of legs still extended, climb the rope, and touch the rafter before descending to the original position.

Light-hearted laughter filled the gym and our days. Yet, nothing could fill the emptiness in my heart. However, there was one medicine the military surgeons repeatedly prescribed. "Trust in the Lord, Sam."

When I was growing up, my mother and father instructed me in faith and persistence. I remembered them saying: "Trust in the Lord, Sam." "Did you pray about it, Sam?" "You'll just have to wait on the Lord, Sam."

Mom always taught me that trust and prayer were gifts from the Lord. Was suffering a gift? What kind of cruel joke was that? Never before was I forced to use my gift of strength and determination as I did now.

Eighteen hours after leaving New York, the train lurched, and the massive iron wheels pulled the train away from the Cincinnati station. Surprised angels fell in heaps of colored organza and precious gemstones before they could compose themselves.

By now, the train was almost empty except for me, and there were only thirteen miles to go before arriving home.

Home. What did that mean to me now? Both Mom and Pop died while I was in Europe. I did not receive word until after their funerals, so I did not get to say goodbye. Now, I had no one. No one to greet me at the station. No one to hold me when I quaked in fear through nightmares. Nothing. Why go on living?

"Serenity?" whispered Curiosity. *"Did you hear Sam's heart? I think Sam might need help."*

"Yes, I heard," sighed Serenity. *"I hate to hear of anyone losing their will to live. It is so sad."*

"Shall we report this to Sir?" Curiosity asked with tears in her eyes.

"I think Sir knows, dear," replied Serenity.

"Mista Sam?"

A kind voice interrupted my thoughts. It was Nathaniel, the porter. I looked up at my friend with glazed eyes. We had been friends since boyhood, and now it seemed Nathaniel was my only friend.

"Mista Sam, the engineer, he is a friend of mine. I done axed the engineer to stop as close up to the old porta house as he can git. That old house is been empty fer some time now. The railroad done give me that house as part of my pay. Me and my woman is in a little house up to town now. You's right welcome to use it ifn you wants."

"Thank you, Nathaniel," I replied, forcing my depression to release my throat and voice. Then, just as quickly, I sank back into contemplative depression.

Chapter 2

Fear not, for I am with you; Be not dismayed, for I am your God. I will strengthen you, Yes, I will help you, I will uphold you with My righteous right hand. Isaiah 41:10

With the backdrop of a winter moon, the piercing sound of the train's whistle ripped open the midnight silence of Florence, Kentucky, signaling an unscheduled stop. Seven hundred Florence residents slept safely in their beds, unconcerned that Cincinnati's last train of the day carried one of their own home from the war. I would have to learn to live with my pain and suffer through it alone.

As promised, the train engineer stopped as close to the porter's house as he could, and I got off.

Four disoriented angels tumbled from the train and observed from a safe distance.

Because the track curved away from the small cottage, I still had to walk a short way. As the train pulled out, the engineer blew his whistle, wishing me a safe journey.

Carefully, trusting my prosthetics, I picked my way through the weeds and rocks. A snowy midnight moon illuminated the path while attentive angels twittered around as if directing my steps. At first, I did not sense the angels, but they later became my constant companions, and I could sense their presence, for which I was grateful.

When I reached the porter's house, I was amazed at how small it was. That field stone and oak house built in 1933 by the Civil Conservation Corps looked much bigger and more sinister when we were kids. We thrilled to imagined murder mysteries behind closed doors or secret lost treasure. We shivered as we hoped for promises of blood-curdling adventures.

Tonight, however, the small cabin held only unseen trepidation. As my prosthetic foot touched the bottom step of the worn porch, the rotting wood crumbled and fell in. I fought for balance with flailing arms and a prosthetic foot that threatened to give way. That sensation of falling into darkness gripped me and held more fear over me than any of my night jumps over enemy territory. Had it not been for the unsteady and splintering door frame, I would have fallen to the ground.

The winter moon illuminated the blinding darkness of the night just enough so that, working with one hand, I managed to juggle my duffle, dislodge my foot from the debris that was once the steps, and pull the screen door. With a last jerk, the door's rusting hinges screamed but gave way, nearly knocking me to the ground again.

The floor of the shallow screen porch, once shady and comfortable, was uneven from settling, boards lay rotting, the screens were torn, and fragments of screen lay buried in the dirt.

Once inside the porch, the creaking front door reluctantly opened enough for me to slip my duffle inside. My ears tensed at the sound of the door, scraping over a worn path on the wooden floor. That foreboding sound crawled up my spine.

Once inside, I fumbled in my pocket for a match and struck it on the door frame. A small flame grew from the stingy match head, and the tiny light revealed a lone wooden table in the middle of the floor. A soot-blackened kerosene lamp sat cold and uninviting. Over-turned chairs and pieces of collapsed ceiling timbers created obstacles in my path, causing me to stumble before reaching the table. The match flame went out. Patting the darkness, I reached out my hand and took several blind steps, then touched the glass chimney, nearly knocking it off the table. Startled and cold, I struck another match. It died. Then I struck another and lifted the glass globe, encouraging the dry frayed wick to life.

In the growing light and shadows, I saw a cot in the corner of the room. Folded on top of bare springs lay a stained, threadbare mattress. Nothing about it offered a homey invitation, but I was too tired to worry about whether or not the bed had linen. I simply threw open the lumpy mattress and fell onto it. The vintage bed frame wobbled, and the rusty bedsprings squeaked in protest. Disregarding my usual fear of nightmares, I slipped into a deep sleep. I was much too tired to allow dreams to intimidate me.

"Serenity, dear, do you want to watch over Sam while he sleeps?" asked Hope.

Courage interrupted in near squeals, *"I do, I do!"*

"So do I," added Curiosity.

"So do I," confessed Hope. *"Very well, let's all stay and watch over Sam. Tomorrow, we can make ready his cabin."*

The next morning, I awakened to the sound of birds singing and stretched my aching muscles. Shock returned when I rubbed what remained of my face and remembered the two fingers on the stump of my right hand and my gruesome reflection in the mirror.

I exhaled, watching my warm breath billow in clouds into the chilled early-morning mountain air before disappearing.

As sleep cleared from my brain, I wondered, *Where am I?* Then, I remembered Nathaniel's offer of a cottage I could use.

"So, this is home? Well, it's better than a frozen foxhole. Thank you, Lord," I prayed aloud.

The angels—Hope, Serenity, Faith, and Courage—having awakened hours earlier, flitted around the cold room. As if sensing a faint atmosphere of happiness and positive energy in the cabin, it seemed I felt that a new morning of my life dawned. So, I rolled out of the lumpy bed.

"Burr," I took two steps on the cold floor, and my feet complained. Remembering the debris I had stumbled over the night before; I collected the rotting wood and threw it into the fireplace. Then, coaxed the fire with a single match and rolled up paper. As hungry flames grew, they devoured the rotten wood. Once satiated, the fire turned to golden flames and crackled like the sound of friends laughter. Warm flames cast dancing shadows on the walls of the small sitting room.

As the soothing light revealed once-painted tongue and groove walls, I sat in the only wooden chair, propped my legs on the table, and lit a cigarette. The dark clouds of depression slowly but reluctantly gave way to imagination. What would it take to reconstruct these shambles to their original pristine condition? Reflectively, I asked, "Which shambles?" The shambles of the cottage would be easy to reconstruct. The shambles of my life, not so easy.

Having anticipated Sam's needs, the angels had searched the small kitchen. Faith found a small worn brush and a used cleaning rag stuck in a corner under the sink. Courage found a once-silver-plated spoon, nearly bald from wear, and Curiosity found a long-forgotten can opener languishing in a dark corner of the cabinets. With help from Courage and Serenity, the angels moved the brush and rag to a nail on the cabinet door. Faith and Curiosity lifted the spoon, washed it, and lay it in a drawer. Then the angels flew about the room, taking inventory of what the previous tenants left behind.

After finishing my cigarette, I felt a low grumble within my belly. Turning my attention to the small kitchen, I rummaged through the dusty cabinets to see what they might offer in the way of breakfast and found only a can of Van Camp's beans. On the battlefields, I had eaten more beans than I ever wanted to see again. But now, U.S. Van Camp's beans looked mighty good.

Okay. Now a can opener. To my surprise, I found a can opener and a spoon lying gleaming in the kitchen drawer as if waiting for me. It took several attempts, but almost in empathy, the can opener cooperated with the stump of my right hand. Soon, I sat before a crackling fire, eating beans from the can. Beans never tasted so good. To my surprise, I began to feel at home and enjoy my new oasis.

Somehow, I came to sense the angels closeness throughout the day and intuitively felt the hope and serenity the angels offered. Was I dreaming? Did I really see tiny flashes of color twinkling in the cabin?—Curiosity's opals burned through negative energy, while Serenity's watermelon tourmaline helped increase my joy. Courage offered soothing properties from her emeralds, and Faith's blue tanzanite provided stability. Still, the angel's had not made their presence clear to me.

After a hearty breakfast and renewed spirit, I began to unpack my duffle and plan my day. However, before I could put away my gear, I had to clean the dusty bedroom.

I searched the kitchen cabinets of the tiny cabin, and found a small brush and rag hanging on a nail under the sink. *"The former renter must have left it there,"* I thought to myself. *"But these things were not under the sink when I looked for something to eat for breakfast."*

Thankful for however the brush and rag got there, I set about cleaning the bedroom bureau and drawers so that they seemed to compete with the glow of the dancing fire in the fireplace.

Above the bureau hung a mirror, which I avoided. I did not want my reflection to remind me of the horror that was now my face. I cleaned the mirror anyway. What was the good of vanity?

After cleaning the small house and stowing my gear, I took account of the money left from my last military pay. It was not a king's ransom, but it held possibilities. I considered paying a visit to the bank where I opened an account. I whispered a word of thanks to my drill instructor for instructing us inductees to open bank accounts in our hometowns. Oh, how we draftees moaned, but now I am thankful for that drill instructor's wisdom.

Rummaging in my duffle, I found a piece of paper and a pencil to make a list of things I needed.

"First, I need food. I want lots of food, lots of fresh food. Should I get a refrigerator? No, that would have to wait. I'll have to make do with canned food.

"Does the cabin have gas for cooking? I don't know, but I'll plan on a pot and a frying pan anyway. I'll have to get items for the kitchen: wash pan, dish soap, clean rags. Next, I need personal care items, linen for the bed, towels, and toilet paper. I sure hope the grocery store will deliver." I chuckled.

The porter's house had a tiny sink, tub, and a worn and rusty toilet separating the two equally small bedrooms. With the adjoining doors and shuttered windows opened, a welcomed breeze blew through the dusty cabin and the cobwebs of my soul.

With a few dollars in my pocket and a glimmer of courage, I left the porter's house and walked two miles west into town. What would I find waiting for me there? Would anyone recognize me, and would my deformed face repulse them?

"Sam's going into town!" called Faith. *"Who's going with him?"*
"Me," called Hope.
"Me, too," called Serenity.
"I'm coming," shouted Courage from the porch.

The angels continued to flutter about me. They never left my side.

As I left the cabin, I dreaded what lay ahead of me in my hometown. Yet, my courage returned when I remembered the day the 82nd Airborne Division returned home in New York. Even though I had to watch from the sidelines, I was no less proud and struggled to stand and return the troops' salute to their fallen brothers as the 82nd marched in review.

Today, as I walked the dusty road into Florence, Kentucky, with feigned courage, I whistled the song the military band played that day the returning troops marched, "Hurray for the Red, White, and Blue."

By the time I reached downtown Florence, Kentucky, my steps were quick, my heart soared like a U.S. troop transport plane emblazoned with the familiar bar and star, and I felt that Army courage swelling deep within my gut.

My first stop was at the bank to introduce myself and check up on my bank account.

"Excuse me."

The young woman behind the teller window, Evelyn Morgan, looked up and let out a little gasp. "Oh, my, I…" she stammered. "I'm sorry. May I help you, sir?"

"I hope so," I replied in a matter-of-fact voice. "My name is Sam Burkett. I believe I have a bank account here and would like to check on the status."

The teller continued to stare at me, then caught herself. "One moment, Mr. Burkett," she replied. "I will get the manager for you. Won't you have a seat?"

I sat and waited for a time, noticing the hustle and bustle in the upstairs, glass-encased office and wondered about the commotion. Finally, a middle-aged man wearing a three-piece suit came out to greet me.

"Good morning, Mr. Burkett." The manager reached out to shake my hand, but seeing my finger stumps, he pulled his hand back, not knowing what to do. Finally, he just held the piece of paper he carried and said, "I am Ken Furman, bank manager. I apologize for the delay. We had to do a bit of back-checking to find your account. You were in the Army Air Corps when you open the account. Correct?"

"Yes sir," I replied, now a little concerned. "Is there a problem?"

"Oh, no, Mr. Burkett," continued a nervous bank manager. "Won't you come into my office where we can discuss this in private?"

I followed the bank manager up an elegant flight of stairs. In his office, I took a seat, and the bank manager began to stumble over his words again. "We are a small bank, you see," Mr. Furman tried to offer a weak explanation. "Quite frankly, I am puzzled. How did you come to open an account in our bank?"

"Mr. Furman, this is my hometown. During orientation, the Army Air Corps instructed us GIs to open accounts in our hometown banks. I was under the impression that my military pay would automatically be deposited into my account."

"And indeed, it was, Mr. Burkett," said Mr. Furman reaching into a file folder. "I have here a detailed record of your deposits. Each month, the US Government deposited your monthly military pay of $63."

"Yes, that's correct so far. I kept $15 a month for my incidentals."

Mr. Furman wiped his brow with a silk handkerchief and continued, "Then there was an additional $50 each month for special pay for paratroopers."

"Correct."

"That brought your monthly deposit to $113."

Mr. Furman looked over his glasses for confirmation, then feverishly continued, "From that monthly total, $12.50 was deducted each month to purchase a $25 war bond." Mr. Furman paused again. "That means you have forty-eight war bonds in our vault, each worth $25."

"Yes. I would like those bonds to continue to their ten-year maturity."

"Yes," choked an over-worked manager. He continued clicking the keys of his adding machine. "When the bonds mature in another six years, they will be added to your account in the amount of $1,200.

Until that happens, your total four-year deposits come to $5,544."

"Yes."

"That is a considerable sum, Mr. Burkett, since the median annual family income is only three thousand dollars these days and with the cost of living, their savings might be just $50 a year. Most soldiers send money home to their families for their use. Your account has not had a withdrawal over the life of your account."

"That's because I have no living family. Mom and Pop died while I was overseas," I said, resenting having to explain.

"Just who was your mother and father, may I ask?" pried the bank manager.

"George and Ginny Burkett," I replied.

This time it was the bank manager who gasped and choked. "Oh, I see. George and Ginny Burkett." Mr. Furman paused to comprehend, then asked in embarrassment, "Are you Sammy?"

"Yes, sir, I am."

The expression on the bank manager's face dropped, as did his voice, and he stood. "Sam. I am so sorry. I did not recognize you. That is … I …I . It has been a long time," babbled Ken Furman offering his hand again. This time with a firm but careful handshake. I stood to accept his hand, and he continued, "I do so apologize."

"No need, Mr. Furman. I did not expect you to recognize me. I almost don't recognize myself," I quipped, breaking the tension of the moment.

"Please, Sam. Please call me Ken," the bank manager said, motioning for me to sit again. "And let me assure you, I will do everything I can to help you settle in," stammered Ken Furman, then added, "settle into your home." The banker offered a questioning smile and raised eyebrows.

"That's very kind of you, Ken. For the moment, I have a place to stay. I am in the porter's house on the edge of town. I have a few more errands to run, then I can start setting up my home there.

I was considering renting out my parents' house. I don't want to sell just yet. Monthly rent will add to my bank account. Other than that, I am open to suggestions."

"Miss Riley? Miss Riley, will you come in please?" Mr. Furman called on the intercom.

Miss Riley entered the office and stole an uncomfortable glance at me before taking a seat.

"Janet, will you please draw up a letter of credit for Mr. Burkett for my signature. Mr. Burkett has just come home from the war. I want to make sure he receives a proper welcome."

The letter of credit and introduction that the bank manager gave me was very generous and made my errands easier. People at the bank and drugstore went out of their way to be helpful and made me feel welcome.

My next stop was to the grocery store. While there, Mr. Eddie, my old Sunday School teacher, and his wife came in to do their shopping. When Mr. Cooper, the grocer, introduced me, Mr. Eddie shook my stump vigorously yet carefully, and Mrs. Eddie said, "Well, thank the Lord. Welcome home, Sam."

"Sam, I'll be glad to deliver your grocery items this afternoon," Mr. Eddie offered.

"And I'll bring a pot of chicken and rice," chimed in Mrs. Eddie.

"Mr. Spain," Mrs. Eddie called to a friend and fellow shopper. "Mr. Spain, do you remember George and Ginny's boy, Sammy?"

"Well, bless my soul. Of course, I do. Howdy, Sammy."

Mr. Eddie continued, "Sammy is living in the old porter's cottage down by the railroad tracks."

"Well do tell," exclaimed Mr. Spain. "Do you have a refrigerator in that old shack, Sammy? I have a used one in my store. I can deliver it this afternoon."

Mr. Otto walked in about that time and joined the conversation. "Well, Sam," Mr. Otto said and grinned, "we're mighty glad to have you back home."

Mr. Eddie repeated his news. "Sammy here is living in the old porter's cabin, Earl."

"The porter's cabin, you say? Well, that place ain't had electricity and gas for years. I'll be by to fix you up, son. You gonna be needin' heat and hot water."

Florence, Kentucky was feeling like home again.

As promised, Mr. Eddie delivered my groceries and drug store purchases, and Mrs. Eddie also came with her husband with a pot of chicken and rice, still warm from the stove. Together, the three of us enjoyed a meal of chicken and rice and shared memories.

While Mrs. Eddie put away groceries in the now clean kitchen cabinets, Mr. Eddie and I visited in the sitting room.

"My sakes, Sam," Mrs. Eddie called from the kitchen. "You cleaned these cabinets all by yourself?"

"Yes, ma'am, Mrs. Eddie," I replied. "The government goes to great lengths to teach GIs the right end of a mop and broom," I quipped.

Having served his stint in the military, Mr. Eddie laughed.

"Did you do the bathroom, too, Sam?" she questioned.

"That, too, Mrs. Eddie," I replied with not a little pride.

"We best be goin' before she finds somethin' for me to do." Mr. Eddie laughed again as he stood to leave. "We're mighty thankful to have you back home, Sam. I know your mom and pop would be proud."

"Thank you, Mr. Eddie. Mrs. Eddie, that chicken and rice dinner was wonderful. With friends like you, I may never leave again."

With heartfelt hugs and hands clasped in love, the Eddies left my small abode.

When I was a boy, I considered eastern Kentucky the most wonderful place to be. The tree canopy over Main Street and the distant hills mesmerized and spoke to me. They spoke of a bright green of new spring leaves or of the old dark green color of summer. Wildflowers painted the meadows, and birds of varied colors and songs filled the trees around my house, making it appear that they all competed good-naturedly for the same spaces. Fall thrilled me with its promise of Halloween candies, turkey and dressing, and pumpkin pies followed by the colored lights and tinsel of Christmas. Winter whispered to me, begging me to come out and play in the snow.

Although Florence sat in a low elevation, stories of mysterious coal mines sparked the imaginations of young boys. My pals and I dug into the flat earth on the outskirts of town, pretending to be coal miners. It must have been the danger and fear factor that beckoned us. Despite warnings from the older men of the dreary life of a miner, we wanted to be deep in the mines surrounded by the tantalizing darkness, spiders, and imaginary monsters that caused the hairs on the back of our necks to rise and prickle. Toil-worn bodies and black lung disease meant nothing to us.

Now, returning home, a welcome from old friends reinforced my love of Kentucky. While I was in Europe, the tree canopy over Main Street was removed to make way for commerce in Florence, but I still look at my home and friends through my same boyhood eyes. I will always see Mom and Pop in everything, and Kentucky will always spell L-O-V-E for me, but there was something missing. My heart yearned for my own family. But how can someone who was deformed and handicapped find a true love in such a small town?

Two weeks later, I visited the bank, this time to deposit my Veterans' Affairs disability check. After I completed my business with the head teller, Ken Furman buzzed Evelyn on her intercom.

"Evelyn, please ask Mr. Burkett to come up and visit with me."

"Yes, sir." She turned to me and said with a wink, "You have been invited up."

Willing my prosthetic foot to cooperate, I took the stairs two at a time, stood at the executive door to regain my breath and knocked on the door.

"Come in, Sam," Ken called and stood, extending his hand as

if to an old friend when I entered.

"Thank you for coming up, Sam. I have some exciting news for you. At least I think it's exciting."

"What news is that Mr. Furman?"

"Please, Sam, do call me Ken. Well, I did some checking and found out that the railroad still owns the porter's house. After having my call transferred numerous times, I finally spoke with the top administrator with the railroad. I explained that you were recently discharged from the Army Air Corps, a disabled veteran, and living in the porter's house."

"Forgive me for being skeptical, but what has this to do with me?"

"Technically, Sam, you are a squatter at the cabin. But I later received a call from the Secretary of the Army who also did some checking. The railroad has agreed to give you permission to live at the porter's house indefinitely and rent free."

"That is good news. Thank you, Ken. I like the little cabin, and since I have decided to rent out my parent's house, I would like to stay there."

So, I lived alone in the small cabin for two months, making it my home. God was good. He gave me a place to live and good friends. But my life was still empty.

Chapter 3

You are my hiding place... Psalm 32:7

"*C*ourage! Did you hear that?" asked Serenity.

"*No. I did not hear anything. What was it?*" replied Courage.

"*Sh-h-h,*" whispered Faith. "*I heard it. Listen closely, Courage. It was a small whimper.*"

The west side of Florence in Boone County was rural and one of the poorest parts of the county. Still, the distant hills, trees, and meadows painted the landscape that I loved so well. There was, however, an ugly side, and this ugliness eclipsed the beauty of Kentucky.

State Road 18 ran east and west through Florence and fronted a five-acre parcel to the west where a dilapidated trailer stood on the fringe of the property. One would wonder how anyone could live there, for the frame of that second-hand trailer, nearly destroyed by neglect, showed severe signs of rust. An equally rusted out truck jacked up and leaning from a flat tire added to the squalor.

His drunken eyes blazed in anger as Randall Crews, her high school sweetheart and husband of six years, cursed and swung with insane fury. Saliva and vile words spewed from his mouth. His clenched fist crushed the last of the six-pack, and he flung the wad of aluminum at her, hitting her in the face, adding yet another abrasion to her once peaches and cream complexion. With flailing arms, he drove his massive fist into her stomach, still tender from the last beating. Her bruised lungs exhaled, and she bent over in pain. She could not speak, but she knew from experience that she should not even try. Trying to reason with Randall only intensified his anger and brought more misery.

Rachel trembled in fear and pain but held tight to Joelle, her frightened toddler. Sammy, her five-year-old, stayed close to Rachel. Sammy dared not look at Randall out of fear. During one angry episode, the little boy made eye contact with his father and received a slap to his head just for holding his gaze too long. Although Joelle and Sammy were not usually the targets of Randall's rage, they were victims, nonetheless.

What triggered his fit of anger this time? Did he get fired from his job again? Did he gamble away his paycheck, the only money Rachel would have to feed her family? She knew she dared not ask. Lately, it did not matter what triggered his rage. The result was the same. Rachel lost count of the red welts and purple bruises covering her body. Randall was careful to aim his blows where questioning eyes could not see.

Still doubled over in pain, she covered her head, waiting in terror for the next blow from his clenched fist. She didn't know what was worse, the fierce blows, the wicked anticipation, or the excruciating pain of knowing someone you love has gone mad.

This time, however, the blow never came. Instead, red-faced from anger, alcohol, and depression, Randall shoved Rachel and the children down the narrow hallway of the single-wide trailer home. With each angry push, he shouted untrue accusations and obscenities, products of his tortured mind.

The force of his unrelenting shoves caused Rachel to bounce off the drywalls leaving a trail of blood that oozed from the soft cream-colored flesh that was her elbows. Haphazardly taped joints split, and plaster fell to the floor.

Angels had been resting and talking to the flowers in the Garden. In shocked surprise, Faith immediately rose and said, *"Come, angels! We must go."*

In quaking tears, Rachel tried to clean up the smears of blood on the walls and pieces of plaster on the floor. She still could not make eye contact. She longed to look into his eyes as they had as young lovers, but fear and pain would not permit her now.

Seeing blood smeared over the bare walls further infuriated Randall. He screamed and cursed her and hit her again. then grabbed her by her ears, lifting her from the floor. When Rachel stood, Randall gave her yet another violent shove that trapped Rachel's body against the thin aluminum frame of the back door. The chain hanging from the storm door swung and hit the back of her head, grabbing her hair in a tangled knot.

Rachel would never forget the hateful words and saliva spewing out from Randall's hot, alcohol-soured mouth. His breath burned over her face and seared into her heart. Instinctively, Rachel turned her head. This perceived rejection escalated Randall's fury.

With renewed anger, Randall shoved Rachel and their toddler aside. She winced in pain when the door's chain ripped patches of tangled hair from her head. Then, with rage-induced force, Randall jerked the door open, yanking the top hinge from the frame.

The last thing Rachel saw was Randall's black, hate-filled eyes as he pushed her and their children out the door.

When she stumbled down the wobbling wood and iron steps, Rachel lost her hold on Joelle, and the crying toddler fell to the frozen ground.

Randall slammed the lame door closed with such force that it bounced against the now warped door frame. Three months of packed snow from the roof fell in torrents and covered Rachel's aching body. She blanched as she wiped her mouth with the back of her hand and tasted the warm, sticky, metallic ooze.

Rachel heard the baby crying, and she instinctively forgot about her own pain.

She had heard the heart-stopping sound of a slamming door many times before, but this time, it was different. This time the victimized door slammed with such intense fury that it hurled its reverberating sound through the barren trees, standing long defoliated by the harsh winter. This time, the sound was permanent. Except for her children, Joelle and Sammy, Rachel's life felt as barren as the ghostly tree branches surrounding the trailer home.

"The babies! Faith! Where are the babies?" shouted a terrified Curiosity. Upon finding the toddler and the five-year-old lying several feet from Rachel, Curiosity hurried to them. *"Oh, babies, it's going to be okay. You are safe now. Jesus loves you."*

Working desperately to dig out from her icy entombment, Rachel searched with bruised eyes and called for her children. "Joelle? Baby? Sammy, where are you?" She crawled on her hands and knees to find where her baby girl had fallen and scooped the toddler up in her arms. Then she heard Sammy's moans. With Joelle clinging to one arm, she crawled to Sammy and comforted the brave little boy. Rachel raised herself on a tender, skinned, and bleeding elbow and wiped away his tears with her tattered t-shirt. "Come on, babies, let's hurry to our safe place."

"Don't Daddy love us anymore?" asked a bewildered and frightened five-year-old Sammy.

With her son's words, Rachel went limp and buried her face in the boy's snow-covered neck, again allowing hot tears to melt the powdery snow.

When Rachel was able to speak again, she told Sammy, "Baby, Daddy don't know what he's doin'." She didn't know how much her empty words actually brought comfort to her sweet boy.

Through her pain-induced haze, Rachel knew she must move to safety to protect herself and her precious little ones. Remembering the words she had once read in the Bible, Psalm 32:7, she found strength from deep within her heart: "You are my hiding place;

you will protect me from trouble and surround me with songs of deliverance." Reaching still further into her soul, Rachel willed her stiff muscles to move and encouraged the children to run. "Run quickly, quietly. Run to our place."

Over the years, branches and vines had covered young sapling trees bending them to the ground and forming a burrow. In that thinly veiled safety, Rachel had stored candles and matches in a mason jar. In an old, waxed vegetable crate, she stowed a jar of peanut butter, graham crackers, a spoon, and a kitchen towel. With experienced forethought, she had squirreled away a ragged tarpaulin that Randall would never miss. At least there, she and the children could sleep, and the tarp would keep them warm and dry.

Rachel continued to encourage the children to run. "Run to the safe place, Sammy! Run!"

Four angels flitted around and ahead of the running children, lighting their way and adding positive energies for the scared little ones.

Once Rachel and the children were in their "burrow," she covered the chilled, hungry children with the tarp and fed them graham crackers and peanut butter.

"Sammy, can you tell God thank you for the peanut butter crackers?" Rachel whispered through sore lips.

"God is great. God is good." Sammy fought back his tears, then continued. "Let us thank Him for our food. Amen."

With the snacks consumed and little fingers licked, she lay down with Joelle and Sammy and pulled the tarp over the three of them.

The angels hoovered around Rachel and the children, keeping vigil, and spreading their soothing energies of hope and joy.

"Sleep, my dears," crooned Faith.

A cold winter moon illuminated the snowy landscape, the earth shook, and freezing air magnified the sound of the train's whistle. Steam billowed in front of the hot machine before disappearing under the racing steel wheels.

The last sound Rachel heard before drifting off into a fitful sleep was the train's whistle. That sound sent shudders through the length of her body before burrowing into her heart. Forever, the sound of a train in the distance would represent fear, loneliness, and pain.

Chapter 4

The LORD shall preserve thy going out and thy coming in from this time forth, and even for evermore. Psalm 121:8

That night had been hard for Rachel. Before she fell into a fitful sleep, her whole body tightened every time she heard a twig snap or an animal rustle in the forest. She hated herself for her cowardice, but she did not want to face Randall and his anger again. Distinction between fearing him and hating him was becoming blurred, and she was not sure if she could hold up under Randall's wrath one more time. She had to be strong for her children.

As the sun brightened the winter sky, Joelle was the first to awaken, and the baby whimpered. Rachel marveled at how such a baby could survive a profound trauma and still be so sweet.

"Shh-shh-shh," Rachel comforted her child and pulled the sleepy baby close to warm her. "It's okay, sweet baby. Come over here and snuggle with Mommy. I'll get you warm. We're going to be okay."

"Pretty," whispered Joelle as she whimpered and pointed at the angels.

"Yes, my sweet. You are so pretty." Rachel, not being able to see the angels, did not understand Joelle's reference.

"Mommy?" Now Sammy was awake, worried, and hungry.

"Yes, my sweet? Come here, my love." Rachel held out her arm, inviting the five-year old to cuddle, and Sammy eagerly moved into his mother's free arm and snuggled down.

"Mommy, I'm cold, and I'm hungry. Can we have some breakfast?"

"Soon, sweetheart," this brave young mother lied. "What would you like for breakfast?"

"Pancakes and syrup!" Sammy nearly shouted.

"Pancakes and syrup, it is," she lied again. "First, let's get you and Joelle to the potty."

Sammy shrieked. "Where am I going to the potty? There's no potty out here!"

"See all those trees, Sammy? You just pick the one you like. Joelle and I will not look," Rachel said with weak merriment. "Then we will go on an adventure."

With that, Sammy scampered off in a giggle to find just the right tree.

As the angel, Curiosity started to follow, Faith pulled her back with the admonishment, *"Even little ones need privacy, Curiosity, dear."*

After a near wilderness potty experience for Sammy and a kitchen towel diaper for Joelle, Rachel gathered her little ones to start their adventure. "What do you say we walk into town and have breakfast at the drugstore?"

"Milk!" Joelle squealed.

"Yes, you can have milk, and Mr. Sammy can have pancakes."

When Rachel stood, her muscles screamed, but she still tried to brush the wrinkles out of her dress, then ran her bruised fingers through her hair. *I'm glad there is no mirror*, she thought to herself. *I don't want to see the effects of last night's beating, nor see what an old-looking woman I have become.*

Despite the traumatic night, the walk into town was happy.

The sun was bright, making for a crisp day, and the angels flew and hovered around the children in joyful frolic.

There was no snow on the dirt road, except for a few snowdrifts here and there. Rachel left her fears and the deep snow in the woods. She relied on her faith in God to face a new day.

Sammy picked up pieces of flint and threw them into the weeds along the road, hoping a rabbit would scurry out. Joelle begged to walk and tried to keep up with her big brother. After several plops in the dirt road, she had second thoughts about this walking thing and returned to the safety and comfort of her mother's arms.

With great courage, a tired mother and two hungry babies walked together the mile east into town. As they walked, Rachel prayed a silent prayer. *Lord, thank You for keeping us safe last night. Thank You for our safe place, and thank You for this beautiful day. Now, Lord, you know my babies need breakfast. Sammy has his heart set on pancakes, and Joelle needs some milk. I don't need much, although a cup of coffee would be nice. Thank you, Lord.*

"Mommy, look! A bunny!" exclaimed Sammy. "Two bunnies. Three bunnies!" he continued to squeal.

"Oh, my, yes." Rachel laughed. She was surprised that she could still laugh. "I guess they are out to find breakfast, too. Let's go, mister. You don't want to be late for pancakes."

Supported by the faith in her heart, her hope increased, although she had no idea what she would do after the babies finished their breakfast. She had no money. *Lord, keep me strong,* she continued to pray.

The small bell over the door tinkled as she walked into the diner with Sammy and Joelle. To Rachel, however, the small tinkling bell was more like a loudspeaker announcing, "Here comes a freeloader!" With downcast eyes, Rachel glanced around quickly, afraid that someone had heard the announcement,

The breakfast bar at the drugstore was busy as usual. Plates rattled, silverware clanked, and Roger, the sweat-drenched breakfast cook, called out, "Order up." The smell of warm bacon was so inviting and tempting, but Rachel would see that her babies ate their fill, and she would stick with coffee. She could not endure the humiliation of not being able to pay for more than that.

"Good morning, miss," the waitress greeted Rachel when she walked in with the children. Gloria, a middle-aged woman, stout of figure, bustled around her tables pouring coffee and chatting good-naturedly with the customers. Her white dress swished against her stockings, and her white oxford shoes made squeaking noises as she walked on the clean tile floor. "Sit anywhere you like. Do you need two booster seats, dear?" Gloria asked as she topped off half-full coffee cups.

"Yes, ma'am," Rachel replied, with still downcast eyes, scanning for condemnation.

As an experienced waitress, Gloria brought over coloring paper and crayons for the children and a cup of hot coffee for Rachel once they sat.

With great admiration, I watched Gloria's kindness and sympathy for this young mother's courage.

"What can I get you this morning?"

"Pancakes!" shouted Sammy, then remembering his manners, slumped his shoulders and sat back in the red booster seat.

"And milk for the pretty baby?" asked Gloria.

"Milk," babbled Joelle, returning Gloria's smiles.

"Yes, please," replied Rachel in a near whisper.

"Pancakes! Pancakes! I'm going to have pancakes," Sammy sang, banging his silverware on the table. Joelle joined in the glee with giggles and a spoon. However, Rachel could not laugh or sing. The world was weighing too heavy on her shoulders.

Serenity hovered over Rachel, sprinkling the tired mother with energies from Watermelon Tourmaline from the angel's gown to calm the tired mother's mind and emotions. Courage showered Rachel with energies from Jade to uplift and soothe Rachel's heart.

The other three angels—Faith, Hope, and little Curiosity—darted from table to table as if taking stock of the possibilities. Then Faith saw me. The angel abruptly stopped in mid-flight. Hope and Curiosity could not stop in time and plowed into Faith's back. Curiosity giggled, thinking it fun.

"Look," Faith whispered, pointing to me. *"There he is. See the man sitting by himself? That's who God the Father sent. I just know it is."*

"I see him," replied Hope. *"Let's see what Sir is going to do."*

The three angels flew back to where Serenity and Courage hovered over Rachel and added their energies of faith, truth, heaven, strength, and courage.

Gloria carried a big tray above her shoulder and, with a big smile, trotted over to Rachel's table. Her friendly laughter, swishing dress and her squeaking shoes announced her arrival.

"There you go, young man," Gloria said as she placed a stack of hot, buttery pancakes and milk in front of wide-eyed Sammy. Gloria also set a small bowl in front of Joelle with a smaller cup of milk. "Here you go, little missy. Here is your very own pancake. The way your brother is shoveling in those pancakes, I don't think he is likely to share."

"Thank you," Rachel whispered and managed a guilty smile up at Gloria before lowering her eyes again.

"Can't I get you something to eat, dear?"

"No, ma'am," Rachel replied, knowing she could not pay for even this little bit.

"Well, eat up, me hearties!" Gloria said, winking at Sammy.

"Sammy, will you say our blessing?" Rachel admonished her hungry son.

"Oh, I forgot," said a repentant Sammy with a mouthful of pancakes and a trail of syrup running down his chin. "Do you think God will forgive me?"

"I'm sure He will. Now say our prayer, please."

Before she finished her coffee, Sammy had gobbled up the last of the pancakes. He sat back on the booster seat and rubbed his tummy and burped.

"Excuse me?" his mother corrected.

"'Cuse me," replied Sammy obediently, albeit with devilish eyes.

"Good boy. Do you feel better now?" she asked.

"Uh-huh," replied Sammy.

"Yes, ma'am?" his mother corrected again.

"Yes, ma'am," whispered Sammy, this time with downcast eyes.

"Let me take these plates out of your way," said Gloria, bustling around the table. "How about a bag of hot biscuits and bacon to go?"

"Oh, no, ma'am," Rachel protested. "You have already been so kind."

"Well then, you have a nice day," sang the kind waitress.

"But … but what about our check?" Rachel asked, knowing she could not pay it.

"Oh, that?" said Gloria, brushing at the air with a free hand. "A gentleman over there took a shine to your little ones and paid for their breakfast."

"Oh," Rachel whispered, consumed with shame. She was ready to bear the guilt of not being able to pay for the breakfast, but this? This act of kindness caught her by surprise.

Before leaving the table, Rachel dipped a napkin in her water to wipe sticky syrup off Sammy's face and Joelle's hands and helped the children out of their booster seats. Then, with a sorrowful countenance, she turned to me. I know she meant to say, "Thank you," but instead, she gasped and then turned red.

Sammy, also taken aback, peeped from behind his mother's

skirt, while Joelle merely pointed.

Once she composed herself, Rachel managed to say a sincere, "Thank you for paying for our breakfast. I am so sorry I reacted in such a rude manner."

"That's quite alright," I replied. "I'm glad I could help." Trying to change the subject to ease her embarrassment, I continued. "Where you off to this mornin'?" I asked reaching for my hat and nodding thanks to a smiling Gloria.

As I opened the door, the bell tinkled again, this time, a little more cheerily.

I took Rachel's elbow and walked on the outside of the narrow sidewalk. Sammy skipped, trying not to step on any cracks. Joelle toddled behind.

"My name's Sam Burkett," I introduced myself.

"Hey! That's my name. Mommy calls me Sammy, but my name is really only Sam," the five-year-old announced with pride. "What's wrong with your face?" the boy blurted out.

"Oh, Sammy!" Rachel gasped in embarrassment. "Hello, Sam. My name is Rachel. I can't tell you how much I appreciate your coming to my rescue," she said, extending her small hand and trying to cover up her embarrassment.

"Oh, ma'am, people have been kind to me since I came home. The least I can do is pass that kindness along. Besides, you looked like you needed a little kindness," I said, smiling at the weary mother.

Then I turned my attention to the boy skipping behind, counting cracks. "Well, Sammy, to answer your question, I was in the Army Airborne Division, and ..."

"The Airborne!?" exclaimed Sammy. "Wow! Did you fly a plane? How big was your plane? Did it go real fast?"

"No, I didn't fly the plane, but I jumped out of it," I said to add to Sammy's excitement.

"You jumped? Out of a plane? How fast was it going? How high did you jump?" Sammy's fast-fire questions rewarded my prompt. And that was that. Scars were forgotten, stubby fingers no longer mattered. Sammy just met a real hero.

I laughed and let Sammy continue jumping over cracks.

"You were in the Airborne?" asked Rachel.

"Yes, ma'am," I replied without fanfare. "There were thousands of us GIs in the European theatre. Many of us nearly froze in a German forest. Some of the GIs did freeze to death. I was one of the lucky ones."

"I am so sorry, Sam. By the way, thank you for your service to our country," Rachel replied.

"Thank you, ma'am. What about you?"

"Me? Oh, nothing as heroic as your story," Rachel said, trying to avoid the question.

"You know, ma'am, I don't mean to intrude in your business, but no woman should be beaten," I said.

Rachel's bruised eyes grew wide with surprise, fear, and shame. She did not reply but looked over her shoulder suspiciously, searching for terror.

For the next few minutes, Rachel and I walked along in silence. Then I asked, "Where are you going, Rachel?"

She sighed deeply before replying, "I don't know. I'm just trusting the Lord."

"I have a little cottage on the west side of town. It's not much, but you and the children will have a room to yourselves. Let me share it with you," I encouraged.

"Oh, Sam. I do appreciate your generosity, but how would it look? I'm a married woman."

"No, Rachel. You are a charming woman attached to a horrible man. I would not call that a marriage. As for how it would look, let's let the Lord handle that, okay?"

Rachel—tired, hungry, and frightened—gave way to her fears and nodded her thanks.

"Can we stop at the grocery store before we go home? There

is something I need to do."

"… before we go home." Those words melted Rachel's bruised heart.

Sam held the door for Rachel, and just as she was about to step into the grocery store, an unkempt man with an offensive odor, carrying two six-packs of beer bumped into her and scowled.

Rachel looked up and was about to say, "Excuse me," then she stopped and recoiled.

I felt Rachel tense when she leaned into me, and before I heard her gasp. I saw her shock and took her elbow with calm strength. "In you go, kiddos." I guided her and her children into the grocery store.

I said nothing to the man. But the man scoffed and spat on my shoes as he passed.

Once she was in the grocery store and regained her composure, the smell of fresh Merita bread ignited Rachel's taste buds. She smelled fresh corn, apples, and meats. She seemed to act as if she stepped into Heaven.

"You and the kids can look around while I talk to Mr. Cooper."

"What if …" Rachel protested.

"There will be no ifs," I assured her. "I won't be long." I walked down the aisle, then disappeared.

As she passed the fresh vegetable display, Rachel reached out to touch the golden tassels on the ears of sweet corn. The tassels were still fresh and silky, quite a contrast to the ruff-looking husks. Next, she touched green beans, and her memory transported her home, where her mother snapped beans, mashed hot potatoes, and fried chicken for dinner.

Sammy made every step Rachel made and mimicked her every move. However, instead of touching the corn gently, he stuck his thumbnail into one of the kernels.

"Mommy! The corn spit at me," Sammy said in giggles.

"Oh, Sammy," his mother scolded firmly but gently. "We are not supposed to damage the vegetables. Now no one will want to buy that corn." But she had to admit the fresh corn smelled, oh, so good.

"You can buy it for us," squealed Sammy with delight.

"Oh, Sammy …" Rachel released a pensive sigh.

Just as Rachel was scolding Sammy, I returned with the owners of the grocery store in tow.

"Rachel?" I spoke softly so as not to frighten her.

Rachel turned almost in shock, then beamed, "Oh. Yes, Sam. Aren't these vegetables wonderful?" she asked returning from her memories.

"Rachel, this is Mr. and Mrs. Cooper. They own the grocery store and have invited us to their church."

Immediately, Rachel blushed with embarrassment and wondered what these good people thought about her.

"Rachel, dear, we are so sorry for your trouble. You don't need to be afraid or embarrassed. We have all been through tough patches at one time or another," said Mrs. Cooper, reaching out to Rachel.

With Mrs. Cooper's kind words, all of Rachel's emotions flooded from her heart, and she fell into Mrs. Cooper's arms and wept.

"There, there, dear." Mrs. Cooper tried to console Rachel. "You've had hard times, haven't you, dear? Well, it's over now. You have friends here, and no one will look down their nose at you as long as I am around."

"And no one is going to hurt you as long as I am around," I assured Rachel.

Rescuing the moment, Sammy burst out, "Do you know Sam? My name is Sam, too, but Mommy calls me Sammy."

The angels bounced and fluttered as only angels do.

Chapter 5

I have loved you with an everlasting love.
Jeremiah 31:3

---

our excited angels tumbled and giggled as they entered the realm of the Garden. The angels flew in an excited pattern of I'm-first-no-I'm-first. Silk organza ruffled in the air, and gemstones flashed.

"Sir, Sir," called a breathless Curiosity as she fluttered much too fast to God the Father. She wanted to be the first to share the angels' news.

"Well, here are My angels." God the Father held out His gentle hand to catch the glowing balls of giggling light. *"What is all the excitement about, Curiosity, My dear?"*

Before Curiosity had time to reply, Faith answered. As was her manner, she took a deep breath, paused to control her giggles, then began in a more subdued but still giggly manner. *"When we went back to earth, we did as you asked ..."*

Not meaning to cut Faith off, Curiosity exclaimed, *"We watched and listened."*

Waiting patiently for her turn, Serenity announced, *"First we met Sam ..."*

"He's a GI from World War Two," interrupted Courage.

Serenity gave Courage a side-ways glance, then continued. *"Poor Sam. He was so depressed. He did not want to live."*

Faith beamed. *"Then we met Rachel ..."*

"And her children," squealed Curiosity.

"And now they are happy together," Serenity shouted. Surprised and ashamed by her outburst, Serenity covered her mouth with her tiny, crisscrossed hands.

"Very well done, My dears," God the Father praised His angels. *"However, you might want to go back. There is more to do."*

"More?" all four angels asked at once. *"More to do?"*

"Yes, My dears. Just before you arrived with your wonderful news, I heard a groan. Would you like to check it out for Me, please?" asked the omniscient God the Father.

"A groan?" Curiosity began. *"We did not hear ..."*

"... a groan," finished Serenity.

"We must go back, angels," agreed Faith.

As he pulled himself up on the side of the bed, Randall's head throbbed, and his stomach wrenched in dry heaves. It had taken several days for the alcohol to wear off, yet he was still groggy and disoriented. He reached for a nearly empty can of warm beer and downed it, then fell back into the filth that was his bed.

Randall lay on dingy sheets that reeked with vomit and sweat. Yellow bile, the outward evidence of an alcoholic liver, further stained and smelled his sheets.

Fumbling for the alarm clock on the nightstand, Randall squinted through his pain. In the stark evening light, the clock glowed six-o-clock.

This time of day had always been melancholy for Randall, and now his sickness magnified his mental anguish. His stomach ached; his head throbbed; and his whole body quaked in an alcoholic tremor. Where was Rachel?

A dim, jagged light pierced through dirty curtains, once torn in anger and now hung by threads. Randall strained to recognize strange dark shapes in the room, that during the day, would be familiar.

Trying to recall recent events, he pressed his hands against his throbbing head. He could not understand the blackouts in his memory. As Randall stumbled to his feet, his diseased blood rushed to his head much too fast for his condition. To keep from falling, he steadied himself on the second-hand bureau. The worn and rotting legs of the bureau caused the furniture to rock, and Randall fell.

"Rachel," Randall called out, sobbing. "Rachel," he yearned. "Rachel, I need you."

Knowing little else to do, the angels—Serenity, Compassion, Grace, and Peace—hovered about Randall, showering the sick man with the energies from their gemstones.

"What do we do, Compassion?" asked Courage.

"I'm afraid, dear, there is little we can do."

"Should we call Sir?" asked Grace.

"Sir knows, dear," replied Peace. *"Don't you remember that Sir always knows even before we do? We must just wait on Him."*

"It's so hard to wait," lamented Compassion.

"I know, dear. But if we tried to do anything, it might not be the right thing to do. Let's let Sir do the right thing," Serenity counseled. All the angels shook their heads in agreement.

The wind picked up as the dim light of dusk turned to night. Wet snow fell, and the lame door slammed against the siding of the trailer home. Randall's head throbbed with each slam, and he held his head, pressing his palms against his throbbing temples, trying to fight the urge to puke again.

"Is someone there? Who is it? Who's there? Rachel?"

"It is I, Randall," said a soft Voice.

"Who is it?" Randall asked again, still in an alcoholic stupor.

"Don't you remember Me, Randall?" replied the kind Voice. *"We were once friends."*

"Friends?" Randall answered, blinking to clear the haze. "We were friends?"

"It's Sir," Grace squealed.

"Yes, dear," whispered Peace.

"I once heard a mortal sing a song about being friends with God. Perhaps this would make Randall feel better," whispered Curiosity.

"Will you sing it for us, dear?" asked Grace.

How long has it been since you talked with the Lord
And told Him your heart's hidden secrets
How long since you prayed, how long since you stayed
On your knees til the light shone through
How long has it been since your mind felt at ease
How long since your heart knew no burden
Can you call Him your friend
How long has it been since you knew that He cared for you

"That is beautiful, Curiosity," replied Grace. *"I am sure it will make Randall feel better."*

The soft voice spoke to Randall again. *"Yes, My dear one. We were good friends once."* A gentle hand touched Randall's throbbing head. It felt cool and comforting. It felt familiar and kind.

"Rachel," Randall muttered.

"Randall, you said you loved Me, and I cared for you. I still care for you, Randall. I still love you with an everlasting love," assured The Voice.

"Go away! Go away," yelled Randall, holding his cramping stomach, burping, and lying in a fetal position on the floor.

"Randall, you need to go to the hospital. It is time for you to remember who you are. It is time for you to account for what you've done. But don't be afraid. I will be with you."

Randall groaned and passed out.

Although Rachel continued to mourn the lost love she once

shared with Randall, she did her best to make a home for her children and Sam.

One afternoon, as Rachel was busy cutting vegetables for stew, she turned around just in time to witness Sammy punch Joelle.

"Sammy! Don't you dare hit your sister," Rachel called out, perhaps overreacting, but it was too late.

Sammy had punched and pushed his little sister down. Joelle lay on the hardwood floor on her back, unhurt, but crying crocodile tears, hoping for sympathy.

"Sammy!" his mother shouted in terror. "Go to the bedroom. I will deal with you later."

Sammy hesitated. He wanted to rebel, stamp his foot, and scowl at his mother, but then he abruptly stopped. Something made him stop and remember *that* night, and he ran to the bedroom in tears.

Rachel picked up Joelle and cradled the baby, singing softly. The toddler sniffed back tears and snuggled into her mother's chest.

"Hello," I called out as I entered the cottage. An atmosphere of tension hung over the room like a thick, dark cloud. "What's happened?" I asked.

"Hello, Sam," Rachel replied, obviously shaken. "Sammy just had a tantrum and shoved Joelle down. I overreacted. He's in the bedroom feeling sorry for himself."

"May I go talk with him?" I asked.

"Please do," replied Rachel, trying to calm Joelle and herself. "I don't think I can talk to him calmly yet."

"We men will have a talk," I said, trying to lighten the tension.

Sammy stared at the ceiling as he lay on his pallet. His hands pillowed the back of his head, and his right leg, bent at the knee, supported his left leg. Both legs rocked back and forth as a mother would rock a cradle to comfort her child.

I knocked at the door and peeped in. "May I come in?"

Sammy did not answer.

"I thought we could have a man-to-man talk. Is that okay?" I asked gently before entering the bedroom. "What happened out there today, Sammy?"

"I was bad," Sammy replied repentantly but without crying.

"Oh?" I asked, taking a seat next to Sammy on the floor. "How did that come about?"

Sammy shrugged his shoulders but would not look at me.

"You must have been upset. Is that right?"

Sammy answered with another silent shrug.

"Can you tell me what made you upset?" I prodded.

"I dunno," whispered Sammy.

"Well," I began, "it doesn't matter now. But I would like for you to remember so that you won't repeat it. Right?"

For a moment, there was silence.

"Sam, am I like my daddy?" Sammy asked in a tearful whisper.

That question coming from a little five-year-old stunned me, and for a moment, I could not speak. "Well, then, Sammy, I did not know your daddy, but I know you. And I think you are a wonderful young man and a wonderful brother. As for being like your daddy …" I paused and searched for the right words. "We are all like our parents in one way or another. Take me, for example. My mother had a beautiful voice, but I cannot sing. Pop was a fine carpenter and could build or fix almost anything. I can fix things as long as I have instructions. Pop was also a quiet man, and I take after him. Mom was loud and jolly, but that's just not me. I'm certain if you ask your mommy, she will tell you wonderful things about you. She will also tell you wonderful things about your daddy. The important thing is to find your daddy's strengths and pattern yourself after those. Forget about his weaknesses until you need to change your actions or attitude. Do you understand, Sammy?"

"I think so," said Sammy sniffing up a tear.

I asked gently, "Do you think you need to ask for forgiveness,

Sammy?"

"Ask who?" Sammy asked with a sense of dread.

"Well, first we ask God to forgive you, then we ask Joelle and your mommy to forgive you."

"I don't know how. If I ask God to forgive me, how do I know He will?" asked an apprehensive Sammy.

"Well, let's see. You are talking to me right now. Right? And we are friends. Right?" I continued.

"Yes." Sammy sat up on his pallet now.

"Well, you talk to God just like you talk to me. You talk to God the way you would talk to a good friend," I explained.

"But what do I say, Sam?" Sammy pleaded with a broken heart and misty eyes.

I thought a while, then said, "I will share with you the prayer I learned in Sunday School many years ago. You can say any words, as long as you are sincere. But these words go like this:

"Gracious and forgiving God, you are so good and kind. You are my friend. I have not been kind. I have not loved You with my whole heart. I have not loved my sister the way I want to be loved. I am sorry. Will You forgive me? I want to be Your friend. Amen."

"How do I know God will forgive me?" asked a trembling Sammy again.

"Because, Sammy, God is Love. Are you sorry for what you did, and you don't want to do it again?"

Sammy shook his head vigorously.

"You ask Him to forgive you, and when you are sincere, and because God is Love, He *will* forgive you. It's just that simple," I comforted and reassured my namesake. "Do you want to tell God you are sorry, Sammy?"

Sammy nodded his head and burst into tears.

I cuddled Sammy close to me then said, "Okay, let's talk to God. Dear gracious and forgiving God …" I began.

With that prompt, Sammy prayed, "Dear God, I have been

bad. I don't want to be bad. I did not love You, and I did not love Joelle." Again, Sammy sobbed into his small hands, then continued as only a child can. "God, forgive me. I want to be your friend. I'm Sam, but Mommy calls me Sammy."

When the child finished his prayer, Sammy stood and grabbed me around the neck in a baby bear hug.

"All better?" I asked.

"Yes. God forgives me, I know He does 'cause I can feel it in here," Sammy said, pointing to his heart.

"Do you want to apologize to Joelle and Mommy?" I prodded.

"Yes, I do," said a lighter-hearted Sammy. "Do you think Mommy will forgive me?"

"If God forgives you, I am sure Mommy will forgive you, too. You see, sometimes Mommy has to ask God for forgiveness, just like you and me," I assured Sammy.

"Mommy has to ask God for forgiveness?"

"Yes, sir. We all do. And you know what?"

"What?" Sammy asked.

I hugged my namesake closer and said, "God always forgives."

Over several days, Sammy was a happier child again. However, he still pondered whether he was bad like his daddy.

"Poor little boy," I observed. "That is a lot for a child to bear."

"It is a lot for any of us to bear," agreed Rachel, "but it's so comforting that God does forgive us. I think Sammy has learned that, too."

"By the way, Rachel, I saw Doc Proctor at the grocery store today," I began gently. "Doc said he admitted a man to the hospital last night. From the description Doc gave, this man sounds like the man we bumped into at the grocery store. Your husband."

Rachel tensed and gasped, then drew away.

I continued. "I think you need to go see him."

Rachel sat stunned, then shook her head and said again and

again, "No, No, No."

"Rachel," I continued softly, "I must admit, I went to the hospital today and spoke with him. Although I never knew him before, he said he is sorry for what he put you through. His remorse sounds genuine."

"I can't. I can't," Rachel said, weeping and turning away from me. "I'll go with you if you like," I offered. "Go talk with him, Rachel. Give him a chance to ask your forgiveness. Besides, it will be a good example for Sammy. I will see if Mrs. Cooper will sit with Joelle."

The following morning was excruciating.

As we walked to the hospital, Rachel could hardly speak. I could only imagine the questions that must have whirled in her head. She told me she had conflicting emotions about seeing Randall. Did she still love him the way she did when they first married? Would the hurt he caused overwhelm her? Would she be able to forgive him? Would she be able to forgive herself? Most of all, would God forgive her?

We stood in the elevator together.

"Run! Run! Run," the elevator motor seemed to say to Rachel, and that's all she could think at that moment. She squeezed Sammy's hand, hoping for an escape. Conflicting thoughts drug her spirit down as she willed her trembling legs to move, then she took the first brave step off the fourth-floor elevator. Her shoulders were tight, and her feet were hesitant and heavy with fear. Although lighting in the corridor was bright, the long dark passage ahead to room four-twenty-five looked foreboding and menacing. As if in a slow-motion nightmare, Rachel hesitated then reached out a trembling hand to touch the door.

Just as Rachel's hand touched the door, a nurse came out of the intensive care unit. As the door started to close, Rachel stepped into the dark room. She gasped and stepped back, but there was no escape. The shock of seeing Randall lying pale and silent in the hospital bed nearly sent her to her knees. Ventilator tubes protruded from his throat under his chin. A heart monitor beeped, and tubes and other pieces of medical equipment covered his body. The sounds of hospital machines counting down life's seconds and the smell of death sent shivers over Rachel's body. Randall looked old. Although poison yellowed his skin with jaundice, he looked pallid. This man did not look like the man she once loved.

l

It was evident that fear and a little hate gripped Rachel's heart in their poison talons. I could see she wanted to turn and run, but Sammy held her back.

"Daddy? Daddy, it's me, Sammy," whispered the brave five-year-old.

Randall's eyes opened slowly. Thin slits revealed yellow eyes coursed with red veins, and the dying man held out his hand to his son. "Sammy. My son," Randall's voice labored through the ventilator's rhythm.

"Daddy. Mommy is here," Sammy said, pulling his mother close to the bed.

It took all her willpower, but Rachel finally spoke. "Hello, Randall."

"Rachel. I thought you would not come," wheezed Randall.

"I came," is all she could utter.

"Rachel, I must tell you," began Randall, then coughed, dislodging a mass of thick congestion. She tried to stop him. "No, darling, I must tell you how sorry I am. Alcohol poisoned my brain and changed me. Please believe me, in my right mind, I would never hurt you or the kids. Can you forgive me? Will you forgive me?"

"I ...I ...," Rachel stammered.

"I had a Visitor last night," Randall continued, forgetting that it had been nearly eight nights ago. "I think it was God. He was gentle and loving. He said He still loved me. I know I don't deserve it. How can He love me after the way I treated you?"

"God talked to you, Daddy?" asked an astonished Sammy. "I talked to God, too, Daddy. I asked God to forgive me for pushing Joelle like you pushed Mommy. And you know what? God forgave me."

So touched by his young son's words, Randall could not speak for a moment. Then through his wheezing breath and tears of love and remorse, he said, "I know, Sammy. God forgave me, too."

"How do you know God forgave you, Daddy?"

"I feel different in here," Randall said, touching his heart with a thin, jaundice-stained hand restrained by an I.V..

"Me, too!" exclaimed Sammy.

"Do you think Mommy will forgive me, Sammy?" asked a repentant Randall.

"Our friend, Sam, told me God is Love, and that sometimes Mommy has to ask God to forgive her. My friend said if God forgives Mommy, she should forgive you, too," said the five-year-old in his child-like faith.

"Rachel?" Randall coughed and choked. "Will you forgive me?" He reached his tube-laden hand out to his wife.

Rachel paused. Her next words were halting but then tumbled from her lips as cleansing water tumbles over river rocks. However, she never touched Randall. "I forgive you, Randall. You get well so that you can come home."

"No, Rachel," Randall whispered in a failing voice. "I will not get well, but I will go Home."

Rachel let those words wash over her heart, releasing a flood of tears. "Oh, Randall, my dearest, I love you," she said, falling onto his chest.

"I love you, too, Rachel," Randall admitted, stroking her golden hair. "You are a good wife. I don't deserve you." Randall stopped to catch his breath, coughed, and continued. "Thank you for loving me, Rachel. Thank you for your forgiveness."

Rachel and Sammy stayed with Randall while he slept. When a nurse came to take Randall's dying vital signs, I entered quietly and stood by Rachel's side. I touched her elbow and said, "Come, Rachel, we must go home."

As she exited the hospital's revolving doors, the morning sun shone bright as if radiating through her weary heart, and she heard a train whistle in the distance. Shading her strained eyes from the sun that glinted off the snow, she took a breath and squeezed Sammy's hand.

"I hear a train, Mommy," exclaimed her son with joy.

"Yes, sweetie. I hear it, too."

"Are you afraid anymore, Mommy?"

"No, sweetie. I'm not afraid. Are you?"

"No, Mommy. I like it when the train talks to me."

"The train talks to you?" Rachel asked in astonishment. "What does the train say to you?"

"It says nice things. It says, '*I love you, Sammy. I will keep you safe.*'"

"I think those are beautiful words, Sammy. God does keep us safe, and we have a little home. I don't know for how long. But let's enjoy it while we can."

The train whistle sounded again in the distance as it traveled on the outskirts of town.

"Thank you, Train," Sammy almost yelled. "I love You, too."

Rachel didn't understand.

Chapter 6

Rest in the LORD, and wait patiently for him ...
Psalm 37:7

When we left the hospital, Rachel, Sammy, and I walked down the dirt road in silence, but the silence was not uncomfortable. Instead, we walked as dear friends, eager for the sweet oasis of the little porter's cabin.

Finally, in a gesture as protector, I turned to Rachel and said, "Rachel, why don't you and Sammy go on ahead to the cabin? I will stop and pick up Joelle from Mrs. Cooper. You need to rest."

"Thank you, Sam. I think a rest would be nice. I would enjoy lying on the cool sheets and let the peace and quiet of the cabin swaddle me."

"Me, too, Mommy?"

"Yes, my sweet. We will both take a nap together."

"Bye, Sam," my little namesake called back to me.

"Bye, Sammy. Take good care of Mommy."

I stood for a moment, watching this brave woman and her son walk on stress-heavy legs. The dust of the dirt road billowed about their feet, looking as if they were walking on soft clouds to Heaven.

"Thank you, Father. Surround Rachel in Your arms of Love and let her rest."

When Rachel and Sammy were out of sight, I turned my attention back to picking up Joelle.

As I walked through the mahogany double doors of Mr. Cooper's grocery store, the little bell tinkled. I could not help but believe this gay tinkling sound was the beginning of a new chapter in our lives.

"Hello, Sam," Mrs. Cooper greeted me. "Are you here to pick up …" but she was interrupted before she could finish her question.

"Sam! Sam!" the toddler squealed.

"… Joelle?" Mrs. Cooper laughed and finished her question.

"Yes, ma'am."

"Sam. See," Joelle called, dragging me to the back room where she was playing. "Book, Sam. Read?"

"You have that book at home, sweetie. Can I read it to you when we get home? Why don't you pick up the toys and put them away?"

Joelle toddled from toy to toy, and when her arms were full, she went to the toy box and dumped them in with unrestrained noise. Then she went back to find the baby doll. She cuddled and rocked the baby and tippy-toed to the toy box, kissed the doll, and gently laid her down. *What a loving mommy*, I mused. *She has a good role model.*

"Here is Joelle's bag, Sam. She is as good as gold," said Mrs. Cooper as she kissed Joelle goodbye.

"Thank you, Mrs. Cooper. I appreciate your watching her for us. See you Sunday."

"Goodbye, Sam. Give my love to Rachel and Sammy."

"Home?"

"Yes, baby girl. We'll go home now. Mommy and Sammy are taking a nap, so we must be quiet."

"Nap!"

"Okay, sweetie. It has been a long day for everyone."

When Joelle and I walked into the cabin, the sweet fragrance of ancient timbers greeted us, and the clock on the mantle chimed 3 o' clock. There was no happy noise to greet us. I peeped into the second bedroom to find Rachel and Sammy snuggled up together with just a crisp white sheet covering their bodies.

In the early part of the twentieth century, hardwood was the material of choice to frame a porter's cabin. As I stood in the doorway of the tiny bedroom, taking in this tranquil scene, the soft, vintage fragrance of heart pine wafted over me, bathing my heart and soul with that romantic fragrance of the railroad. Sixteen-inch pine timbers made a solid structure and floor, and swinging wooden shutters covered the sparce windowpanes to keep out the cold.

The west-facing window of the second bedroom stood open, letting in the clean, spring air. Outside, new green leaves of the sycamore tree danced in the March breeze, and the soft, pointed leaves made the afternoon sunlight twinkle throughout the tiny bedroom and over the beautiful dreamers. Rachel stirred and pulled the clean sheet over Sammy's shoulders, then drifted back into her own dreams.

As I watched her sleeping eyes flutter, I whispered, "I hope they are happy dreams, Rachel. I hope you will find those dreams in the little cabin."

Joelle and I found milk and graham crackers in the kitchen and settled in the overstuffed second-hand chair to read.

"The end," I said to Joelle, as I finished reading the book. "How about you and me make dinner for Mommy and Sammy?"

"Dinner? Milk?"

"Yes, sweet pea, you can have milk for dinner, and Mommy can have hamburger soup and biscuits."

"Biscuits!" cried the sweet baby girl.

As I expected, the fragrance of hamburger and vegetable soup and hot biscuits woke Rachel, and she stumbled into the kitchen, mumbling her apologies. Her golden hair was mussed, and her face bore creases from crisp sheets. She was beautiful.

"Well, hello, sleeping beauty. Did you rest well?"

"Yes, I did. Thank you, Sam. I'm sorry I slept so long. You have dinner ready." Rachel lamented as she brushed the golden strands of hair from her eyes.

"Your feast, ma'am," I quipped as I pulled out the sturdiest ladder-back chair for her. "Do you want me to get Sammy up?"

"Yes, please, or he will not sleep tonight."

No sooner had the words left her mouth than Sammy shuffled in with bare feet and snuggled into Rachel's arms. I didn't mind that Sammy ignored me. It thrilled my heart watching the mother and son in this tender moment.

I ladled the hot soup into brown glazed pottery crocks and set out the hot buttery biscuits like my mother taught me. Rachel and I had coffee while the children each had milk.

"Sammy, would you like to say our blessing?" I asked.

A still sleepy Sammy shook his head.

"Okay. Let's pray. Thank You, Lord, for this day, for Your strength, and wisdom. Thank You for bringing us back to the cabin safely and for warm soup and biscuits. In Jesus's name. Amen."

Sammy, finally a little more awake, repeated, "Amen."

My heart thrilled as I watched Rachel and the children devour their soup. Did I dare to say, I watched my family? No. Not yet.

It was too soon. *Thank you, Lord, for this time we have together. Help us to watch and listen as you direct us in Your will.*

It was two weeks later on a Wednesday that Rachel walked to the school to pick up Sammy. As I sat reading and Joelle played around my feet and chattered to her baby doll, the screen door burst open, and Sammy rushed in from school. Tears streamed down his dirty face, running rivers of mud on his cheeks and down his neck. Before I could speak to him, the Kindergartener slammed the door to the bedroom where he slept.

I looked at Rachel in surprise. "What's wrong?" I asked.

"You better talk to him. I think this is a man-to-man thing," Rachel replied.

"What's up, Sammy-man?" I asked the distraught little boy. I expected Sammy to burst forth with a detailed explanation as usual but not this time. I had to move slowly and gently to find out what bothered my Sammy-man.

At last, when he cried out most of his tears, he turned his head to me and snuffled. "The kids at school say you are a freak."

"Oh? And what did you say?"

In a baby-gruff tone of defending his best friend, Sammy blurted, "I told them you are a war hero!"

"Thank you, Sammy," I said rubbing his tense little back.

"And they said that you are not my daddy," Sammy buried his head in his mother's pillow and sobbed.

It took several minutes for the right words to come to me to console Sammy. "Well, Sammy, that's true. I am not your real daddy, but I would like to be. I would love to have a son just like you. You are brave and kind and honest. Those are valuable traits of a wonderful son. Maybe one day God will make it so that I can be your real daddy, and you can be my real son."

The sobbing and snuffling quieted, and Sammy sat up and asked, "Really?"

"I hope so. We will have to ask God and then wait to see what He will do. Do you want to pray with me about it?"

"Yes, sir," Sammy whispered through his last tear.

I picked up my Sammy-man and held him on my lap, and we prayed together. "Most gracious and loving God, you know the prayers of our hearts even before we say them. Father, God, comfort Sammy. Give him the assurance that You are in control of all things. Thank you that Sammy is brave and kind and honest. A boy like that, I would love to call my real son. Amen."

Then, to my surprise, Sammy prayed, "God, will You make Sam my real daddy? I love him. Amen."

We ended our prayer with a daddy-bear and baby-bear hug.

"Does anyone want milk and cookies?" we heard Sammy's mommy call from the kitchen.

"I do!" we answered in unison.

When it came time to go to bed, Rachel fluffed up the pallet on the floor for Sammy and tucked Joelle in the bed next to her. I had just finished my bath, threw on my bathrobe, and hopped on one foot to my room. When I pull down the sheets, the hair on the back of my neck stood on end. When I looked up, I saw two little eyes staring at the stump of my amputated foot. Sammy said nothing, he just stood and stared, then smiled before turning and going back to his pallet.

As I thought about that private moment Sammy and I shared, I felt accepted. There were no questions, no shocked gasps, just acceptance, and that was that.

After everyone was in their respective rooms and the lights were out, I could hear Rachel's muffled crying. She cried and prayed, then cried again. Her prayers were not only for herself, her children, and Randall, but they were for me. What did I do to deserve the prayers of such a gentle woman?

Chapter 7

... as long as he sought the Lord, God made him to prosper. 2 Chronicles 26:5b

Another warm June Monday morning brought hot weather to Kentucky replete with a plethora of songbirds, black flies, mosquitoes, and fresh fruit, and, of course, fruit flies.

Mr. Meadows owned the field adjacent to the dirt road leading into Florence where he grew peaches, blueberries, and rhubarb. Wild blackberries also grew along the fence row. However, those blackberries held no fascination for me, for I remembered hearing stories of rattlesnakes waiting in the blackberry brambles for their prey.

Summer in Florence, Kentucky also brought armies of school weary children, ready for summer vacation.

Oh, there was another thing summer brought to Florence, Kentucky.

"Get out of my room!"

"Wa-a-a-a!"

"Mommy! Mommy, Joelle took my best Lego! Get out of my room!"

Shrill screams from a not so dainty baby girl filled the air of the small cabin.

"Mama!"

On those occasions, I usually found an errand to run in town and took Mr. Sammy with me to give Rachel a break. It was during those times that I enjoyed Sammy's company and our man-to-man talks.

This day was no exception. Sammy found so many wonderful things along the road, things that I overlooked or considered so common that they did not warrant a special look. But for Sammy, everything was special.

"Look at that giant grasshopper, Sam. His green and red stripes are so big. He must be a foot long. Sure wish I had a mason jar."

"You know, Sammy, if you try to catch a grasshopper, he will puke brown juice on you."

"Eww. What if I don't grab him very hard."

"Well, you know, Sammy, all of God's creatures have a job to do, just like you and me."

"What kind of job do grasshoppers have, Sam?"

"Well, let's see," I said, stalling for time to develop the best reply for a little boy. "Grasshoppers must have babies who need food. The daddy grasshopper hops around all day searching for the best patches of food. Then he has to hop all the way home to tell his family."

"Wow! I never thought about that 'afore."

"You wouldn't want to keep daddy grasshopper from feeding his family, would you?"

"I guess not," the lad said thoughtfully. "Have you ever caught bugs, Sam?"

"Oh, a time or two, but my mom always made me turn them loose."

"Women just don't know how to have fun, do they?"

I laughed, and Sammy kicked at a clump of dirt, and we walked quietly for a time.

Then, a little further down the road, Sammy's demeanor changed when he remembered penny candy waiting for him at the grocery store. His eyes twinkled, and he cheered, "Do you think Mrs. Cooper has any jaw breakers?"

With the prospects of jaw breakers, our steps quickened. Sammy lost all thought of catching grasshoppers and focused on heading for the grocery store, and I tried to keep up with a now six-year-old.

I had to chuckle when we reached the grocery store. Sammy was out of breath, but he still made quick work of putting his whole weight behind the heavy wooden door, then stepping back to let me enter.

Mrs. Cooper was busy behind the check-out counter installing a new roll of tape into her adding machine.

"Good morning, Mrs. Cooper."

"Good morning, Sam. And here's Sammy primed and ready for summer vacation. Hello, Sammy. Are you going to Vacation Bible School next week? I'm teaching your age group. It will be fun."

"Hello, Mrs. Cooper," Sammy answered politely while surveying the massive glass-encased mahogany counter for candy.

"I just got in a fresh supply of penny candies, Sammy. Do you want to have a look?"

This news left Sammy breathless, but he managed to say, "Yes, ma'am."

"Come over here, then."

Not everyone received an invitation to go behind the counter for a private glimpse of the glorious penny candies. I watched as Sammy's eyes widened and his tongue worked overtime, licking his lips.

"You may have two pieces, Sammy. Any two pieces you want," instructed Mrs. Cooper, trying to hide her laughter.

Sammy forgot about jaw breakers when he saw bright red fire balls. A thread of drool escaped from between his lips at the anticipation of the stinging sweet candy. For his second piece, and as an afterthought, he chose a tootsie roll. "Thank you, Mrs. Cooper."

"You are very welcome, Sammy. You are such a polite young man. It's a joy to share my candy with you."

"Uh huh," was all Sammy could manage, already savoring

the red fire ball.

Then Mrs. Cooper turned to me. "And what can I do for you Sam?"

"I have a list, Mrs. Cooper," I said, handing it to her. "I also have another errand to run. Can I pick up these items on my way back?"

"Certainly, Sam. I'll have them waiting for you."

"Thank you, Mrs. Cooper. Okay, Sammy-man. Let's hit the road. We have to go to the bank."

On the short walk to the bank, Sammy started to ask a question, but as he did, the fire ball, now much smaller and no longer red but white, shot over his red stained teeth and fell into the dirt. Sammy mourned the unfinished fire ball for about two seconds before tearing into the tootsie roll.

When we arrived at the bank, Sammy shoved the last of the tootsie roll into his mouth and licked his fingers. Then, he pushed on the heavy glass door. I shook my head in dismay, then remembered what it was like to be six. If Ken Furman, the bank manager needed Sammy's fingerprints, he would have a good set on the door. I chuckled and entered, acknowledging Sammy's efforts.

As Sammy and I walked through the door, a soft breeze of cool air invited us in. I didn't know what there was about a bank that smelled so good. It was like the drugstore, but with its own essence. The drugstore smelled of a pleasant combination of body fragrances, iodine bandages, and Life Boy soap. The bank had none of those, so maybe it was all that money—some crisp and fresh from the Mint, but mostly old and worn with their own stories to tell.

As soon as Ken saw Sammy and me, he left his grand executive desk enclosed behind glass windows and hurried down the stairs to greet us. Unlike the first time we met, Ken did not stare and wince but grabbed my stumpy right hand in a firm greeting. "Hello, there, Sam."

"Hello, Ken. You remember Sammy?"

"Sure do. Hello, Sammy," Ken Furman said, shaking Sammy's

hand without reacting to the sticky tootsie roll fingers. "It's good to see you again. Have you come in to make a deposit, Sammy?" Ken quipped.

"No, sir. But I think Daddy Sam has some money."

"Well then," Ken chuckled, "Sammy, why don't you go over to Miss Evelyn's window and ask for a bunch of pennies and paper wrappers?" Ken motioned to Evelyn Morgan, the senior teller.

Evelyn knew exactly how to entertain little ones while the grownups talked business. She escorted Sammy to a table and a small red wooden chair in the safe deposit vault and gave him a cloth bag full of pennies. The bag, once white, was now dirty from holding years of coins.

"Sammy, can you put fifty pennies in this wrapper and seal it up tight? Maybe you will find a 'steely.' Here is another wrapper."

"What's a steely?" Sammy asked wide-eyed.

"Daddy Sam, is it?" Ken asked, turning back to me with a twinkle in his eye. There was no condemnation there, only admiration, for Ken knew of Rachel's situation and of my giving her and the children a safe place to live.

"Yes, Ken. Can you believe it? It makes my heart glow every time I hear those words. I just wish they were really my family."

Sensing my emotion, Ken quickly changed the subject and asked, "What can I do for you, Sam? Let's go into my office and visit."

As Ken sat in his executive chair, the springs of the leather, brass studded chair sounded a welcoming squeak and emitted a clean, leather scent. Ken motioned for me to take a seat. The matching, thick brown leather of the executive guest chair was cool and comfortable. When I sat, it felt like an old friend embracing my entire body.

Ken exhaled and continued, "What's on your mind, Sam?"

"Well, Ken, I saw in the newspaper this morning a list of properties that the bank foreclosed on. I am especially interested in one piece of property, the …"

"The Randall Crews property?"

"Yes. How did you guess?"

"I have eyes," Ken grinned. "You know, Sam, that old single wide on the property isn't worth much. I'm not even sure you could call it livable. What are you planning to do with it?"

"I'm not sure, Ken. I'm leaving my options open, waiting on the Lord to let me know what to do next. I just thought it would be good property to have for the future."

"Do you think she will want to live on that property?" Ken asked.

"Well, if we have many mornings like this morning, she might just send the children off to live there," I laughed.

"Bad morning?" Ken asked.

"Normal."

"I understand, Sam. When my children were small, I had my share of normal mornings, too." Ken paused, then called his assistant on the intercom. "Miss Riley?"

"Yes, sir."

"Will you please bring in the list of properties the bank holds?"

When Miss Riley brought the thick manilla folder, I couldn't help but stare at its bulk.

"Okay, Sam. Let's see what we have that you might be interested in," Ken said, laying out property descriptions and photos.

"I didn't know there were so many."

"Remember, Sam, the bank holds mortgage loans from over the entire county. You will find an assortment of properties from retail to office space, to farm parcels to single family homes. Here. Here is a picture of the Randall Crews property."

I tried not to gasp when I saw the photo of the single wide trailer home in disrepair. "I can't believe Rachel lived in that, Ken. I want her to have something better."

"I know you do, Sam. And I believe you will. Do you want to take out a loan or pay cash?"

"What is your asking price?"

"The bank's investment in the five acres of land is $200, the trailer home was worth the same when it was new. Today, you could pick up the land and what's left of the trailer home for $250 if you pay it off today. Do you want to pay it off or take out a mortgage?'

"I'll pay cash."

"Miss Riley, will you come in, please, and bring the Randall Crews property file?"

"It's still on your desk, sir."

"Oh, yes, so it is. Thank you, Miss Riley." Turning to Sam, Ken continued shuffling through folders on his desk. "Seems someone else was here today inquiring about this property."

"What was that you said? Someone else was looking at that property?"

"Yes. I'm afraid I cannot divulge any information about that, but it's a moot point because he could not come up with the money."

"Oh," I said contemplatively, then continued. "You know, Ken, since I will probably not find a regular job in this area, let me talk to the Lord about also investing in some of your other properties."

"Any time, Sam. I think I see how your mind is working. Just remember not to be too overly generous."

Just as I was completing the paperwork, Sammy came running in to the manager's office. "Daddy Sam! Look!" Sammy displayed a wrapper of pennies in each little hand, still sticky with tootsie roll.

"Wow! That's a lot of pennies. How much do you have there?"

"A *hundert*. There's fifty pennies in this one, and fifty pennies in that one," exclaimed Sammy.

"Do you know how many dollars that is, Sammy?" asked Ken Furman.

"Uh?"

"You have your first dollar there, young man. Would you like to make a deposit?"

"No way! I'm giving these to Mommy."

"Oh, Ken, I almost forgot. I want to cash this VA check, keep out $100 and deposit the rest."

"I'll be right back, Sam." Ken went to the teller's window himself to cash Sam's check. When he returned, Ken had a worried look on his face and seemed to be a shade paler.

"Here you are, Sam," Ken said, handing the envelope of cash and deposit slip to me. "Sam, I don't mean to be an alarmist, but that man who was here earlier looking at the Crews property is still out in the waiting area. I thought he had gone."

"That's not unusual, is it, Ken?"

"Usually, I would say not, but this man looks as if he has no business being in a bank. I don't mean to stereotype, but this man is wearing dirty clothes, smells like an outhouse, and needs a haircut and shave. The hair on the back of my neck tells me he is up to no good. Watch yourself, Sam," Ken advised his friend.

On the walk home, my namesake and I engaged in a more serious man-to-man talk.

"These pennies are really heavy," Sammy hinted.

"Burning a hole in your pocket already?"

"Huh? What can Mommy buy with so much money?" asked Sammy.

"I imagine she can buy a whole lot of love."

"I'd rather have roller skates," added Sammy in six-year-old seriousness.

"Where are you going to roller skate?"

"You can take me to town, of course, and I can roller skate on the sidewalks," chirped Sammy.

"Hmmm."

When we men arrived home, Sammy ran inside the cottage, slamming the door. "Mommy! Look what I got!"

"Shhh," whispered Rachel with a slender finger to her lips. "Joelle is down for her nap. What is this?" Rachel asked, admiring Sammy's handiwork.

"It's a *hundert* pennies Miss Evelyn gave me at the bank."

"Did you put all those pennies in that wrapper all by yourself?" asked a proud Rachel.

"Uh huh."

Rachel raised her eyebrow and wrinkled her nose questioningly.

"Yes, ma'am." Sammy replied obediently. "Me and Daddy Sam went to the grocery store. I got a red hot and a tootsie roll. Daddy Sam just got groceries. Then we went to the bank. That's where Miss Evelyn gave me the pennies. I got to sit in the vault and everything!"

"It sounds like you men had a whirling good time," Rachel said with a wink. "What have you there?" she asked me, peeking into the grocery bag.

"Oh, the usual."

Rachel took out a package of del monte steak, a couple of baking potatoes, and a package of fresh green beans. "This doesn't look like 'just the usual' I've seen around here."

"I thought you needed a little 'not so usual.' You've had a hard day, Rachel."

"What's the occasion?" Rachel asked, trying not to be ungrateful.

"Today we saw a big grasshopper. Sammy got to go behind the counter to look at all the penny candy, and Sammy called me Daddy Sam, and I cashed a check," I said, handing the cash to Rachel, "so I'm celebrating. Oh, yes. I bought some property."

Chapter 8

When the righteous are in authority,
the people rejoice ...Proverbs 29:2

It had been a month since I last visited the bank and bought the Randall Crews property. I had already forgotten Ken's concern and advice, "Watch yourself, Sam." That was in June. Today was July 15th.

"That was a delicious lunch, Rachel. Thank you." I rubbed my full belly and exhaled a satisfied sigh.

"You're welcome, Sam. Sammy, would you like this last apple wedge?"

"Will you peel it for me?"

"Peel it for you?" Rachel asked. "You've already eaten three unpeeled wedges."

"Yes, but I want this one peeled," pleaded Sammy.

"Okay. Your wish is my command," Rachel conceded and went to the kitchen. "Sam, would you like another piece of apple?" Rachel called.

"No thank you, Rachel. I couldn't eat another bite."

When Rachel returned to the small dining area, Sammy greedily reached for the apple wedge before leaving the table.

"Rachel, I need to go into town. Do you want me to take the children?"

"Oh, boy!" shouted Sammy with visions of penny candy in his head.

"That would be wonderful, Sam. Thank you. I want to mop and wax the floors. They should be dry by the time you get home."

"Come on young 'uns. We'll go to town."

I picked up Joelle and started for the door with Sammy.

"Bye, Mommy!" Sammy shouted with a mouth full of apple before running out the screen door, letting it close with a slam.

Joelle just grinned and waved, looking over Sam's shoulder.

Rachel tied up her golden hair in a black and red bandana and grabbed her pail, mop, and dust rag. As she worked, she sang, "To God Be The Glory." The fragrance of pine filled the small cabin, and everything that could shine, gleamed.

As her usual cleaning pattern moved into the kitchen, she stopped to straighten the familiar porcelain plaque she had hung on the wall above the gas range. On a whim, Sam had bought that plaque for her at the dime store, and she had been so proud of the inexpensive plaque painted with pastel flowers. Now, every day, it reminded her about how blessed she was and how safe she felt in this cabin with Sam. She smiled to herself when she read the words again, "Bless This House."

Rachel's next thought was of Randall. It did not happen immediately, but after Randall died, Rachel felt that those years of fear and sadness were in the distant past. Yet, fear and anxiety still plagued her. Wasn't she happy with Sam and the children? Yes, she had not been this happy in a long time, but those old memories still filled her heart and would not let her go.

Although Rachel could not see or hear the angels, she felt their soothing presence. The angels played around her, darting over her shoulders and around her feet, spreading their energies of courage, hope, joy, and peace.

Rachel had just finished mopping the kitchen floor and threw the dirty water out the back porch, then turned the pail upside down on the floor, when there was a knock at the front door.

As if sending a warning to Rachel, the cicadas buzzed outside in a cacophony of sound in the humid July air. But Rachel thought nothing of it.

The angel, Curiosity, flew from the kitchen to the living room window to peep out. Curiosity shrieked, *"Courage! Don't let Rachel open the door."*

Remembering God's warning that the angels were not to interfere with people's decisions, Courage was helpless to stop Rachel.

Rachel opened the living room door and walked onto the porch, still carrying her wet mop, and wiping her hands on her apron. "Yes, may I help you?"

"Well, hello there, sweet thang," said a stranger in a much too familiar tone.

"Excuse me?"

"Sir! Sir!" called Hope. *"Sir, we need You."*

At that moment, Hope heard the sound of the 11 o' clock train's whistle in the distance. The train was lumbering at a normal speed. Hope and Courage continued to listen and called again, *"Sir, please hurry,"* yet there was still no urgency in the train's movement.

"Sir! Hurry, Sir!" cried Hope.

"You don't remember me?"

"No. Should I?" Rachel replied, reaching for the metal hook, blackened from age, and placed it into the corresponding eye of the screen door. She didn't like the looks or feel of this stranger at the door, and she was grateful for the latch, no matter how blackened and old.

"I'm Austin. Austin Pierce. You know, Randall's pal from the gas station," Austin announced, trying to be charming.

I was at the bank discussing investments with Ken Furman in his executive office when I heard the train's whistle. Although I had no other appointment in town, something urged me to turn the clock on Ken's desk to read the time.

"Eleven o'clock. Ken, I'm sorry, but I have to go. Can we discuss this further another time?"

"Of course, Sam. Is something wrong?" my friend asked.

"I just heard a train whistle and need to go home. I know it sounds strange, but the train whistle seems to always alert me to trouble. The whistle speaks to me."

"Hearing a train whistle in Florence is not unusual, Sam."

"I know, Ken. I don't always hear the trains in Florence, but when I do, I pay attention. I'm afraid something might be wrong. I have to go home."

In an uncharacteristic move, I stood quickly and turned to leave, nearly knocking over the heavy leather chair. Ken stood with me and voiced his concern.

"Let me call the sheriff for you, Sam. At least he can give you a ride to your house and check on things. I'll call Mrs. Cooper to come get the children."

"Thank you, Ken. You're a true friend."

"I'm sorry. No, I don't remember, and Randall is dead," Rachel said in a stiff voice.

"Yes, I heard. Too bad. That's why I'm here. Randall and me, we had a pact that if anything happened to either of us, the other one would take care of his family," Austin lied.

Even through the screen door, Rachel smelled Austin's pungent body odor and sour breath of stale beer. Dirt and urine soiled his clothes, and he needed a shave. He certainly did not look like someone Rachel would want to know.

"Oh, excuse my appearance. I just left work," Austin lied again. "Can I come in?"

"No."

"Now that's not being very friendly, ma'am. I just come to take care of you is all."

"As you can see, I don't need taking care of," Rachel retorted, lifting her mop in a defensive manner.

"Oh, ma'am. I think you do. Why don't you let me in, and I'll show you how I can take care of a lady real good." Austin grinned, showing his yellowing teeth and brown gums stained from tobacco juice.

"Go away. Please go away," Rachel screamed and went inside. With fear running cold in her veins, she slammed the living room door and turned the dead bolt lock.

So shaken by this encounter, Rachel could only stand in the middle of the living room, leaning on her mop, breathing shallow rapid breaths. Fear, and not a little disgust, paralyzed her body and mind.

Faith and Hope stayed close by Rachel's side while Courage flew to the front door and back to Rachel, then back to the door again.

The noise of the pail falling down the steps shocked Rachel's mind back to the present, and her blood chilled when she remembered that she had left the back door open. She ran to the kitchen. However, by the stench that overpowered the sweet pine scent of her clean kitchen, she knew that the stranger was already inside.

"No! No! No!" she screamed. "Go away. I don't know you, and I don't want you here."

"Sir! Sir!" Courage called again while Faith sat on Rachel's shoulder. Serenity and Peace hovered about Rachel, trying to bathe her with their gemstone energies of courage and peace.

It was too late. Austin was in the kitchen, moving toward her with hungry, evil-looking eyes.

"Aw come on, sweet thang. Randall told me what fun you can be, and I just want to keep my end of the bargain."

"I said no!"

"And I said yes," Austin snarled as he snatched Rachel by the waist, digging his grimy fingers into her flesh through her thin cotton dress. He pressed his filthy body against hers, but she was too repulsed to scream. She just held her breath.

Courage and Hope tried to defuse the assault, but God the Father's admonition not to interfere kept them from releasing their full power over Austin. So, all the angels could do was to flutter around Rachel, showering her with calming energy.

With her body bent away from his stench, Austin forced Rachel to walk backward, trapping her against a counter.

"I've got a cute little trailer just waiting for us. You know where it is. It's the one you and that no account Randall lived in together. Now it's mine, and you're mine. We can make a sweet little love nest," Austin said, breathing his foul breath into Rachel's face.

"Sir! Where are You?" a desperate Serenity called to God the Father as she joined her sister angels in their protection of Rachel.

"I am here, My dears. I am in control," replied God the Father. *"Although the situation might seem grim, this is My plan for Rachel. I will not let harm come to her. Wait and see."*

Austin forced his sour mouth over hers, as Rachel fought desperately, trying to keep him from taking control of her body, starting with her lips. The taste of Austin's stale beer and tobacco mouth caused her to gag and choke up bile.

When Austin nuzzled Rachel's neck, his steel-like stubble dug into her neck and chest, adding additional pain. Again, he breathed his foul breath in her face as he ripped the top of her dress, searching greedily for her soft warm flesh. His hands were coarse and uncaring. In shock, she gasped with pain when his calloused flesh and dirty fingernails touched her.

The angels, though believing the words of God the Father, cringed in disbelief at the vicious attack. They continued to flutter and hover over Rachel, while still holding themselves back, as God commanded.

Rachel strained without success to push Austin away. "Stop! Let me go! Get away from me! Why are you doing this to me?" She thrashed and screamed. "Why do men like you do this to women?"

"Because I want you, and I take what I want," Austin spat in his deranged logic. "Now that your tramp of a husband is gone, I am taking possession of what I want," he growled with another vicious forced kiss, sour and repulsive.

Rachel fought to fend off her maniac attacker while trying to grip her now ripped cotton dress. Desperately, she grappled over the kitchen counter that entrapped her, searching for something to protect herself. Shock began to cloud her thoughts, vision, and hearing, yet she still fought with her attacker.

"Remember Sammy. Remember Sammy's apple," shouted Courage.

Rachel's hand frantically felt the top of the counter. After several attempts, her hand closed around a familiar object, and she closed her eyes as tight as she could.

Reeling in the euphoria of his impending conquest, Austin loosened his grip to kiss the revealed flesh of Rachel's shoulders. In that moment, Rachel released her arm and swung with as much force as she could. The resistance of the blade ripping through Austin's shoulder sickened her further. The sound and feel was not unlike a blade splitting through a watermelon.

Austin released his grasp and yelled in pain, spewing foul words, breath, and sputum over Rachel.

When she opened her eyes, she saw her favorite butcher knife, the very one she had peeled Sammy's apple with, lodged in Austin's shoulder. Then Rachel saw the look of disbelief, pain, and hatred on Austin's face, and the butcher knife protruding from his chest.

Only the wooden handle and copious amounts of blood were visible.

Strengthened only by God's Spirit, Rachel reacted with more courage and tenacity than she ever had before. "Get out! Get out of my house!" Rachel screamed and pushed Austin toward the door. When she was with Randall, Rachel would never have had the guts to say those words or act with such defiance, but now, years of anger exploded, and she reacted.

Austin, gripped in pain and delirium, stumbled, then his body spun, slamming his chest into the wall, burying the blade of the knife still further into his chest. He yelled and spouted obscenities as the searing pain intensified.

Rachel searched and grasped blindly for another weapon. In her terror, her clawing fingers upset the porcelain plaque she had hung on the wall above the gas range. The plaque swung precariously on its nail and tinkled against the cast iron skillet hanging next to it. She didn't think of the comforting words printed on the beautiful plaque, instead her searching fingers grabbed the cast iron skillet, and in one motion, she threw it. The heavy skillet hit Austin's head above his eye, ripping open a deep wound. After hitting its mark, the skillet fell with a heavy bounce and a ring of victory.

Blood sprayed from the gaping wound on Austin's head. With each pump of his heart, dark red blood spurted across the kitchen, covering the once clean kitchen floor with sticky red nastiness. As the blood gushed from the now black and blue throbbing wound, it matted Austin's filthy hair to his head and intensified his stench.

The intruder spun again, holding his shoulder, staggered, and stumbled out the kitchen door, then down the steps. Without remorse, Austin spewed out slurred curses. "I'll be back, sweet thang," he heaved through painful and labored breaths. "And when I do, I'll take care of you and your two brats." A blood trail followed Austin to his rusted-out truck. As he staggered, Rachel could only stand at the kitchen door, bent over, willing her fear-paralyzed lungs to breathe. Angry red scratches covered her face and arms, and her ripped dress hung from her soon-to-be-bruised shoulders, exposing the softness of her breasts. Still, Rachel clenched her fists in fury, glaring at her attacker in defiance.

It took several agonizing attempts for Austin to start his old Ford pickup truck, cursing and pumping the gas with each failed attempt. Finally, the truck engine backfired and sprang to life. Austin backed out of the dirt driveway, throwing up gravel and a cloud of dust, still cursing and glaring at Rachel with evil red eyes and wiping blood from his face.

"Don't come back. Don't ever come back!" Rachel screamed, slammed the door, and bolted it. Blood rushed from her brain, the room spun, and she passed out, hitting her head on the edge of the counter. When she hit the floor, the remaining blood from her wound mingled with Austin's.

The angels hovered over Rachel, crying but praising God for His protection.

The sheriff's car pulled up in front of the cabin, and I jumped out.

With fear clenching my gut, I grabbed the screen door but found it locked. I knocked frantically. When there was no answer, Larry and I ran to the kitchen door and found it locked as well.

"Something's wrong, Larry. Rachel never locks the doors."

Sherriff's Deputy Larry Perry called in his report before breaking the window of the kitchen door. I could do little else but stand by in panic mode, but my quaking mind and body strained to do more.

Just as Larry reached in to turn the deadbolt lock, Rachel sat up, shaking the cobwebs from her mind. When Larry entered, he announced himself, "Boone County Sheriff's Department." Rachel stumbled in delirium to the door shouting, "No! No! Go away!"

My heart and head spun in relief hearing her voice, and I pushed my way past Larry and grabbed Rachel just as she fainted again.

Larry called in his report and asked for an ambulance. A few minutes later, in his official capacity, Doctor Proctor parked the ambulance in front of the porter's house shortly after the call.

Following a cursory examination of Rachel's body, the doctor found no evidence of foul play, just scrapes, bruises, and shock.

"Thanks for coming, Doc."

"Sorry it has to be under these circumstances, Sam," replied Doc Proctor. "Even though there is no sign of trauma, Rachel might need to go to the hospital overnight for tests and observation."

"I'll go with you, Sam," offered Larry. "I will need to take her statement if she is up to it."

"I understand. Can I ride with her, Doc?"

"Of course. Larry, will you call the hospital to alert them to Rachel's arrival. We will meet you at the emergency entrance," the doctor said.

After several long hours, the hospital staff admitted Rachel to a room, and Larry returned to ask questions about the attack. "Rachel," Larry began in a whisper, "do you feel up to answering some questions?"

Still woozy from the sedative Doc Proctor gave her, Rachel replied with a slurred voice, "I will try, Larry."

"Did you know your attacker?"

"No. I never saw him before, but he talked as if I should know him."

"How did he find you at the porter's house?"

Rachel held her throbbing head and tried to remember.

"I think I can answer that," I offered. "The day I was at the bank, I spoke to Ken about a piece of property. When I left the bank, I noticed an unkept man watching me, but I thought nothing of it. He must have followed me home."

"Did you ever see him before, Sam?"

"No. Never, but come to think of it, Ken said a man was asking him about the same property just before I arrived. Ken may have more information."

Larry wrote down this information and touched his hat before leaving. "Thank you, Rachel. Rest well, ma'am."

Doc Proctor came back not long after Larry left and checked Rachel's vital signs before saying good night to her, then turned to me. "Have the hospital call me if you need me, Sam. Oh, what about the children?"

"Ken asked Mrs. Cooper to take them. I'll pick them up on my way home. Thanks, Doc."

I sat with Rachel and watched as she drifted off to sleep. The sedative calmed her, and she looked peaceful.

The angels sat on Rachel's shoulder and fluttered over her bruised body.

"I love you, Rachel."

"I knew it! I knew it!" whispered Hope in an unmuffled voice and danced in the air with her sister angels.

Larry arrived at the bank, looking official in his crisp, green Sheriff's deputy trousers and white shirt as Evelyn was just opening the bank.

"Is Ken in, Evelyn?"

"I think so. He usually comes in early on Tuesdays. Come on in, Larry. I'll let Ken know you are here."

As Larry took a seat, the freshly oiled leather of his thick black belt and holster squeaked. That sound of official law enforcement equipment and Larry's aftershave resonated throughout the bank in a strong yet friendly essence.

When Ken came down the stairs from the executive office, Larry stood. His equipment rubbed against each other, again creating that official leather-on-leather sound.

"Good morning, Larry. Come on up."

Larry took the stairs three at a time, and Ken waited until the two men were behind closed doors before, he spoke. "This is shocking. Just shocking. Have a seat, Larry."

"Ken, can you tell me what transpired the day Sam came in to talk about the Crews property?"

"I'll tell you what I can without divulging any confidentialities," offered the bank manager.

"At this point, Ken, I don't think confidentialities play a part in this investigation." Larry paused, then continued. "Sam said there was another person asking about the property. Can you tell me his name?"

Ken shuffled through files, looking extremely uncomfortable. Then, as he picked up a document said, "Ah. Yes. Here's the file. It was a Mr. Austin Pierce, address unknown, asking about the property. He spoke as if he knew Randall and Rachel. As I recall, he left my office disgruntled that I would not turn the property over to him."

"Turn the property over to him? Are you sure? He didn't want to purchase the property?"

"No. He thought I was just going to turn the property over to him because of an alleged agreement he had with Randall. When I told him the property was for sale and the sale price, he left in a huff."

"Where is he now?" asked the deputy.

"I don't know. He just left. This man was a little incoherent. He smelled of alcohol and mumbled something about how he didn't need to buy the property anyway. He said, 'Possession is nine tenths of the law.' It sounds as if he is living there, without permission, I might add."

Larry wrote this information in his notebook, then continued with the investigation. "Can you tell me what happened yesterday when Sam was in your office?"

"Yes. We were discussing … Well, I cannot tell you what we were discussing, but he looked at the clock on my desk and rose abruptly saying he had to go home. That was quite unlike Sam. He did say that he heard a train's whistle and had to go home. That's when I called you."

"Hearing a train's whistle in Florence is not unusual," commented the deputy.

"That's what I told him, but Sam said whenever he hears a whistle, he pays attention."

"Curious," murmured Larry as he wrote in his notebook. "I think I will take a ride out to the property and check it out. Since the bank owns the property, do you want to go with me, Ken?"

"Well, technically, the bank does not own the property any longer. Sam does. He bought it a couple of days ago. He might want to ride out with us."

"Let's go," said Larry, snapping his notebook closed.

"I think it would be wise to go in separate cars," Ken suggested. "I'll meet you out there."

Larry drove out to the porter's house to pick me up.

"Yes, I would love to ride out with you," I said. "The only problem is, can the kids go?"

"As long as they stay in the cruiser," instructed Larry. "Let's just hope there is no confrontation."

"Confrontation? What confrontation could there be?"

"You never know, Sam. We don't know if this guy Pierce is stable or if he has a gun or not. Do you want to take that chance?"

Sam's lips moved as if he was talking to someone, then replied to the deputy. "Yes. The kids will be okay."

On the ride out to the property, I talked with Sammy and Joelle, warning them of danger without frightening them.

"Oh, boy!" shouted Sammy. "A real police investigation."

"Boy," Joelle mimicked.

"You understand, you two, you must stay in the car."

"Yes, sir," Sammy responded with disappointed eyes.

The angels—Curiosity, Courage, and Hope—entertained and protected the children while the deputy and I went to the trailer. The angels sang songs, told the children stories about Jesus and God, and answered all their childish questions.

Deputy Larry knocked on the door and announced his official presence. "Boone County Sheriff. Open the door."

Inside, we heard muffled sounds of movement, then someone opened the door just enough to peep out.

"Austin Pierce?"

"Who wants to know?"

"I'm Deputy Sheriff Larry Perry. I'd like to ask you a few questions."

"Just a sec."

He closed the door, and the next sounds we heard were the slamming of the back door of the single-wide trailer home and running feet.

"He's running!" Larry called. Larry and I gave chase.

Just as Pierce ran past the squad car, he glanced back over his shoulder. At the very moment Pierce looked backward, the back door of the cruiser swung open. Austin turned his head around and ran into the corner of the heavy cruiser door, splitting open the fresh wound over his eye. Austin cursed and fell.

Larry arrived with gun drawn just before Austin regained his wits to run again. "Austin Pierce, you are under arrest." Larry cuffed Pierce and jerked him to his feet.

"Oww! Hey! On what charge?" Pierce spat.

"Trespass, suspicion of rape, breaking and entering, and assault."

"I never raped anybody."

When I reached the cruiser, I knelt down and scooped Sammy up in my arms, smothering him with kisses.

"You are quite the little deputy, Sammy," Larry said, ruffling Sammy's hair.

"The angel helped me do it," announced Sammy.

Larry disregarded Sammy's reply as a little boy's imagination and quipped, "You need to submit an application to the department."

"In a few years maybe," I protested, hugging Sammy tight again.

Chapter 9

I will say of the Lord, "He is my refuge and my fortress My God, in Him I will trust." Psalm 91:2

I was at the hospital at 11 a.m. and spoke with Doc Proctor.

"Sam, the emergency room doctor verified my preliminary exam. Rachel suffered a concussion when she fell, but there were no signs of rape, just bruises and abrasions. I'm afraid that her biggest injury is not physical. These injuries may become evident as time goes by. Watch her, and let me know if she needs further attention."

"Thanks, Doc. Can I take her home now?"

"I think that would do her the most good, Sam. She will heal better once she is home. By the time the nurse has the discharge papers processed, I will be ready to drive you home."

"Thanks, Doc. She is a tough little girl, but I don't think she's ready to walk two miles to the porter's house."

While we waited for her discharge papers, Rachel and I talked about her event.

"Rachel, the sheriff's deputy arrested Austin Pierce and is charging him with trespass, assault, and attempted rape."

Rachel just shuttered and looked away.

"Larry told me that Austin is wanted on five other warrants, one out of state. The State of Ohio will extradite Pierce after his trial here in September. You should never need to see or speak with him again."

"Good!" Rachel spat with venom in her voice.

I was at a loss for words and felt that this conversation was DOA when the ward nurse popped in, wearing her crisp white uniform, nurse's cap with her nursing school's distinctive design.

"Good morning, Mrs. Crews," the nurse chirped as she entered. "You are all checked out. I just need you to sign these discharge papers." She handed Rachel a pen and the papers, then turned to me and whispered, "Sam, here is a copy of the doctor's instructions. Call us if you notice any change in her behavior."

Once we got back to the cabin, ladies from the church brought casseroles, platters of fried chicken, and homemade desserts. Pastor Johns stopped by a time or two to pray with us. Of course, Sammy and Joelle were the best medicine for Rachel. Joelle knelt on the bed next to Rachel and attentively plastered Band-Aids over her mother's body, and Sammy just snuggled her.

Rachel was healing, physically, anyway. She still had mental healing to do. It seemed like every time she heard a noise, she jumped, tightening into her fight-or-flight response. I tried to comfort and reassure her, but most of the time, she just pulled away from me and shut me out.

After what seemed like a long time, Rachel's physical wounds were finally fading, but emotional wounds, even old wounds left from Randall, continued to surface. Occasionally, Rachel's words and actions were irrational and caught me off guard, but I said nothing and let her have time and space to heal and counted my blessings.

Having Rachel and the children living in the second bedroom of the porter's cabin this last eighteen months had been the happiest I could remember. I had someone else to think about instead of just myself and my own injuries. It was like a new life for me. Yet, both Rachel and I still needed time to heal and find our lives again.

We attended church together, almost like a family. We went

to the grocery store together, almost like a real family. I felt my happiness was complete.

Although Rachel's mental health was still tenuous, she went the extra mile to make the cabin clean and comfortable. She was industrious beyond my imagination, and I tried to tell her often how much I admired and appreciated her. However, I could tell that something besides her attack was weighing on her mind, so, one evening after one of her wonderful suppers, I carefully quizzed her.

"That was an excellent dinner, Rachel. Thank you. You are a good cook and take care of us so well."

"Thank you, Sam. I am pleased to do my part. It's not much, but I love doing it for you," she said but then quickly amended, "doing it for the children. They love being here with you, too. I think it's the first time both of them have felt safe."

"What about you, Rachel?"

"Me?"

"Yes, are you happy to be here? Do you feel safe?"

I could see the hesitation in her eyes and felt my stomach tighten. For a moment, I thought I would be sick. What is this strange feeling?

When Rachel started talking, she relaxed and revealed her true feelings.

"Yes, Sam. I am very happy to be here and feel safe, but ..."

"There's a but?" My stomach wrenched tighter.

"Sam, I don't want you to think I am ungrateful, but I think the children and I need our own place. Letting us stay here has been a blessing, but we ... um ... I cannot impose on you forever."

"Impose? Rachel, there is no way that you are imposing on me. Just as the children are happy to be here, I am happy to have you here, too. I hope I have not given you the impression that I felt imposed upon. If I have, I apologize."

"Oh, Sam, no." Her eyes filled with tears. "You have been so kind to us. That's just it. You have been too kind. I don't deserve to be here—to be safe—to be loved so much."

"What is this? How can I be *too* kind? Don't you realize I need you as much as you need to be here? You have helped make my own healing bearable. I don't mean to sound melodramatic, but Rachel, you and the children are my reason for living. Please don't take that away from me."

"But Sam, I have nothing to contribute to the …"

"Wait just a minute. You just contributed a wonderful dinner."

Rachel's thinking that she was a burden to me was irrational. How could I convince her otherwise? *Lord, help me*!

" … but I did not help pay for the groceries. I did not help pay for the electricity, or the gas. I am still just a freeloader." With those words, Rachel buried her face in her hands and sobbed.

I just sat there, helpless. I felt like a boob.

Sammy interrupted my thoughts. "Mommy, I'm ready for bed. Will you come tuck me in?"

He seemed to always have the right words at the right time.

"Coming, sweetie," Rachel replied, sniffing back a last tear. "I'll look for a place tomorrow, Sam."

She left the room, and my world crashed around me. Rachel was leaving. What would I do? What would *she* do? How would she take care of herself? My mind alternated from an upward whirl of blinding lights to a fathomless vortex of blackness.

"NO!" I cried aloud.

"No, no, no," a tiny voice mocked me. "Yes, yes, yes."

I scooped Joelle up in my arms and buried my grief in the folds of the baby fat of her neck.

A train whistle sounded in the distance.

"Down," Joelle said, wiggling from my embrace.

"Yes, sweetie. Have you had your bath?"

"Bath! Water! Bubble!"

Listening to Joelle's excited expectation of a warm bubble bath, the black vortex that gripped my soul relinquished its hold for a fleeting moment, and I felt a tiny hand grip the stump of my finger.

"Bath. Sam, bath."

I must be strong. She needs me. "Okay, missy. Are you a big girl?"

"Big! Me."

"Okay, let's see if big girl, Joelle, can tinkle in the potty." I placed the precious tot on the potty and turned to start running warm water into the old claw-footed bathtub. I froze. My grief returned, and all I could manage was a blank stare at the rust stain of the vintage tub and the worn surface of the once chrome faucet. The black vortex began dragging me down, down, down. *Help me, Lord!* I cried deep from within my soul.

At first, I did not hear Joelle's sweet voice, that voice that relied on me to keep her safe. That voice that called for help when she fell. That voice that enchanted me to the point that I became mush.

"Sam, done."

"I'm sorry, baby girl. Ready for the tub? Good job! You tinkled in the potty just like a big girl."

"Big! Me."

I placed the naked little toddler into the bubbles and was relieved when Rachel walked in.

"I'll take over. Thank you, Sam."

The squeeze through the bathroom door was tight, and as I slipped passed Rachel, I smelled her scent. My heart wanted to lean into her and take her into my arms. Instead, I choked back the not-so-silent mummers of my grief and went outside.

The second train rumbled down the black tracks, and the whistle blew.

"Sam?"

Drowning in my grief, I did not hear my name called.

"Sam? Are you listening to Me?"

I shook my head, letting the cool evening air cleanse my mind. "Yes. I'm listening." As my wits returned, I shook my head again, but this time asking, "Who am I talking to?"

"Have you already forgotten, Sam? On the battlefield, who told you to hold on, that I would keep you safe? When you came home on the train, Who provided the porter's cabin for you? When you went to the bank and the grocery store, Who prepared the way for you? When you needed someone, Who led Rachel to you?"

"Lord?"

"Yes, Sam. Just as then, I am with you now. I am in control, and I have a greater plan for your life. Do you trust me, Sam?"

"Yes, Lord. I trust you."

"Then have no fear, My son. Here, take My hand."

Chapter 10

*O give thanks unto the God of gods: for his
mercy endureth forever. Psalm 36:2*

After I walked and talked with the Lord, I gathered up all
my courage and went back inside the cabin. In the second bedroom,
I found Rachel and Sammy on the pallet reading a bedtime story.
Sammy tried so hard to be his mommy's little man and protector,
but on the pallet, he looked so vulnerable and small. Joelle was
already asleep in the middle of the bed. The baby girl looked so
sweet curled up with her beautiful hair spread over the pillow and
two fingers in her heart-shaped mouth. Rachel and the children
had become a big part of my life in such a short time. What would
I do without them?

"Rachel, we need to talk."

Rachel's voice cracked, and she stopped reading. She hesitated,
then looked up at me with tears in her eyes. "I don't think there's
anything to talk about, Sam. I have brought nothing but trouble to
you, and the children and I need to leave."

An anxious breath escaped my tense and trembling lips.
"Trouble? You have not been any trouble. Oh, you had that incident
with the assault, but that was not your fault. You didn't create that."

"But it followed me, Sam. Trouble will always follow me."

"That is only one occurrence," I protested. "Where will you
go? How will you live? Who will protect you? You and the children
have brought me such happiness I have never known before. I
want it to be me who takes care of you. I want it to be me who

gives you a home. You say you have not contributed anything to our household, but I never asked you to. Lots of wives stay home and take care of the family without contributing anything other than love and stability."

"But, Sam … I'm not your wife."

Those words pierced my heart, and my mind went black. When I finally regained my composure, I knelt beside her on the pallet and whispered, "But I want you to be, Rachel, with all my heart. Will you marry me?"

Rachel looked away, unable to answer. Her silence spoke volumes, at least it did to me. Why did she hesitate? What was her battle? Did I make her feel unworthy?

Sammy jumped up from the pallet and flung his arms around my disfigured neck. "I will!" shouted Sammy. "I love you, Daddy Sam."

"Me," came a sleepy little echo from the middle of the bed.

"There. See. I have two votes of confidence."

"Can I think about it, Sam?"

"I don't see what there is to think about, but, of course, you can think about it. Just let me know when you're ready. Until then, please stay. I will happily provide for you."

With relief spreading through my whole body, I clasped Rachel in my arms. Our tears mingled as one, and the angels danced around us.

Over the next few weeks, I could tell that Rachel was thinking about my proposal. Her face was happier, she sang again, and I basked in my family.

"My family. My family," I repeated those words throughout the day. My heart filled with sunshine, and Rachel looked strangely at me when I giggled out loud. *Thank you, Lord. You are always faithful.*

November brought Thanksgiving, and I had much for which

to be thankful. My joy continued through December, making Christmas the most spectacular I can remember. We cut a small tree from the forest that surrounded the cabin and decorated it with popcorn and homemade paper decorations that Sammy and Joelle had made. I had never experienced such joy.

The celebration of our Lord's birth was always special to me, and I knew it by heart and the truths it held for everyone. My spirit soared when Pastor Johns read the Christmas story from the Bible, but now, it brought new meaning to my life. The music was uplifting and inspiring. Yet, I felt envious of a weary Joseph and exhausted Mary in the cattle stall with their newborn. They had a family of their own.

On Christmas morning, I experienced a new thrill. Sammy and Joelle awoke to presents under the small tree. Gifts were modest, but the love and joy were extravagant.

January brought the beginning of a new and joyous year for my family.

Chapter 11

---

*Thus says the Lord to you, 'Do not be afraid and do
not be dismayed at this great horde, for the battle
is not yours but God's. 2 Chronicles 20:15*

As God's angels—Faith, Serenity, Compassion, Courage, Curiosity, and Grace—played in the Garden, they again experienced that familiar something … They had always felt safe, joyous, and loved. But now, however, they felt needed.

"Courage? Do you feel that? asked Grace. *"Someone needs help."*

"I do feel it. Curiosity, do you feel it, too?"

"Yes, I do. We need to talk to Sir. He always knows."

So, the gentle angels flew across the calm waters, moss-covered rocks, and grass of the Garden, searching for The Creator. When the angels found God the Father, it was Faith who boldly approached Him.

Following Curiosity's example, Faith addressed God the Father. *"Sir? Sir, we angels feel that someone needs help."*

"Well, well. It's little Faith."

"Yes, Sir, and all my sisters are here as well. We need your help again."

"Yes, My dears. I am aware of the need. It is one of my youngest, Kayla. She is in desperate need of love, strength, and healing."

Curiosity, with eager anticipation, asked, *"What shall we do?"*

"Well, first, I will arrange for Sam to find Kayla. Then you angels can help Sam from there. But, be not afraid, I will always

be there, too," said God the Father.

"Will Sam be able to hear us and speak to us?" asked Grace.

"Yes, My dear. Sam has been through his own struggles and has remained faithful. I have given him the Spirit of discernment. He can communicate privately with you but will remain discreet. He's waiting for you now along the train tracks."

"What about Rachel?" asked Hope. *"Will she be able to hear and see us, too?*

"When the time is right, My dears," replied a loving God.

"Thank you, Sir," shouted Curiosity as she looked over her shoulder and waved while flying off to catch up with her sister angels.

After breakfast, Rachel and I sat on the porch, enjoying the cool June morning. A gentle breeze blew, rustling the leaves of the old sycamore tree. The gentle sound of Joelle's chatter bathed my soul in warm joy.

A train's whistle in the distance interrupted my euphoria.

"Hear the train whistle, Rachel?"

"Yes, Sam. Before I met you, that sound meant pain and fear. Now, I rather enjoy it."

"As do I. Although I hear the whistle every day, sometimes I listen more intently, because The Voice comes."

"The Voice, Sam?"

"Yes, Rachel, The Voice started speaking to me when I first came home from the war. We have become good friends."

"You know, I remember Sammy said the train's whistle spoke to him, too."

The whistle blew again. I knew it was for me.

"I'm sorry, Rachel. I need to go."

"Go where, Sam?"

"I'm not sure. I just need to go."

"Of course you must, Sam. Do you need my help?"

"Thank you, Rachel, dear. Just stay here and watch after the baby. I will be back as soon as I can."

An overwhelming power led me to walk along the railroad tracks from the porter's house west toward Florence. Trusting The Voice that shaped my life, I had stopped questioning Its power, for I felt safe in Its presence and care.

A short time into my walk, the piercing whistle and rumble announced the train.

"Yes, Lord?"

The whistle blew again.

"I understand."

Then, the red light of the caboose disappeared out of sight with one more sounding of the whistle.

"Yes, I will go right now."

Along the dirt path next to the train tracks, The Deceiver was there, trying to intimidate me.

"Help me, Lord," I prayed.

As I walked, a movement in the now hot Kentucky dirt startled me. The ground under my feet became alive. Orange legs dug and scraped through the dirt to excavate their bodies. As each gruesome black armor-plated head surfaced, red menacing eyes glowed, and antenna protruding from their flattened heads waved in the air as if searching for prey.

Soon, millions of Brood X cicadas infested every surface of the ground and brush along my path. When the creatures took flight, the swarm blackened the sky. Hard armored bodies hit me in my face, and prickly legs clung to my clothing and hair. Then, the deafening sounds began. Everywhere, the cicadas' red eyes glowed, and their brown membranous wings buckled and raked over each other to create a cacophony of hissing sounds. It was hot, and the dry air magnified the menacing sound. The Deceiver was cunning and dangerous. Who else would use these harmless insects to distract me from the task at hand?

"Lord, give me strength. Lead me where you need me," I called out. I realized my shoulders were tense, but I walked on. Instantly, the deafening hissing of the cicadas became a quiet hum, and a warm breeze soothed my soul.

The intense afternoon sun burned down on the flint rocks that filled the railbed, then glinted back into the hot, still air. Several yards away, the refracted light created swimming lights that rippled in the heat. I cocked my gray fedora to shade my burning eyes and saw a mirage in the distance. The distorted objects appeared as a mystery of dancing lights which beckoned me closer.

With halted steps, I inched forward, afraid the dancing lights might disappear. A dry dirt devil stirred the hot air and played with the rain-deprived grasses at the edge of the path. The brim of my fedora turned upward. I squinted. In a natural reaction, my arm shaded my eyes against the flying dirt and debris. As the breeze blew, the grasses bent and separated like a man would part his hair. Now the wind changed and bent my fedora downward, briefly obscuring my vision. Another quick rush of air and the dry grasses swished, separating the grasses again, this time enough for me to get a glimpse of an object that lay crumpled in the burning soil.

As the dirt devil moved away and vanished into the hot dry air, I noticed one of the dancing lights stood beside me. It was Serenity. She asked, *"What is it, Sam?"*

Curiosity moved next to Serenity from the shadow of the grasses and lifted the dirty material that covered the shape. Then recoiled and gasped, *"It's a girl."*

"What are we to do?" asked Compassion.

With my mind racing, trying to recall my rescue experience in the Army Air Corps, I replied, "I need to get her to the cottage. Grace, will you and your sister angels straighten her dress so I can pick her up?"

"Of course, Sam."

Not knowing what the girl needed, the angels danced over the maiden, hoping the gemstone energies would be a comfort and help.

As I struggled with my balance to pick up the injured girl, I braced myself to lift her. Instead of the shifting of weight I expected, I lifted her easily, for there was no weight to her.

Faith fluttered over the girl's face, listening for the sound of life. *"She is barely breathing, Sam."*

"Hurry, Sam! Hurry!" exclaimed Courage as she flew ahead of me.

Despite the heat of the day, the short walk home was easy, but I carried the girl gently for fear that I might dislocate her bones.

"Rachel! Rachel, come quick," I yelled.

At the urgency of my call, Rachel opened the screen door and stepped aside, wiping flour from her hands. The delicious aroma of chicken and dumplings should have tempted me, but my attention was on the girl.

Without considering what was wrong with the limp form I carried, Rachel directed me, "Lay her on the children's bed, Sam. I'll get some warm water and bathe her."

During the bath and change of clothes, the girl did not stir. Her reddened temples were sunken into her skull, as were her black-ringed eyes. As Rachel uncovered the girl's emaciated body, I saw that her stomach had no form and had fallen into her body cavity. Quickly, Rachel covered the skin and bone body with one of her own clean shirts. Even though Rachel was petite, her shirt hung about the pathetic form.

Fear intruded into my thoughts. However, I quickly dismissed fear and remembered that The Voice would not send me on a mission such as this if there were no hope. So, I held the bones that were the girl's hands and prayed.

Rachel brought warm potato soup, but with the first spoonful, the girl choked and gagged. Rachel stepped back and whispered, "We should let her rest."

"I'll keep an eye on her. Where is Joelle?"

"She's in the kitchen playing with potatoes and spools of thread," Rachel replied in a calm voice.

"No need to disturb her. Let her play."

"Curiosity and I will go play with her, Sam."

"Thank you, Grace. That will be a great help."

Hearing Sam's words, Rachel looked quizzical. *Who was Grace?*

Later that afternoon, Sammy came home from school, expecting milk and cookies. Instead, he found a curious form in his bed. In typical seven-year-old fashion, Sammy stood, staring with saucer-sized eyes at the bones beneath the blanket.

"Who is this?" Sammy demanded. "Why is she in my bed?"

"She is a young girl who needs our help, Sammy. Can you go help Mommy?"

"Yes, sir," agreed Sammy, taking several steps backward but still staring at the intruder.

A few nights later, Rachel came to me with her concern.

"Sam?"

"Yes, 'm?"

"Sam, with the girl in the second bedroom, the space is getting crowded, and I think Sammy is feeling uncomfortable."

"Yes," I chuckled. "He has mentioned to me that there are too many girls in his room."

There was a pause.

"Sam?"

"Yes, 'm?"

"Would you mind if Sammy sleeps in your bedroom? I can fix a pallet for him on the floor."

"No need for a pallet, Rachel, dear. Sammy can sleep with me. I will enjoy his company, and we can have bonding time talking about serious manly-man things."

"Thank you, Sam."

As Rachel fed and bathed Sammy and Joelle, I watched the

young girl and prayed. I knew nothing of how sick the girl might be, and nothing about young teenage girls, for that matter.

Through the night, I prayed, asking the Lord for wisdom and guidance.

The next morning, I awakened to sounds of choking and vomiting. The girl's dry heaves must have been excruciatingly painful. I had no idea when she last ate, but it was clear that she had nothing in her stomach. I listened further and heard Rachel fixing breakfast for Sammy and Joelle, so I went to the girl.

"Good morning. I'm Sam Burkett. You are in my home. I found you along the train tracks. Do you remember how you got there?"

She shook her head but said nothing.

"Can I get you some water?"

Another shake of her head.

"Can I get you some food?"

That question evoked a violent shaking of her head and the wrinkling of thin skin that covered her boney face.

"Would you like to rest?"

This time, she shook her head in the affirmative, so I wiped her face with a cool cloth and straightened her covers before leaving the room.

"Rachel, I think I need to get the doctor. This girl is not well."

"I know, Sam. If it's what I think it is, I have gone through the same thing. It is a disease, a horrible disease that attacks not only the body, but the mind and soul," Rachel lamented. "Yes, you must get the doctor. I'll stay with the children."

"You're a wonderful mother and friend," I praised Rachel and kissed her on the forehead. "I'll be back as soon as I can."

I had to wait for Doctor Proctor to finish with his regular patient, but he soon appeared with his familiar smile. "Hello, Sam. How's the family?"

When I was a kid in Florence elementary school, Doctor Proctor was just starting his practice. Through the years, he was a good doctor, a faithful believer, and a good friend.

"Morning, Doc. The family is well, thank you, but I do have a medical emergency I need your help with."

"Oh?" Doc said, raising his eyebrows in a questioning manner. "What kind of emergency, Sam."

"It's a young girl."

The doctor raised his eyebrows again but said nothing.

"I found her beside the railroad tracks not far from my place. I have no idea who she is or where she is from. I only know that she is ill and needs help. I will pay for any expenses and take responsibility."

"That's mighty kind of you, Sam, but are you sure you want to take this on?" asked Doc.

"Yes, I'm sure. I must. You see, Doc …"

"No need to explain, Sam," Doc said, waving me off with sympathy and a hint of admiration. "I know." Doc then turned to his nurse. "Patty, will you cancel the rest of my appointments and lock up for me?"

"Yes, sir, Doctor. Hi, Sam."

"Hi, Patty. You and Doc make a great team."

"You are a pretty good member of our team, too, Sam," Patty said with a knowing wink.

"Does everyone know about my ministry, Doc?"

"Yes, Sam, they do. The whole town has watched you since you came home from the war. They admire you for your strength and bravery. Your astounding generosity to Rachel sealed the admiration of the whole community."

"I'm not looking for praise, Doc."

"I know, Sam. We all know."

When Doctor Proctor pulled his car up to the porter's cabin,

I got out first. Sammy came running with outstretched arms. A gaggle of angels flitted about the seven-year-old. "Daddy Sam!"

My heart soared. "I love hearing him call me that, Doc. I will never get enough of it. How do I live up to it?"

"Just do what you do, Sam. Sammy will soon notice your gifts and generosity."

I swooped the seven-year-old into my arms, and four angels continued to swarm about us, while three others flew to the cottage door. As I smothered Sammy with kisses, he was oblivious to my scarred lips and face and missing pieces of my nose.

"The girl is awake, Daddy Sam. I have been helping Mommy take care of her."

"That's splendid, Sammy. I brought Doctor Proctor. Say hello to the doctor, Sammy."

"Hello, Doctor Proctor. Are you going to make the girl well?"

"I'm going to try, Sammy."

"Good! Because Mommy and me prayed about it," exclaimed Sammy as he now skipped ahead of us, with the angels, Curiosity and Faith, close by.

Rachel opened the screen door, wiping her wet hands on her apron. "Hello, Doctor Proctor. Thank you so much for coming."

"My pleasure, Rachel. Now where's my patient?

Doc walked into the children's bedroom where the angels Grace, Compassion, and Serenity, were waiting.

"Hello, young lady," the doctor introduced himself. "I'm Doctor Proctor. Sam tells me you might need a good doctor. He found me, instead," the doctor quipped. "Hope you don't mind."

Without a word, she turned her sunken face to the wall.

"Well, let's see if I can hear your ticker," said Doc.

At first, the girl protested, pulling one bony arm around her chest and pushing the stethoscope away with the other.

In sympathy, Grace watched the doctor try to help the girl. Then, Grace remembered God the Father's words, *"Children, the elderly, and the very ill and dying can see and hear you …"* So Grace leaned against the bed and asked the girl, *"Won't you let the doctor help you, Kayla?"*

"I would like to help you, Miss," said the doctor with a gentle voice. "Can I do that?"

"It's okay, Kayla," soothed Serenity. *"Let the doctor help you. He's our friend."*

Slowly, the girl relaxed but still said nothing.

"Yes, sir. I hear it, there. It's ticking loud and strong," lied the doctor. "May I hold your wrist?"

Again, the angels hovered about, encouraging the frightened girl, and reluctantly, she surrendered her bony wrist to the doctor's gentle hands. She seemed pleased that Doc did not criticize or accuse her.

"Yep. Just as I thought. There it is. You have a pulse," Doc joked.

The angels, although concerned for the emaciated girl, giggled at Doc's humor.

After the quick examination, Doc walked outside, and Rachel and I followed.

"It's not good, Sam. I estimate she is five feet seven inches tall and weighs maybe eighty pounds. At her height, she should weigh one hundred fifteen pounds. Eighty pounds is only thirty percent of what she should weigh. Her heart is barely beating, and her pulse is dangerously slow. Her hair is thin and brittle, and her teeth are in bad shape. She's dehydrated and in desperate need of nourishment. A foul odor emanates from her body. From all indications, this poor girl is suffering from anorexia, an eating disorder common to many teenagers."

Even though Rachel suspected the diagnosis, she reacted with a gasp and leaned onto my shoulder.

"What do we do, Doc?"

"Well, Sam, first, I would recommend we take her to the hospital."

In a quick reply to Doc's recommendation, Rachel spoke up with angst in her voice, "Doctor, I know from experience that anorexia is a serious and hard-to-cure disease, but can't we keep her with us and try to get her to at least drink water?"

"Well Rachel," the kind doctor cleared his throat and hesitated before continuing, "against my better judgement, you can watch her for a while and see if you can get her to eat and drink. If that does not happen, she will need to go to the hospital. There, she will receive fluids to rehydrate her. She will have access to healthy food. Whether she eats or not is up to her."

After listening to Doc's explanation, the angels returned to the girl and sprinkled their gemstone energies over the pathetic body. They continued to talk with the girl and encourage and comfort her.

"What causes anorexia, Doc?"

"It's hard to say, Sam. The onset could be brought on by any social, mental, or psychological stimuli. A divorce, pressure at home, bullying at school, peer pressure. Our society puts tremendous pressure on young girls, and older girls for that matter, to be thin."

"How can we help, Doc?"

"First, don't criticize her. Don't pressure her. That can make it worse. Offer her food and water, but don't pressure her to eat or drink."

"I know from experience, Doctor Proctor, that anorexia is a serious and hard-to-cure disease," Rachel shared.

"Yes, Rachel. Sometimes even the best doctors cannot cure anorexia. The patient must come to grips with what is disturbing him or her. The cure must come from within the patient's psyche or soul. We will do the best we can."

"Thank you, Doc. We will stay in touch."

Doc dropped his head and squeezed my arm as he left the cabin.

The next morning, Rachel and I agreed that I should attend

church with the children. She would stay with the girl to eliminate any maleficent gossip. I argued that God would not allow that to happen, but Rachel's faith and common sense won.

"Let's not tempt the Lord with our poor judgement, Sam. We both know there are people who love nothing more than to gossip and discredit God."

"You're right, as usual, Rachel. I'll get the kids ready for Sunday School."

When the children and I left for church, Rachel and the angels returned to the young girl's bedside. The angels fluttered around the girl, whispering encouragement into her ear and sprinkling her with gemstone energy.

All during Bible study and church service I prayed, asking God to show me what to do for the girl. *Give me Your wisdom, Lord. Help me to do what is right.*

Pastor Johns read the text taken from 2 Chronicles 20:1-30. His sermon emphasized verses fourteen, fifteen, eighteen, and nineteen:

Do not be afraid or discouraged because of this vast army. For the battle is not yours, but God's.

Jehoshaphat bowed down with his face to the ground, and all the people of Judah and Jerusalem fell down in worship before the Lord. Then the people stood up and sang praises to the Lord, the God of Israel, with a very loud voice.

I read the passage several times before I understood. The Lord said, "Do not be afraid. For the battle is not yours, but God's."

Pastor Johns went on to explain, "The people of Israel praised the Lord for victory even before they went to battle."

On the way home, I mused to myself, that is true faith. I could not wait to share it with Rachel.

When the children and I arrived home, the house was unusually quiet, and fear rose in my throat. I had to rebuke myself and The Deceiver for allowing me to be afraid. Had I already forgotten the Scripture Pastor Johns shared with us?

Do not be afraid or discouraged because of this vast army. For the battle is not yours, but God's.

Then, the angel, Faith, came to me, *"The girl is resting, Sam. Do not be afraid or discouraged. She is still far from well, but she said she would like to try to get well."*

"Thank you, Faith. That is a great comfort to me."

As the children and I entered the front porch, Sammy called out, "We're home!"

Baby Joelle, trying to mimic her brother, squealed and babbled, "Home."

The jolly circus expunged all my fear.

"Thank You, Lord," I prayed.

To add to my joy, Rachel came from the children's bedroom and nuzzled my neck. "Come see," she invited.

Obediently, I followed and found the girl sitting in bed with two angels on her shoulders and one on her feet. There was no smile, but there was no vomiting and sadness, either.

"Thank You, Lord," I said quietly.

"Hello. Remember me?" I asked her.

As if the pain were too great to bear, she carefully shook her head in the affirmative.

"Did you have a good morning?"

She answered with a shrug.

"Well, I did." I turned to Rachel and told her about church service. "I learned an old truth. After we tell God our troubles or the desires of our heart, we should praise Him."

"I know a song," piped in Sammy.

"Alright, Sammy. Will you sing it for us?"

Sammy started off softly, but by the time he finished, he sang with gusto.

"Praise Him. Praise Him. All you little children.
God is Love. God is Love.
Thank Him, Thank Him, all you little children.
God is Love. God is Love."

The angels flitted about Sammy as he sang as if adding their own praises to God. The girl's eyes did not beam, but they did show signs of peace. They were small signs, but peace nonetheless.

"That's wonderful, Sammy," Rachel praised her son.

Then, wanting to be part of the fun, Joelle started singing.

"Pray Pray chil'ren"

"God Love. God Love."

We all laughed. Even the girl could not help smiling, albeit a tiny smile. *We'll work on that. Thank You, Lord.*

Sammy broke the praise moment. "Mommy, what's for lunch? I'm hungry."

"Ok, Sammy, then go set the table," Rachel instructed.

As Sammy ran off to do his task with Curiosity flitting about his head, Rachel called over her shoulder, "Use the good napkins, please."

"While Rachel and Sammy are getting lunch, can you and I talk?" I asked the reluctant girl.

She twisted her mouth and shrugged as if to say, "If I have to."

"Please talk to Sam," begged Courage.

"What's your name? I hate to keep calling you 'the girl'."

She hesitated, shifting her eyes from side to side as if searching for an escape.

"Do you have a pet name, a nickname your friends call you?"

There it was. A light. A tiny light, but still a light. Her eyes changed.

"K ... K ..."

"K? Is that short for something?"

Without realizing that Joelle had not followed her mommy and Sammy into the kitchen, K and I were both startled when Joelle started reciting her ABCs. "A, B, C, K, KK."

"It sounds like Joelle wants to call you KK. Is that alright with you?"

Joelle leaned on the bed, supporting herself with her little elbows and smiled up at the girl while the angels hovered and flitted, giggling for joy.

The girl's smile grew a little, and her eyes almost twinkled. "Thank You, Lord," I whispered to myself. "Okay. KK it is. Sammy!" I called. "Sammy, can you come here a minute?"

Sammy bounded into the bedroom and bounced up on the bed before I could stop him. Oh, well. "Sammy, Joelle thinks the girl's name should be KK. Is that okay with you?"

"KK? KK? Yup, I like it."

"Then we need someone to do the ceremony to give KK her name."

Almost before I finished my sentence, Sammy hopped off the bed and ran to the kitchen, again closely followed by angels. In a split second, he returned and hopped on the foot of the bed.

"Whatcha got there?"

"This is my magic wand. You have to have a magic wand to give someone a special name," replied Sammy in all sincerity.

"What a good idea." It was Rachel standing in the open door. She had just come in to join the fun. "Do you know what to say, Sammy?"

"Sure." In typical Sammy style, he hopped down from the bed and stumbled over my feet to reach KK. Then, he held out the wooden spoon and lightly touched KK on the head. "I hereby, and forever more, name you KK! Now, let's sing 'Happy Birthday' to KK."

Leave it to Sammy to put on the finishing touches. While the singing was not particularly good, and Joelle did not get all the words, the atmosphere was joyous. By the time we finished singing, the girl, I mean, KK, had tears in her eyes and a hint of a smile on her lips. *Thank You, Lord.*

Rachel, nearly overcome by the emotion, rose and said, "I need to finish getting lunch ready," Rachel exclaimed.

As she walked from the bedroom, I thought I saw her wiping tears away and blowing her nose. *Finally, a little emotion,* I mused.

When Rachel called from the kitchen that lunch was ready, the children and angels scrambled. I turned to KK and asked her to join us at the table. She turned her head away from me as if to say, "If I can't see you, I can't hear you."

"You don't have to eat, KK. Just come sit with the family at the dinner table. Rachel has put out some of her clothes for you."

Still, she gave no response, even though Grace, sitting on KK's shoulder, did her best to motivate the girl.

"You know, KK, it would be impolite to refuse your hosts' hospitality. We want you to share in our family as long as you are here."

With those words, "share in our family," KK turned her head and smiled a weak smile.

"That-a-girl. Do you need help getting out of bed?"

"Yes, please," her voice quivered. "Then will you not look?"

"Certainly, I will not."

It took no effort at all to lift KK out of bed. However, it took some doing to help her gain her balance on the bones that were her legs and feet. When I reached out my good hand and the two fingers of my right hand, KK flinched. Then, she looked at me as if seeing me for the first time, and surprise covered her face. I could tell that at that moment, she noticed my scars and amputations. It took several minutes for her surprise to give way to determination, and once she was stable, I turned my head as I had promised.

I watched as Grace flitted and turned summersaults in the air. Her lavender organza gown billowed as she danced, and the amethyst gemstone sparkled with the energy of gratitude.

"Okay, Sam," her still weak voice whispered. "You can turn around."

When I turned around, I almost gasped, as others had done when they looked upon my face. The jeans hung on her body where hips should have been. The shirt, too, hung over her formless bones. Quickly, I found one of Sammy's belts and looped it in the jeans and used the last hole to secure the belt. Then, I unbuttoned the last two buttons of the shirt and tied it up so that the shirttail came just at her knees, making sure it would not make her stumble.

"There, now. All dressed up and ready to attend an elegant dinner."

Extending her emaciated hand to me, KK gave no indication that she understood my humor; she just shuffled her feet toward the bedroom door. After three shuffled steps, she stopped. With labored and shallow breath, she clung to the door jamb. Once recovered, she looked up at me with fright-filled eyes. Then, with subdued determination, she took several more steps. These were the first steps she had taken in a week.

"I've got you, KK," I said as I put my arm around her empty waist.

Grace hovered above KK but was careful not to interrupt the girl's concentration and balance.

I have read that children are intuitive. That turned out to be true with Joelle, for in her own childish way, Joelle sensed that KK needed a kind friend.

As we entered the kitchen, Joelle squealed. "KK! KK, sit," the three-year-old invited, patting the chair next to her.

"You look funny in Mommy's clothes," Sammy blurted out. However, when he noticed Rachel's disapproving scowl, he back peddled and said, "Hi, KK."

Baby chatter and fairy giggles tumbled over the lunch table like bubbling water tumbling over rocks in a small stream.

"Sammy, please don't kick the chair," Rachel admonished.

"Milk, Mommy! Milk," demanded Joelle.

"Mommy, do you know what our Sunday School story was about today?" asked Sammy with genuine enthusiasm.

"Cheer o's," Joelle demanded next.

"Well, no, I don't. What was the story?" Rachel said playing along.

"It was about Jesus."

Again, I watched the angels when they heard the name of Jesus. They all paused from what they were doing and listened reverently as Sammy told the story. It was apparent to me that the angels never tired of hearing stories of Jesus.

Sammy continued, "Jesus touched a sick little girl and made her well, and she got up and played."

At the end of Sammy's story, the angels continued their flitting and flying about, spreading energies of joy, harmony, and wellbeing.

"Sanbich! I want dat," shouted an impatient Joelle and pointing her tiny finger at the top sandwich.

"That's a wonderful story, Sammy. Can you save that story in your heart and remember it when you need it?" I prompted.

"Yup. I have a friend at school who is sick a lot. I'm going to tell that story to her," Sammy announced.

Rachel winced at Sammy's informal reply but ignored his poor manners. She didn't want to discourage her son from sharing the Bible story.

Trying to turn everyone's attention to the lunch Rachel prepared, I praised her. "This looks wonderful, Rachel. Thank you."

"You're welcome, Sam," Rachel replied in an almost shy manner. "I know how you like tuna sandwiches."

When I said, "Let's say Grace," everyone became quiet, and I enjoyed the sensation for a moment before I began. "Thank You, Lord, for Your love and care. Thank you for our family and for KK who has come to be with us for a time. Bless her, Father, and give her strength and courage. Thank You for delicious tuna sandwiches and milk. In Jesus's name. Amen."

When Rachel offered a sandwich and milk to KK, I sensed that the girl fought back a gag. But KK did smile when Joelle slid a soggy Cheerio to her. A thrill ran from my arms to my heart when KK gingerly picked up the Cheerio and placed it on her tongue.

"Thank You, Lord," I whispered.

As usual, there was not a crumb of tuna sandwiches left, and the last slurp of milk noisily disappeared.

"Down," Joelle asked.

"Yes, ma'am," I replied and released Joelle from her highchair with a kiss. "Time for a nap, baby?"

"Nap. Nap, KK."

"Well, KK, I guess you are going to take a nap," I chuckled.

After I helped KK to her feet and she balanced herself, Joelle ever-so-gently grabbed one of KK's boney fingers and slowly led the girl to the bedroom.

"Play, KK?" Joelle asked.

"I will read to you," offered KK.

"Thank you, Lord," I said again. "Five words. One Cheerio and five words."

Rachel, coming into the bedroom from cleaning up from lunch, smiled. It was good to see her smile again.

With a toddler's glee, Joelle ran to her bookcase and grabbed her tattered Golden Book of Bible Stories.

"Read."

As Rachel and I peeped in to witness the reading, I could feel Rachel's emotions surge as she leaned next to me. KK and Joelle lay in bed together, Joelle with two fingers in her mouth snuggled up to KK. The angels, Courage and Compassion, sat with the new friends, sprinkling them with gemstone energies. Compassion sat on Joelle's head while Courage sat on KK's shoulder. Before KK finished the story that Joelle knew by heart, the baby was asleep.

"Thank You, Lord." Then, I remembered the Scripture reading this morning:

Do not be afraid or discouraged because of this vast army. For the battle is not yours, but God's.

Over the next few days, and into the next week, KK read many books, some multiple times, even though Joelle let her know when she made a mistake. The girl devoured at least a cup of Cheerios, one at a time. Then, Joelle orchestrated the next step.

Joelle slid off the bed and trotted into the kitchen where Rachel was starting the evening dinner. Several angels followed, skipping and dancing around the happy tot.

"Mommy, duice."

Rachel poured apple juice into Joelle's sippy cup and offered it to the baby.

"Mommy. Duice. KK."

A surprised Rachel poured a tiny bit of apple juice into a red plastic cup and handed it to Joelle.

"Mommy," Joelle stomped. Her tiny black patent shoe emphasized her exasperation. "Straw."

Again, Joelle's request shocked Rachel. "I'm sorry, baby. You're right. She needs a straw. Do you want a blue, white, or pink straw?" Rachel asked.

"Pink! Tanks you, Mommy."

Pleased with her accomplishment, Joelle trotted to the bedroom, spilling a trail of apple juice along her way.

Little Curiosity followed Joelle but lagged behind. Looking all around to see if anyone was watching, Curiosity put her tiny finger in the droplets of apple juice then into her mouth. I could hardly muffle my laughter when the angel's eyes popped.

"Sam," Rachel called in a soft, amused voice, "come see."

We followed the trail of juice from the kitchen to the bedroom where we found Joelle and KK sitting on the floor playing with a tea set I had picked up at the thrift store. We were both amused to see that Joelle poured apple juice from her sippy cup into the tiny metal teacups.

"Pray," instructed Joelle.

"Me?" asked an astonished KK.

"You, pray."

KK prayed the only prayer she knew, "Thank You for the world so sweet. Thank You for the food we eat. Thank You for the birds that sing. Thank you, God, for everything."

"'men. Drink."

Rachel held her breath as she watched. With hesitation, KK put the tiny cup to her lips but could not bring herself to drink. She choked back a gag.

"I wouldn't want to drink it either," I said with a whispered chuckle.

With those words, Rachel gave me an elbow in my ribs.

"Straw?" asked Joelle, the polite hostess.

"Yes, please," replied KK.

Joelle got on her hands and knees to retrieve the pink straw from where it had rolled under the bed and, with a smile, handed it to KK.

"Sip. Little."

Following her hostess's instructions, KK placed the pink straw to her lips and sipped.

"Good?"

"Yes, thank you. Mmm. Delicious," KK said in play.

"Good. Cheerio?" asked the hostess.

"Yes, please," KK answered.

I could tell that her reply was just to be polite, that she dreaded eating even a Cheerio.

Again, Joelle scouted the bedroom floor until she found two

Cheerios: one for her and one for KK.

After taking her seat on the floor, Joelle politely handed KK a lint-coated Cheerio.

"Toast," Joelle said. "Eat."

Together, Joelle and KK sipped tea and ate "toast" while Rachel and I clandestinely watched just outside the bedroom door. If someone were to listen closely, they might have heard our spirits soaring.

The tea party continued for three minutes, Joelle's attention span. Yet, that was enough time for KK to eat a Cheerio and sip two ounces of apple juice.

"Thank You, Lord," I offered my praise again. "Thank you, Joelle."

Over the next two weeks, KK's transition to Cheerios and apple juice was a difficult one.

Rachel, in her caring-mother's way, told me that after many tea parties, KK lay in the bed holding her stomach and moaning.

When I started listening closer, I heard KK get up many nights to throw up. But, having nothing in her stomach, cramping dry heaves tortured her. They must have been painful. On those times, I thought I heard the gentle encouraging whispers from the angels, Serenity and Courage. Finally, I was able to fall asleep knowing that the angels stayed close by her side. Serenity's gemstones showered energy of strength and healing over KK.

One difficult night seemed to be a turning point. I heard KK in the bathroom trying to throw up. From my bedroom I called to Rachel. "Rachel?"

"Yes, Sam?"

"KK is in the bathroom again."

"I know," Rachel whispered with great sympathy, then continued. "I'll go to her."

I heard Rachel's bare feet shuffle to the bathroom. She knocked on the bathroom door. "KK? Are you okay, sweetie?"

"Yes, ma'am," replied a weak-and-shaken KK. "I'm okay. I just want to go back to bed."

"Okay, sweetie. Let me help you. Here, lean on me."

"Thank you, Rachel. My mother never helped me before."

When I heard those words, they stung my heart, as I am sure they pierced Rachel's.

"I am so sorry, KK," whispered Rachel. "I am glad I am here to help you. There. Lie down, and I will tuck you in."

As Rachel turned to leave the room, KK whispered, "Rachel?"

"Yes, KK?"

"Will you stay with me until I fall asleep?"

"Of course, I will, sweetie. Would you like me to rub your back?"

"No," KK replied curtly, but then changed her mind. "Yes, ma'am."

From my bedroom, I could hear Rachel humming softly as she rubbed the protruding bones that were KK's back. Then, I heard muffled crying.

"What's wrong, KK? Do you want to talk about it?" asked Rachel.

"I don't think I can yet. It's just … It's just that no one has ever been so kind to me before."

"I understand, dear," Rachel whispered. Rachel continued to hum, and I knew she was praying. Soon, everything was quiet and still.

After a time, I think it was two months, Rachel and I earned KK's trust, and she began to talk about herself. During one private conversation, KK told me that her name was Kayla.

"Kayla," I repeated. "That's a beautiful name."

"Thank you," Kayla replied with weak breath.

"How old are you, Kayla?"

"Fourteen."

"When is your birthday? Not the birthday Sammy proclaimed for you."

"June twenty-third. I was not happy at my home —not like I am at yours, Sam. Although I was smart and did well in school, my dad was never happy unless I was perfect. If I made a "B" on my report card, he punished me.

"My mother always called me a 'little fat girl,' and that hurt. I didn't get my period as soon as my friends, so my body didn't slim down, and I didn't have a girlish figure."

When Kayla shared with me about her father's unrealistic expectations and her mother's disapproval, it broke my heart.

Out of curiosity, and to protect myself, I asked Kayla about her parents. "Where are your mother and father, Kayla?"

"My dad is in prison. He beat my mom. He killed her," replied Kayla with indifference.

"Kayla," I asked, "do you mind if I ask when you stopped eating? Starving oneself is not a natural thing to do."

Kayla hesitated but then confided, "When I was seven. I remembered my mom and dad fought a lot, and I thought it was my fault. Their fighting scared me. I thought if I could just disappear, they would stop fighting, so I stopped eating. When I lost weight, I was sure I was invisible. Mom and Dad continued fighting, and I continued to believe I was invisible."

It took several long seconds for my brain to process Kayla's story. How could parents treat their child this way?

When my mind cleared, I could understand how Kayla receded into her own world of wanting to disappear. It was no wonder that Kayla succumbed to the emotional, mental, and physical pain of anorexia. "This is a great burden for a little girl to bear. I'm sorry, Kayla." My words felt empty.

When, after several months, Kayla began eating selected foods on her own without having a gag reflex, Rachel's and my hearts filled with thanksgiving. We continued to encourage but never push. We made certain to have available foods that Kayla liked, and Joelle continued to feed Kayla Cheerios.

"Kayla," Rachel called from the kitchen, "would you like to walk to the grocery store with me? You might find something new you would like to try."

"Yes, I would love to go."

Rachel told me later that on their walk to the grocery store, Kayla shared her deepest feelings. "Sam, I felt so honored that Kayla would share her feelings with me. That made me feel important … a person of value."

While we were on our way, Kayla asked, "Rachel, am I cheating?"

"What do you mean, Kayla? Cheating whom?"

"Myself, I guess. For so long I was this invisible girl. That's who I was. Now, that I am beginning to eat, I don't know who I am."

"Oh, no, Kayla. You are not cheating on yourself or anyone. You are just rediscovering the real you, and I like that person. I like that person a lot."

"Thank you, Rachel. I hope I can like that person, too."

"You will, Kayla, dear. You will learn to like yourself, for that's who God made you. God does not make mistakes. God made each of us to be His temple. That's pretty special, to be the temple of God, and He has asked us to take care of His temple."

It seemed that every day Kayla opened up a little more to Rachel and me. The day that she asked about my face and prosthetic foot was a special day. It meant that, now, she was doing the reaching out to us.

"Sam, how did you get your scars? Oh, I'm sorry. Would you rather not talk about it?"

"On the contrary, Kayla. I am happy to share my story with

you. Two years ago, I could not say that because depression had me in its vice grip."

"What happened?" Kayla asked, forgetting about herself.

I took this opportunity to share with Kayla how God led me all through the war and how He continued to be by my side. When I told her of flying over enemy lines in Germany, her attention was riveted to my voice, not my disfigured face.

I must admit that I was pleased when she considered me to be a hero. Although, I was no hero. I just did my job, like all the other GIs. But she seemed genuinely touched while listening to how I suffered through frost bite, amputations, and infections, and still praised God and listened to His instruction.

When I spoke of hypothermia and how God did not intend for us to abuse our bodies, she took notice.

"What's hypothermia, Sam?"

"Hypothermia occurs when your body core drops to ninety-five degrees. You know the normal body temperature is ninety-eight point six degrees."

"What happens when your body temperature drops so low?"

"You die. God did not intend for our bodies to sustain such abnormal conditions. You know, Kayla, our bodies are the temple of God, and we must care for them."

"That's what Rachel said," Kayla mused.

By this time, the angels were sitting with Kayla, listening to my story as if they had never heard it before. I guess even angels never tire of God's grace and miracles.

Even though we had been talking for some time, Kayla still asked questions. I felt that the Lord would lead me to talk to this young girl about God's goodness, so I continued. When I told her about my phantom pain, she wanted to know more.

"What is phantom pain?"

"When my foot was amputated, for some reason the spinal cord and brain did not get that signal that my foot was gone. My brain still sends messages to the nerve that it hurts. That's why it is called phantom pain."

"Does it get better?"

"It did for me with the medication the Army doctors prescribed, but that took its toll, too. My mind and body eventually became addicted to morphine, so I was a prisoner again. The medication that gave me peace, also imprisoned me. When I didn't receive my morphine, pain was severe and relentless, and gripped my mind in fear. I started hearing voices."

"Voices? What kind of voices?" asked Kayla, now wide-eyed.

"Voices of pain and fear. Every minute of the day and night, pain racked my body and mind. Fingertips, no longer there, ached and burned. The nerves in my brain shot needles of pain to my foot: the foot that no longer existed.

"Self-pity became my constant companion. As bad as pain and medication were, the most aggressive, the most relentless voice was depression. Depression was a harsh task master, a constant liar that whispered in my good ear that my life was worthless. Depression fiercely demanded that I give up and die, not caring about me or my pain."

"How did you get over it?" asked Kayla, understanding the evils of depression.

"It was nothing that I did, instead; God did it."

"What did He do?"

"I started hearing another kind of Voice. This Voice was gentle, but I was skeptical. However, after several encounters with this gentle Voice, I soon learned the purpose of these visitations. This Voice only worked for good, for those who choose to listen. Eventually, I learned to speak to The Voice and received truth and even comfort."

I told her of how God provided the porter's cabin, the very

cabin we were sitting in now.

"That was lucky for you."

"It was not luck, Kayla. It was God."

"You don't really believe that do you, Sam?"

Now, the angels began to stir and flutter about Kayla as if fanning her flames of curiosity and belief.

"I certainly do, Kayla. When I started listening to Him, the voices of pain, fear, and depression left me."

"How can that be?" she asked with the same skepticism I once had.

"There are some things we can't explain. We just believe. When I got off the train in the middle of nowhere, the night was as dark as my depression. Between fear that my prosthetic foot would give way and cause me to fall in the darkness and the depression that still gripped my soul, I was a prisoner.

"Depression continued to whisper, 'Who could live a full life with one foot, one hand, three fingers and a horrifyingly disfigured face?' However, the next morning, while rummaging around the cold, dark cabin to find food, The Voice spoke to me. It called my name and compelled me to listen. That moment shaped my life and gave me a purpose and reason to live."

"Do you still hear that Voice?" asked Kayla now, without such great skepticism.

"Yes, and I have learned to speak back to The Voice. In fact, it was The Voice who encouraged me to walk along the train track where I found you."

"The Voice told you about me?"

"Yes. Are you surprised?"

"Yes. Yes, I am. I thought no one cared about me."

"That's depression lying to you, Kayla. The Voice is God's voice, and He cares deeply for you."

Sammy, now home from school, interrupted our conversation

when he came romping into the bedroom.

"KK!" Sammy called, happy to see his new friend again. "I was afraid you would not be here."

"Well, here I am, Sammy. I'm not going anywhere. I have nowhere to go."

Rachel walked into the bedroom in time to hear Sammy blurt out, "Does that mean you're going to eat your supper?"

"Sammy!" Rachel raised her voice in exasperation and embarrassment.

"What?" answered an innocent Sammy.

"I think your mommy means you are not supposed to talk about my eating," giggled KK.

"Bright girl," I said to Rachel with a wink at KK.

After numerous Cheerio and apple juice tea parties, KK welcomed mealtime with the family; although, she still was reluctant to eat little more than what Joelle shared with her.

I have never witnessed a three-year-old helping a teenager to heal. But that's exactly what Joelle did. After a couple of weeks of Joelle sharing Cheerios and apple juice with KK, Joelle shared a tiny broccoli "tree" at dinner. KK hardly noticed that Joelle was feeding her a balanced diet.

"Dinner's ready," Rachel called.

"What are we having for dinner, Mommy?" asked Sammy.

"Meatloaf, mashed potatoes, and peas," Rachel replied.

"Hurray! I love mashed potatoes and peas," called Sammy.

"What about meatloaf, Sammy?" I asked.

"Well, not so much," replied a reluctant Sammy wrinkling his nose.

"Loaf!" squealed Joelle. "Loaf!"

"At least someone likes my meatloaf."

"Sammy," I asked, "would you like to say our blessing?"

"No."

"I'm sorry?"

"I mean no, sir. KK wants to say the blessing."

"May I say the blessing?" Kayla asked, surprising everyone at the dinner table.

"Of course, you may, Kayla," I replied. "Let's bow our heads for the blessing."

"God, this is KK, I mean Kayla. Thank you for bringing me here to Sam's home. Thank you for Rachel and Sammy and Joelle. Thank you for this dinner. I will try to eat it. Amen."

We all replied, "Amen."

"Tatoes, Mommy!"

"Yes, ma'am," replied Rachel with an amused smile and served the baby a teaspoon of mashed potatoes.

"Mommy, tatoes, KK."

Rachel looked at Kayla with questioning eyes, and the surprised girl replied, "Well, just a little, please."

"Mommy, loaf," requested Joelle. "Loaf, KK."

As instructed, Rachel placed a small serving of meatloaf on Kayla's plate. Then Rachel and I were amazed as Joelle placed two peas on KK's plate.

Joelle wiggled in her chair with a squeal and beaming eyes. "Eat, KK. Little. One pea me. One pea KK."

"Look, Daddy Sam. I gots peas in my mashed potatoes," giggled Sammy.

"Yum," squealed Joelle. "Mommy, mine."

The entire family played with their mashed potatoes and peas. Even Kayla enjoyed the game. She managed to eat the tiniest bit of mashed potatoes she could get on her fork, followed by a gagging reflex.

"It's okay, Kayla. Go slow," soothed Rachel. "Would you like to drink some milk?"

"Milk!" shouted Joelle. "Mommy, milk."

Neither Rachel nor I watched Kayla worry with her food, and

she seemed to realize we were supporting her in her recovery.

That night, as the angels slept with KK and the children, we all slept peacefully. *Thank you, Lord.*

Even though she did not eat much, Kayla enjoyed the happy family dinner time. Once she passed the point that she could keep her food down, she enjoyed sitting with the family each day.

Part of our family time was evening Bible study. I made it a point to choose small passages of Scripture that the children could understand. From the Bible, I told stories and prompted Sammy to ponder the Scriptures and ask questions. Even Joelle picked up a few words here and there.

As with most children, Joelle's favorite word was "Jesus." Isn't it curious how little children associate Jesus with love, even before they learn that truth? Oh, that we could do the same so naturally.

Little by little, Kayla, too, started to ask questions and began to internalize the lessons within the Scripture readings. It was apparent that even though Kayla was not hungry for physical food, she was hungry for spiritual food.

As soon as she gained some physical and emotional strength, Kayla went with the family to Sunday School and church. Rachel shared her Bible with Kayla to follow along as Pastor Johns read. Joelle also shared the hymnal, even though the baby always turned to the wrong page, and most times, upside down.

Chapter 12

"Kayla?" Rachel called from the kitchen.

"Yes, ma'am?"

"Mrs. Eddie has invited us to drive with her to Sears in Cincinnati. As soon as I clean Joelle's breakfast off her face and the floor, would you like to go?" Rachel invited Kayla. "The baby needs new shoes."

"Oh, yes, ma'am. I'll be ready in a sec," Kayla replied.

"Good morning, Mrs. Eddie," Rachel greeted her friend. "Thank you for inviting us to ride with you. I do hope we will not be a bother."

"Well land sakes, Rachel. You three are no bother at all. I am glad to have the company. Mr. Eddie worries about me on the road by myself, you know."

Almost as soon as the car started moving, Joelle curled up in my lap and went to sleep. From the back seat, Kayla started asking questions, wanting to know more about my life. When I shared about my life with Randall, Mrs. Eddie reacted with a gasp, even though she knew my story, but Kayla was nonplused. She had witnessed beatings before. There were many times that she watched and listened while her father beat and ridiculed her mother. Yet, the young teenager seemed sincerely touched by my story.

As I continued, Mrs. Eddie wiped her eyes with her hanky when I told how Sammy, a brave little boy, tried to protect me. "Oh, the precious little dear," breathed Mrs. Eddie.

But it was Kayla who had tears in her eyes when I told how Sam came to my rescue and invited me and the children to share his cabin. Kayla was unaccustomed to such love and generosity. However, now that she was the recipient, maybe she would learn to love the One who loved her first.

When I finished sharing my story, Kayla breathed, "Oh, Rachel, you are so strong. I wish I had someone to love me like Sam loves you. I wish I knew how to have your kind of strength."

That was the opportunity I was hoping for and said, "Oh. No, Kayla. I am far from strong. I have battled fear all my life—I still battle it. But, I know that God is always with me. It is with His strength that I survive."

Mrs. Eddie shared her life and how her faith had seen her and her husband through bad times and good times.

Kayla listened with her mouth open. Having one person share their faith is one thing, but when two people share their lives and faith in one conversation, it can be profound.

"Are you and Sam going to get married now?"

"We're going to let God decide that, Kayla. We never know how God works, but we do know that He works for our good."

"Are you afraid, Rachel?"

Those words from Kayla's lips caused me to stop short. I reflected. I blinked, then sheepishly admitted, "I guess I am."

"Why are you afraid?"

I felt another punch in my stomach.

"And a child shall lead them," Mrs. Cooper whispered and smiled at me.

I returned my gaze back to Kayla. It took me several attempts to speak. "I guess I am afraid of failure—of being hurt again."

"But if we know that He works for our good, will He let us fail? Will he let us be hurt again?"

Her words spoke of her own deep feelings. "How do I know that God wants the best for me?"

Mrs. Eddie and I took turns sharing with Kayla how God speaks through the Bible. I shared how in the first century when the Roman government was killing Christians, the missionary Paul encouraged the Christians to have faith in God even when they faced death. He said in the book of Romans:

And we know that all things work together for good to them that love God, to them who are the called according to his purpose.

Kayla was stunned. "But that was thousands of years ago."

"It is the same today. Human beings have not changed, neither has God's love. If we listen to Him, he will tell us what to do."

"You hear God, too? Like Sam?" asked Kayla in amazement.

"We hear God speak to us when we read The Bible."

"How can I hear God?" asked Kayla.

"Well, you've got a good start. Reading The Bible in church helps. Reading The Bible at home is another way to strengthen your faith," encouraged Rachel.

"I want to hear The Voice," said Kayla longingly.

"You will. Just keep reading and listening. The missionary, Paul, writes again, 'Fix your thoughts on what is true, and honorable, and right, and pure, and lovely, and admirable. Think about things that are excellent and worthy of praise.' If you follow Paul's example, you will hear God's voice."

Mrs. Eddie was just pulling into a parking place at Sears when Kayla begged, "Rachel, will you show me how to listen to God's Voice?"

With happy hearts, Mrs. Eddie and Rachel both agreed that they would.

"Kayla, you only have to ask God."

"What do I say?"

"Jesus taught us to talk to God when He said, *'Our Father, who art in Heaven…'*"

Upon hearing Jesus's name, Joelle woke from her nap, stretched, and asked in a sleepy voice, "Jesus?"

Mrs. Eddie, Kayla, and Rachel laughed, then Rachel continued, "So, Kayla, you can say the same thing, but make it more personal. Say, my Father, I want to hear Your Voice. Please speak to me. I am listening. Forgive me for unkind things I have done or for kind things I have forgotten to do. Be my Father and accept me as Your Child."

"Thank you, Rachel."

Filled with overwhelming emotion, Rachel drew Kayla into her arms, and they embraced each other across the car seat. Both held on tight, not wanting to let go, and sobbed. It was as if Rachel could feel the electricity of love and pride flowing between their bodies. Tears continued to flow, and Rachel knew it was God's love and forgiveness.

When they finally loosened our arms, Rachel said to Kayla, "That is another way God speaks to us. God's Spirit can fill our hearts so that we feel His presence."

"Yes, I felt something. But that feeling is gone."

"I know, sweetie. On occasion, I have felt this same mutual spirit of love with other believers, but never quite this strong. We must not let occasional feelings confuse us, because feelings are temporary. But God's love and forgiveness are always with us."

Mrs. Eddie and Rachel wiped away their tears, then Rachel said, "Now, let's go buy new shoes for the baby, and maybe a new dress for you."

Mrs. Eddie agreed to meet back at the car in two hours.

After buying new shoes for Joelle, Rachel directed Kayla to the Girl's Department and picked out several dresses for her to try on. After several minutes, Kayla called for help.

When Rachel went into the dressing room, she gasped. "Oh, no. This will never do."

"What's wrong!?" Kayla shrieked.

"It's too small! You have a figure. Kayla, you have a figure! This girl's dress is too small! Oh, Kayla, you are beautiful," Rachel said as she grabbed Kayla in a big teary hug. "Let's go to the petite department."

Rachel scouted the petite section for a dress, and Kayla again went to the fitting room. "Rachel!"

"What is it, sweetie?" she asked with fear in her voice.

"I like it! I love it!" squealed Kayla.

Rachel eagerly went into the fitting room, "Oh, Kayla, it is perfect. Except …"

"Except, what?" Kayla asked in wide-eyed apprehension.

She whispered, "I think you need a bra."

"Do I? Do I, really?"

"Yes, I think you really do," she replied with a glowing smile.

"May I have a lacy one, Rachel?" Kayla asked with a shrug of her shoulders and a sheepish smile.

"Of course, you may. I don't see why not, darling."

"Don't tell Daddy Sam," whispered Kayla.

"Mum's the word," Rachel replied in surprise. "Oh, Kayla, you are beautiful."

That very afternoon, Kayla gave herself permission to become part of their family.

When she told Sam how Kayla called him 'Daddy Sam,' he agreed that God had truly blessed them. Then, he reflected, "When I was facing my amputations, I never dreamed that I would have a son and *two* beautiful daughters. Now, God has to work on a wife."

Rachel blushed, but secretly agreed.

Chapter 13

Concerning this house that you are building, if you will walk in my statutes and obey my rules and keep all my commandments and walk in them, then I will establish my word with you 1 Kings 12:12

In 1950, through sibling bickering and accidental broken bones, scrapes and bruises, Rachel and I enjoyed every moment of our children's lives. Sadly, though, as all children do, our children were growing up, and we were not ready. We wanted to hold on to those precious baby years. Sammy just turned nine; Joelle considered herself grown at age five; and Kayla, now sixteen, was becoming a beautiful young lady.

With stealth, Rachel entered the living room where I was reading. "Sam?"

"Yes, dear."

"Sam, have you noticed our children are growing?"

I closed my book and gave this dedicated and contemplative mother my full attention and chuckled. "Yes, sweetie. I have noticed. Either our children are growing, or our cabin is getting smaller. What's on your mind?" I asked, providing an opening for her thoughts.

"Sam, do you think we need a bigger house?"

"Well," I considered, "that might be a good idea. What do you suggest?"

"Oh, nothing grand, just a little more room."

"The tenants in my parent's house will be moving out next month, so it will be available. It's a little bigger with three bedrooms, but only one bath."

Carefully, not totally trusting her feelings, Rachel continued, "You have that property on the other side of town."

"Are you sure, sweetie?"

"I think so. That part of my life is over. We could ask God to cleanse and consecrate the land."

Obviously, Rachel had been giving this idea considerable thought. "I think that is a splendid and very brave thing for you to suggest, Rachel, dear. Shall we talk with Pastor Johns about it?"

"You don't mind, Sam?"

"Of course not, sweetie," I said taking her in my arms. "Now, since that's settled, what kind of house do you want to build?"

"Oh, Sam!" Rachel squealed with love and delight, and I delighted in the spontaneity of having her arms around my neck.

On Wednesday night after prayer meeting, we spoke with Pastor Johns about meeting us to consecrate the Crews property, now the Burkett/Crews property. He said he thought that was a delightful idea and would pick us up Friday morning at 9 a.m.

So, on Friday, my family and I stood in the openness of the five-acre property, well away from the unsightly trailer. In the bright Kentucky morning air, we stood, feeling the warm sunshine on our faces, and we listened. I wanted so much for this to be a final cleansing for Rachel, and the trees and birds played their parts in glorious chorus.

Pastor Johns picked up a handful of soil and emptied a portion into Rachel's and my hands. Following Pastor John's example, we let the soil symbolically slip through our fingers as our minister prayed. "Our Gracious God, we come before You in the name of Jesus and in the power of The Holy Spirit. On our behalf, we ask that You forgive any sin that has been committed on or against this land."

Then, with joined hands, Rachel and our children listened as I prayed, "Father, by an act of our will, we choose to forgive everyone who has sinned against us. We dedicate this place to You, Lord Jesus. Come and be the Lord of this land and our lives. Consecrate and sanctify this land, our new house, and our family. In Jesus's name." As a family and with Pastor Johns, we all said, "Amen."

In silence, and with a deep sense of faith, forgiveness, and renewal, Rachel and I embraced each other, then each of the children. I shook Pastor Johns's hand and offered him a nominal gift, which he graciously declined.

Over the next few months, I had much work to do. First, I called Ray Stevens and asked him to remove what was left of the old trailer. Ken had told me that Ray was looking for a structure for his chickens.

"Mighty glad to help, Sam. Besides, this here frame will make a right nice chicken house for my ladies. How 'bout me bringing my tractor over tomorrow?"

"Perfect. Thank you, Ray. I hope your ladies will be happy in their new home."

Next, I called George Jenkins to ask about clearing the land and laying out the footprint for a new house.

"Sure, Sam. Whatcha got in mind?"

"We are not quite sure, George. I was thinking of a 1,800 square foot two-story with four bedrooms, two baths, and a pool."

"A pool?" quizzed George.

"For a teenager, you know."

On Thursday morning, Rachel and I went to the bank to talk to Ken about financing.

"That's quite an undertaking, Sam. From what you describe, the cost of building a house like this would be in the range of $10,000 to $20,000, depending on the amenities. Let's say you want to finance

$16,000. A VA mortgage rate is currently four percent and cannot exceed twenty years. At that rate, the total expenses of taking out a loan would be $7,269.64, bringing the total loan to $23,268.64. That would be a monthly payment of $96 and change."

Rachel gasped in disbelief.

"Will you check the balance in my account, Ken?" I asked.

"Certainly." Ken opened my bank file, and Rachel sat tense, wringing her hands. "Disregarding your war bonds, your account balance comes to $28,545."

I felt Rachel quake, and I squeezed her hand. I did some quick calculations in my head and decided to forego the VA loan and go with a conventional thirty-year loan. "How 'bout if we split the difference. I'll put down half of the $10,000. That should lower our loan repayment cost to $7,637 and the monthly payments to approximately $21.22."

"We can do that. Miss Riley, will you come in please?"

After signing the papers, Rachel sat back in the leather chair. The leather squeaked and released its soothing fragrance. Rachel exhaled, and I took out my check book and wrote a check.

"There. A new beginning." Then I turned to Rachel. "Now, will you marry me, Rachel?"

The next step for us was Kayla's meeting new friends. It was a slow process that took much reassurance, but Rachel and I introduced Kayla to teenagers at church. We took baby steps; and eventually, our beautiful teenager found her place and blossomed.

In the teen Sunday School class, Kayla became acquainted with Mr. and Mrs. Cooper's granddaughter, Trinity. The two girls hit it off right away and became inseparable. If Kayla was not at Trinity's house, then Trinity was at ours. Because the cabin was so small, the girls spent hours walking in the forest or down the dirt road and just talking. I never knew girls could find so much to giggle about.

At church, Trinity introduced Kayla to other girls. Even a few boys seemed interested. Eventually, Kayla received invitations to sleep-overs and birthday parties. When Rachel and I told Kayla that many of her new her friends would be in some of her classes, she even seemed excited to be starting the tenth grade at Florence High School.

"Sam, now that Kayla is going out at night to sleep-overs and such, should we buy a car? I hate to think of her walking two miles to these parties," Rachel suggested.

"Always the sensible mother, huh? Yes, I think that is an excellent idea. Would you like to go with me to the bank tomorrow? I'm sure Ken must know of good used cars for sale. In fact, he might have some repos."

"Do you think it will be okay if we ask Kayla to stay with Joelle and Sammy?"

"Yes," I replied. "I think it would give her a sense of responsibility and purpose."

The next morning, I spoke with Kayla about staying with the children so Rachel and I could go into town. As I anticipated, Kayla was thrilled that we trusted her.

After lunch, Rachel and I walked the two miles into Florence and straight to the bank. As we walked in, it seemed that magically, Ken appeared before our eyes. "Well, good morning. What can I do for you two fine folks today?"

"Hi, Ken. We find ourselves in a very unfamiliar situation," I began with a twinkle in my eye. Rachel gave me a shove in response to my corny joke.

"Well, you've come to the right place, Mr. Bar ... Bar ...," Ken joked. "I'm sorry. What's your name again?" Ken continued, picking up on my humor.

"Burkett," I replied.

"Oh, yes, Mr. Burkett, we have a wide assortment of services that will fit any unfamiliar situation."

"Oh, Ken," Rachel broke in, "we just need to buy a car."

"I see," Ken said, stroking his chin and still in a comical persona. "I guess your family has expanded. Am I right?"

"Correct." Rachel understood the game.

"And this new expansion is perhaps, of the teenage, female persuasion?"

"Right, again."

"Then you will be wanting something economical and conservative."

"Right on," I chimed in.

"Come this way, my friends. I have a little honey that you will just fall in love with."

Ken led us out back to the parking lot speaking in his farcical used-car salesman jargon the whole time. He nearly danced as he pointed out a cherry red, white-top Ford convertible. "This, folks, is just what you are looking for."

With that, we all had a belly laugh that only good friends can enjoy.

"Seriously, Ken," I broke the hilarity, "we need something practical …"

"… and something that young teenage girls would not be ashamed to be seen in," Rachel quickly added.

"I know what you mean, Missus. Just follow me," Ken said, staying in character.

"Now this little beauty was owned by a little old lady who drove her only on Sunday," Ken joked as he drug Rachel by the arm to a four-wheel drive jeep with a camouflage paint job.

Again, we all bellowed in laughter.

"I'm sorry, not quite what we were looking for, Mr. *Formen*."

"Well, then, I'm gonna tell ya what I'm gonna do." Then, Ken dropped his comical character persona and became serious. "How about this black 1946 Ford sedan with low mileage for only $400?"

"Does it come in bright orange?" Rachel quipped.

"No, unfortunately not. But it does come in baby blue with an optional sun visor," chirped Ken.

"Sold!" I shouted.

"Do you think she will like baby blue, Sam?"

"We'll soon see," I said, squeezing Rachel's arm.

With the title and keys in my hand, Rachel and I skipped out of the bank like a couple of kids. On our way home, we stopped at the grocery store and picked up chocolate ice cream to celebrate. I think we were enjoying being parents to a young teenage girl. I hoped it lasted, but from my memory of being a teenager, moods could change on a dime.

We drove home slowly, enjoying this new sensation of having our own car. Rachel was in the center of the bench seat, and I had my arm around her. When the dirt road was clear, I looked at her beaming face, and I kissed her. We were euphoric.

As we drove the baby blue Ford up to the porter's cabin, I blew the horn, and Rachel and I slid down into the seat and tried to muffle our giggles. It was Sammy who first came running out at the sound of an unfamiliar horn, followed by Kayla carrying Joelle.

Like two kids, Rachel and I popped up and yelled, "Surprise!"

Kayla's mouth fell open, and she put Joelle down for fear that she might drop the baby. "Wow!" was all she could say. Her eyes were as big as the "wow" she exhaled.

Sammy, on the other hand, babbled non-stop. "A new car! Is it a Ford? Is it my car? I'm the boy! You can borrow it sometimes, Kayla."

"No, Mr. Sammy. It is the family car," I said winking at Kayla.

Kayla, still standing in one spot, had tears in her eyes. She was afraid to speak, for fear this wonderful dream would vanish. Finally, when she found her voice she sobbed, "Oh, Sam. Is it really for me?"

Feeling like her knight in shining armor, I nodded.

"Oh, thank you. This is the nicest thing you have …" Then she stopped and thought before continuing. "This is one of the nicest things you have done for me." Kayla turned and smothered Rachel and me in hugs and kisses.

"Do you like it, Kayla? The baby blue, I mean." I asked?

"Who wouldn't?" Kayla gushed and fingered the shiny blue finish.

"Now you can go to sleep-overs and parties in style, me lady," I teased.

"Thank you. Oh, thank you, thank you," Kayla whispered into my mangled ear before melting into another puddle of tears.

Chapter 14

For the moment, all discipline seems painful rather than pleasant, but later it yields the peaceful fruit of righteousness to those who have been trained by it. Hebrews 12:11

While April showers bring May flowers, May brought the end of the school and the end of the year dance. I didn't know who was the most excited about Kayla's end of the year dance—Rachel or Kayla. My two girls had their heads together for weeks, and everything was secret. All I knew was that Kayla had a new dress.

On May tenth, the day of the dance, Rachel, six-year-old Joelle, and sixteen-year-old Kayla spent hours in the tiny bathroom, primping and giggling. "Oh, not that way, sweetie. This is the way it goes. How's that?" Rachel stood back and admired Kayla's blue taffeta dress adorned with a matching chiffon sash and bow.

"Do mine, Mommy."

"There," Rachel patted Joelle's cotton dress. The small sleeveless dress with a full gathered skirt was white with tiny pink rose buds. A stiff crinoline under the skirt held the yards of fabric away from Joelle's body so that she looked like a beautiful fairy ballerina. Joelle wanted large open red roses, but Rachel talked her into rose buds that matched her lips.

"I think you need a little rouge and a tiny bit of eye shadow," Rachel said to Kayla.

"Me, too!"

"Here. Here is a beautiful blue. It will bring out your eyes."

"My eyes are brown, Mommy."

"Do you want to wear your hair up or down? How about a swishy ponytail?"

"I want a ponytail!" Joelle squealed with excitement with each of Rachel's questions.

On and on went the girl chatter. I loved it. *My girls*, I mused. *I never thought I would have three beautiful girls.*

"What happens if I need to go to the bathroom?" I teased.

Rachel giggled, then shouted through the door, "Go outside!"

"Don't worry, Daddy Sam," said Sammy in all seriousness. "All you have to do is find a tree you like."

I laughed and ruffled Sammy's hair. "Come on, Sammy-man. Let's get ice cream."

At last, the hour arrived, and it was time to go to the dance.

"Come on, guys," I shouted, "you don't want to be late."

Rachel exited the bedroom first, followed by a giggling Joelle walking in a toe first fashion with her arms held out away from her crinoline skirt. I had to cover my mouth to hide my laughter, but then my mouth dropped. There in front of me stood a beautiful lady dressed in layers of blue taffeta and chiffon. Her auburn hair, tied up with a dark blue velvet ribbon, swished in a sassy ponytail. Another dark blue velvet ribbon topped with a cluster of baby roses, the color of pink angels' wings, adorned her wrist. I was speechless.

"Well?" Rachel prodded.

"I ... I," I stammered like a fool. "You are beautiful, Kayla."

With those few words, Kayla ran into my arms. I recognized Rachel's perfume scent, and my heart swelled with pride. "Your carriage awaits, me lady."

"Pick up your skirt like I showed you, sweetie," Rachel fussed. "It will keep you from tripping. Besides, it shows off all those beautiful ruffles and your lovely slippers."

Even though Rachel was speaking to Kayla, Joelle followed Rachel's directions perfectly, still walking toe first.

"Load up!" I shouted. "Load up, Sammy."

The whole family piled into the baby blue "princess carriage," and we drove into town.

Just as we arrived at the school gym, Kayla had a melt-down. "What do I do? What do I say? What if a boy asks me to dance? Will I forget what you showed me?"

"Now, sweetie, you will be fine," Rachel said, soothing the distraught teenager. "Just be yourself, and you will be beautiful."

"Kayla," I interjected, "can we say a prayer for you?"

"For me?"

"Sure," said Sammy. "Daddy Sam prays for just me all the time," added Sammy in his Sammy-saves-the-day fashion.

"Yes. Thank you … thank you, Daddy Sam."

Her calling me Daddy Sam caught me by surprise and left me breathless for a second. "Then, let's pray. Gracious Lord, we thank you for Kayla's special occasion. Rachel and I thank you for such a beautiful daughter. Now we ask that You go with her, calm her fears, and protect her. In Jesus's name. Amen."

When we all got out of the car in excited commotion, Kayla grabbed me around my neck in a tender hug and said, "Thank you, Daddy Sam. Thank you for such a beautiful prayer. I feel better."

"I'm glad, sweet lady."

"God go with you, Kayla, and have a wonderful time," Rachel encouraged the teenager.

"We will be back to pick you up at about ten."

"Can you make it nine?" Kayla whispered.

"Sure. You don't worry, and have a good time," I said, fighting back "proud daddy tears."

As Kayla turned to go, the angels—Joy, Hope, and Peace—followed our lovely daughter, then, in an excited frenzy, Trinity bounded out from the gym. I thought we would say one last goodbye, but the teens hurried away in a flurry of taffeta, chiffon, and giggles. I did not move to go until I saw the girls safely in the gym. Even then, I had to will my legs to move. Leaving Kayla at the gym was a big step for both Rachel and me.

When Rachel and I returned to the car, I asked, "How about some pie and ice cream when we get home, kiddos?" But there was no answer from the back seat. Rachel turned around to find Sammy fast asleep.

"They are asleep, Sam," Rachel crooned. "I guess all this primping and giggling was too much."

"What a trooper, that Sammy-man," I chuckled. "This is the first of many lessons on the joys of girls."

Rachel gave me a gentle elbow in my ribs.

When we got home, I picked up a sleeping Sammy from the back seat and carried him to his bed. Rachel followed and tucked him in. Then, our bodies gave way to near emotional exhaustion, and we collapsed on the sofa. We sat together, recounting the days, weeks, and years, basking in our joy.

"Rachel, dear, if you want to go to bed, I will go pick up Kayla."

"Thank you, Sam. I'll make another check on the children before I go to bed."

I put my feet up on the ottoman and exhaled a satisfied breath, glowing in the remembrance of Kayla calling me "Daddy Sam."

"SAM! SAM!"

Rachel's calling my name in such terror, shook me to the bone. My euphoria vanished in a heartbeat. "What is it?" I said rushing to her, upsetting the ottoman.

"Joelle is not here!"

"What?"

"The baby is not here, Sam!"

"I'll check outside. She must still be sleeping in the car."

When I returned to the cabin with empty arms, Rachel broke down. "Oh, Sam! Sam! Where is our baby?

Fearful images of a six-year-old walking home on the dark dirt road gripped my stomach. I had to stop my mind from imagining all the horrors that might happen to her. I trembled in fear when I remembered how on the dirt trail to find a young Kayla, the Deceiver tried to stop me with all his evil powers. "I thought you had her," I said, trying not to sound accusatory.

"No, I thought you had her."

"I was carrying Sammy, remember?"

"Oh, Sam. Where is she?" Rachel ran out of the cabin letting the screen door slam behind her. "Joelle? Joelle! Joelle, where are you?!" Rachel called, turning in panicked circles where she stood.

"I'll circle the cabin," I offered in a weak breath.

As I was trotting back to the front of the cabin, Rachel fell limp into my arms, sobbing in near hysteria. Holding her quaking body, I asked into the air, "Where are the angels? In the happy, pre-party celebration, I forgot about the angels."

Then, my mind went back to Sunday morning, when Pastor Johns read Psalm 4:1.

Answer me when I call, O' God, defender of my cause;
You set me free when I am hard-pressed;
Have mercy on me and hear my prayer.

At that moment, I heard a train whistle. In my desperation, I don't know how I heard it, but I stopped and listened.

"Sam? Sam?"

I recited verse three of Psalm 4:3

Know that the Lord does wonders for the faithful;
when I call upon the Lord, He will hear.
Tremble, then, and do not sin

"Yes, Lord?"

"Sam, go to the gym. It's almost time to pick up Kayla."

"Rachel, we need to go back to the gym."

"Back to the gym?" Rachel answered in disbelief. "We can't go back to the gym now!"

"Yes, Rachel. The Lord told me. We must go back to the gym."

"I'll get Sammy," the brave mother said through her tears.

Rachel carried a sleepy Sammy to the car in his red and blue airplane pajamas, and we drove the two miles in silent agony.

The blue "princess carriage" had not come to a complete stop before Rachel bounded out. My heart dropped to my feet at the thought of her falling under the tires of the still moving car. "Stay in the car, Sammy."

Sammy curled up in the back seat and went back to sleep.

In a desperate trot, I followed Rachel as she ran in a panic into the gymnasium. Then, she stopped short and gasped. My eyes bugged in disbelief, but I was grateful, nonetheless.

There on the gym floor was our six-year-old, Joelle, dancing with one of the senior boys, who stooped over to Joelle's eye level. Her happy ponytail, tied in a dark blue velvet ribbon, bounced to the beat of the music. Another surprise, surrounding our baby were all the angels with their silk organza dresses rustling and their gemstones sparkling with delight.

"What is this?" I blurted.

"*Sh-h-h,*" Rachel whispered, leaning her weary body into mine.

Kayla was standing talking with friends. When she saw us, she hurried over and hugged us. "She's okay," the teenager said. "Joelle slipped away when Trinity came to greet me. *The baby* said she wanted to make sure I would eat."

Just then, Joelle, out of breath from happy exertion, came up to Kayla, grabbed her sister's hand to pull her to the banquet table. "Kayla, you need to eat someth … " , Joelle saw us. Blood dropped from her face, then rushed back again, and she blushed at the thought of "being caught in the act."

"Come, Joelle," I said taking our daughter by the hand. "Mommy will take care of Kayla."

Joelle's hand tensed in mine until I led the trembling girl to the dance floor and twirled her around. Fear and panic faded, and we had a wonderful night together while Sammy slept in the car.

Thank you, Lord, I whispered to myself.

"You are most welcome, My son."

The next day was Sunday, and I was up early talking to the Lord. "Of course, I can't let Joelle's willful act go unpunished, but my heart aches at the thought. What should I do, Lord?"

When I heard Joelle stirring in the bedroom, I called, "Joelle?"

"Yes, sir?" our little daughter answered from the bedroom.

"Baby, will you come here? We need to talk before we go to Sunday School and church."

With slow, apprehensive steps and slumped shoulders, Joelle shuffled out of her room, still in her thin Sleeping Beauty nighty.

"Did you have a good time last night?" I asked.

"Yes, sir."

"So, did I, but you know, Joelle, you scared your mother and me to death. You should not have slipped away from us, no matter what your good intentions were."

"Yes, sir."

"You know I have to punish you, don't you?"

"Yes, sir," Joelle replied in a contrite whisper and a trembling lower lip.

"Come go with me?"

Joelle had watched many times as Sammy walked out back with me. Those times, she knew her brother was in trouble, but she never knew what his punishment was. This time, it was her turn to go out back, and her anxiety was at its peak. She did not know what to expect.

The angels—Compassion, Faith, and Wisdom—flew quietly

around me, while Curiosity and Courage stayed by Joelle.

As we walked, I talked to the frightened little girl without knowing exactly what to say. "Joelle, you frightened your mother and me last night," I repeated. "We didn't know where you were or what might have happened to you. I know you just wanted to take care of Kayla, but you should have asked permission, don't you think?"

"Yes, sir," Joelle replied with downcast and misty eyes.

As we walked along the path behind the cabin, a breeze rustled the leaves in the tree canopy, causing the morning sun to twinkle like diamonds. The songbird's morning greetings filled the trees, but I didn't think Joelle heard them. I could almost hear her frightened heartbeat. We walked along in anxious silence for another while, then stopped. "Well, I think that about does it."

Joelle's pent-up breath escaped, and her eyes looked as big as saucers. I bent down on one knee, grabbed her in my arms, and said, "I love you baby girl."

"I love you, too, Daddy Sam."

We wept in each other's arms, then, in relief, walked hand-in-hand back to the cabin. "Listen to the songbirds, Daddy Sam. Don't they sound happy?"

Pastor Johns's text that morning was from Proverbs 3

Don't reject the instruction of the Lord, my son; don't despise his correction.

The Lord loves those he corrects, just like a father ...

Joelle snuggled under my arm, and I held her close.

Chapter 15

Love suffers long and is kind; love does not envy; love does not parade itself, is not puffed up; does not behave rudely, does not seek its own, is not provoked, thinks no evil; does not rejoice in iniquity, but rejoices in the truth; bears all things, believes all things, hopes all things, endures all things.1 Corinthians 13:4-7

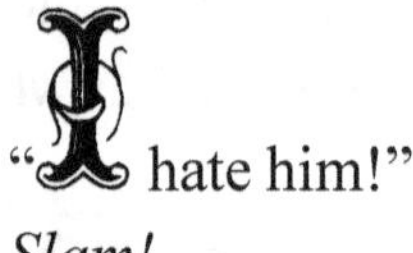

"I hate him!"

Slam!

The sudden exclamation of disgust and slamming of the screen door interrupted my reading and prayer. "Whoa, there. What's wrong?"

"I don't want to talk about it! I hate him!"

"You hate whom?"

"I don't want to talk about it! He's a jerk."

I knew exactly whom Kayla spoke of. It couldn't be anyone but Roger. Roger Billings, a senior in high school, caught Kayla's eye at the school dance, and he asked her to go steady a month later. Going steady was a big deal in Florence, Kentucky. To be crude, supply and demand was an issue, as was location. There were more girls than boys in Florence, and the distance between them was too far to walk. If someone did have a car, there was nowhere to go. Although Roger was one of the lucky few and thought it little inconvenience to drive out to pick up Kayla at the porter's cabin, he was short on time. His work schedule kept him pretty busy.

Hearing the commotion, Rachel came in from the kitchen.

"Must be boy trouble," she beamed. "Our little girl is growing up."

"Yes, but why does she have to grow up so noisily and with such venom?"

"Because our hormones and you men drive us to it," Rachel winked.

"Do you want to go talk to her, or do you want me to?"

"I better go. This is a girl thing."

Rachel tiptoed into the bedroom where Kayla was sobbing. "What's wrong, sweetie?"

"I hate him, Rachel!"

"I know, sweetie. We girls all go through this, sometimes multiple times. Is it Roger?"

In the 1950s, boys in high school fit in one of three pigeonholes: teddy bear, nerd, or jock. Roger was a nerd. He was tall and lanky, and his arms seemed disproportionately too long for his body. However, the size of his heart outmatched the length of his arms. His black slacks, sinched at his waist with a brown belt, rode up to reveal not-so-cool-socks, and his size ten feet, clad in PF Flyers, appeared to flop as he walked. He did not go out for any of the high school athletics, but he was the captain of the math club. The talk of Florence High was that Roger planned to go to the University of Kentucky in Lexington and study engineering.

By this time, the angels—Compassion, Serenity, and Grace— were in the bedroom and fluttered between the overwrought teenager and Rachel.

"Roger? How did you know?" Kayla asked in surprise.

"Oh, sweetie, I have eyes. I see how you and Roger sit together in church, look into each other's eyes, and whisper," Rachel said with compassion and understanding. "Did he physically hurt you?" Rachel asked with trepidation.

"No. Of course not. Roger is too sweet and kind," Kayla whispered, softening her tone. "It's just"—she paused to sob—"it's just he won't let me make a decision."

Sensing a need for her energy in the bedroom, the angel, Wisdom, left Sam and joined her sister angels, Compassion and Serenity, as they hoovered about Rachel.

"Well, what decision did you disagree on?" Rachel pried.

"I wanted to go to The Pink Rose Restaurant, and he wanted to go to the Burger Barn. So, we argued, and we ended up going to the Burger Barn."

"Well, sweetie, maybe you need to look at this from Roger's point of view. Roger has a job after school at the drugstore, doesn't he?"

Kayla nodded through her tears.

"I rather doubt if Roger makes much money at the drugstore."

Another nod with a long sniff.

"Isn't The Pink Rose a little expensive?"

"Yes, ma'am. But it was …"

Rachel interrupted, "I'm not sure there is a good 'but' there. Yes, it was your birthday, and you wanted something special."

Kayla began to brighten a bit, knowing that another woman understood.

"Do you think Roger was being stingy?"

"Yes!"

"Oh, sweetie, you must consider Roger's feelings. When you were at the Burger Barn, what did you do"

"I guess I … pouted."

"What did Roger do?"

"He played my favorite song on the juke box, we danced, he bought me a large chocolate ice cream float instead of a small one, and he put his cherry on top of my whipped cream."

"I'd say that was a lot of acts of love, wouldn't you?"

Kayla was silent.

There was a knock at the screen door.

"I'll get it," I shouted, as if anyone would listen, Then I lay aside my forgotten book.

"Hello, Mr. Burkett."

"Hello, Roger. Won't you come in?"

When I opened the door for Roger, the angel, Courage, rushed in ahead of the nervous young man.

Considering the anguish on Roger's face, I tried to be sympathetic and invited the young man into the living room to take a seat. "Tough times, Roger?"

"Yes, sir."

I chuckled and tried to console a distraught teenager. "You're young. You will have lots of tough times ahead of you. I'm still going through them myself."

"What do you do, sir?" asked a forlorn male teenager.

"Well …" I paused to think. What do I do? "You just have to be a man and let this thing run its course." *What a lame thing to say,* I admonished myself. However, Roger seemed to understand and appreciate my answer. "Rachel is talking to Kayla now, trying to make her feel better and understand."

"I didn't mean to hurt her, Mr. Bur …"

"I know, I know," I waved in the air and tried to reassure Roger. "Depending on the moment, sometimes we men walk into a booby trap, and most often, *we* are the booby."

Roger gave a weak smile.

"I suspect it will all be better in a little while. Just give her time."

I saw Rachel coming from the bedroom and said quickly, "Oh, I have something I need to look after, Roger. Will you excuse me?"

Rachel took Kayla by the hand and led the downcast young maiden into the living room.

As soon as he saw Kayla—I'm sure he saw Rachel, too but it didn't register—Roger stood and shifted from foot to foot, as all we men do in the presence of the lady we love.

"Hello, Roger. So nice of you to call," Rachel said, trying to break the ice.

"Hello, Mrs. Bur- …Mrs. Crews. Hello, Kayla."

That's all it took. Kayla dropped Rachel's hand and ran into Roger's arms.

"Well, I have something I need to attend to," said Rachel, and she joined me in the kitchen from where we listened.

The two young teenagers sat quietly for a moment with all of the angels surrounding them. The atmosphere was syrupy thick and sweet.

"I'm sorry, Kayla."

"Oh, no, Roger. I'm sorry."

There was an awkward silence.

"Roger, thank you for a wonderful time at the Burger Barn."

"I'm sorry I couldn't take you to The Pink Rose, Kayla, it's just that …"

"I understand, Roger. Rachel and I had a talk, and I realize I was selfish."

"Oh, no, Kayla, you are not selfish. I was cheap."

"Oh, no, Roger. You are so sweet and kind, and I … I …"

"Kayla, I have something for you."

"For me?" Kayla asked in surprise, forgetting how, the night before, she wanted something special for her birthday.

Roger reached into the pocket of his corduroy jacket and presented Kayla with a tiny box wrapped in a pink bow. "Happy Birthday, Kayla."

As is common to most women, Kayla burst into tears and fell on Roger's shoulder.

Roger must have thought to himself, *Mr. Burkett didn't tell me what to do now*, but the brave young man rallied and held Kayla, then said, "Open it."

Between tears, sniffs, giggles, and wiping her nose, Kayla slowly and gingerly opened the tiny box. When she lifted the lid, she gasped, and the tears rolled again.

"Here, Kayla, let me help you put it on."

Kayla turned and lifted her beautiful auburn hair for Roger to fasten a tiny heart-shaped locket around her neck.

"Oh, Roger. It is so beautiful," Kayla crooned.

"Will you forgive me, Kayla?"

"Oh, no, Roger, will *you* forgive *me*."

Rachel and I held each other while the teenagers sat in romantic silence. At last, when it seemed the silence lasted a little too long, Rachel and I joined the embarrassed teens in the living room.

"So," I interjected, "does anyone want ice cream?"

Chapter 16

A friend loveth at all times...Proverbs 17:17

Our summer activity increased with commotion and sounds of a hectic, happy family. Our new house was finally ready.

Rachel rushed about in a tizzy, trying to orchestrate packing the cabin and supervising delivery of shipments from Sears and Western Auto. After Rachel and the girls finished packing all the boxes of toys, clothes, and kitchen pots, pans, and dishes, there was hardly room to move in the tiny cabin. It's amazing how much stuff a little family accumulates in just a few short years.

Mr. Eddie and Mr. Cooper drove up to the porter's cabin in an old black Ford pick-up truck. Mr. Cooper made a wide turn and coaxed the gears into reverse. The old manual transmission ground its teeth and complained, but finally, the faithful truck whined as it backed up to the cabin. With their help, Sammy and I loaded multiple boxes of our family's simple possessions. Rachel and the girls had already gone ahead in the car, carrying dishes and linen. I knew Rachel could hardly wait to tear into the delivery boxes, even though she had ordered the household items herself. Today would be like Christmas.

Mr. Eddie took me aside and whispered, "Our ladies have made a special surprise for your moving day." This filled me with joyful anticipation, but there was little time to ponder what surprise the ladies might conjure up. Besides, I wouldn't want to spoil the ladies' surprise for Rachel.

When the building of the house began, I requested the builders to frame the southeast facing kitchen window with a trellis. I envisioned passionflowers and morning glories twining together to fill and bedazzle the white trellis to greet Rachel each morning with hues of blue and purple. Fluttering butterflies in assorted shapes and colors completed my daydream and my special gift for Rachel.

When we men, Sammy included, arrived at the new house, the girls hurried out to meet us. Rachel wanted us to share in a glorious welcome to our new home together. When my family and I saw our new farmhouse-style home, we stood, gaping at the beauty. The two-story farmhouse stood tall and gleaming white. Overlapping vertical circles formed the railings of a full-length porch. Grand rectangular columns, also painted white, supported a tongue and groove ceiling. This ceiling, painted with historic blue, offered the perfect tranquil welcome to wide oak double doors stained the color of burgundy wine. Brass hardware, complete with a brass kickplate, finished the gleam of our front porch.

Mrs. Cooper and Mrs. Eddie had already added their special surprises. Terra-cotta pots filled with red and pink geraniums graced each of the seven steps leading to the porch while four hanging baskets of Boston fern hung full and green from the horizontal frame of the porch.

As if in their own welcome, summer wildflowers dotted the field around the farmhouse. Yellow black-eyed Susans, purple cornflowers, and red flocks danced among banks of native grasses playing in the breeze. At the back of our five acres stood a small forest of Kentucky shade trees along with flowering dogwood here and there. A split rail fence completed the rustic look. Honeysuckle made its home on the fence and bathed the air with its sweet essence, a stark contrast to the barren trees Rachel remembered years ago. All remnants of the old trailer were now gone, providing a new home for Ray Stevens's chickens.

I heard in the distance the soft sound of a train's whistle and smiled. *Thank You, Lord.*

When Sammy and I entered the house through the wide double doors, we found that Rachel and the girls had already unpacked some of the home furnishings Sears and Roebuck delivered a month earlier. Boxes, tissue, and packing material covered the wood floors.

In much fanfare with the predictable *oos* and *ahs*, Rachel pulled white Pricilla curtains from their boxes.

"I guess it's my job to hang curtains." I said with a sly grin. Rachel just shrugged and smiled her sweet, knowing smile.

When Mr. Eddie brought in the last of the boxes, we all sat on the floor, exhausted but exhilarated. Looking around me, I admired the new dining room table and chairs, a China hutch, and buffet. The southeast facing bay window glowed in the afternoon sun.

"Wouldn't a pot of African violets look nice on the windowsill?" I asked.

Rachel looked at me in surprise, as did Kayla.

"What? You didn't think I knew about flowers?"

Laughter relaxed our weary bodies.

As Mr. Cooper and Mr. Eddie started to leave, I gave each of them ten dollars with a firm handshake with my stubby fingers and my heart-felt gratitude. "You don't have to do this, Sam," said Mr. Cooper.

"I know I don't, but then you didn't have to do all this," I said, motioning to the chaos of boxes.

"We're just glad to help out, Sam. It makes us feel like part of your new home."

I watched and waved goodbye as my friends drove back to town.

Loud laughter, squeals, and giggles led me to the back of the house and through the screen door. I stood in the shade of the porch and beamed as I watched Sammy and Joelle explore the new pool. I had to admit, the water reflecting the blue Kentucky sky did look inviting.

"Lunch time," Rachel called. I had to stand aside from the stampede of two frolicking children. But I didn't mind, for my heart was so filled with joy.

"What's for lunch? I'm starving."

I turned, expecting to see Sammy patting his empty belly, but to my surprise, it was Kayla.

"Cheerios?" I quipped.

"How about tuna sandwiches?" a wise and thoughtful Rachel interjected.

When we all sat around our new dining room table with fresh tuna sandwiches, my heart soared higher.

"Let's pray. Our Father, thank You for our new home, new dining room table, new curtains. Thank You for my family and tuna sandwiches."

Sammy finished, "Amen."

Again, I heard the train in the distance, and smiled.

After three months, Rachel was still unpacking and placing home furnishings. She placed a chair here next to an end table adorned with silver candlesticks. She stood back and studied the placement, then moved the chair to the other side of the end table. She placed a yellow checked throw pillow on a blue chair, then changed her mind and replaced it with a purple embroidered pillow. She repeated this activity in each room. Worn out from just watching, I went to the den to find my old favorite chair, but I continued listening to Rachel's happy occupation. She was in her element, consumed with joy.

Kayla was in her room, admiring the canopy bed and ruffled pillows. Then, she went to the bureau and primped in front of the wide mirror. What more could a young teenager wish for, unless it was for a special friend who came often to swim? Roger was a frequent guest when his work schedule allowed. It was a wonderful summer.

Joelle hummed as she played with her dolls, brushing their thinning hair and changing their limp clothes. Changing doll clothes gave Rachel a much-deserved break from picking up dozens of little dresses that Joelle tried on, then tossed aside. As always, the angels, Joy and Curiosity, stayed close by as Joelle played.

The soft humming that filled the house warmed my heart. Then Sammy came in to stand beside my chair where I was reading.

"Daddy Sam?"

"Sir?"

"Are we *effluent?* "

Well, that did it. I lost the text I just read. "What do you mean, Sammy? Where did you hear that word?"

"From Trey. Trey said people with a new car, a new house, and swimming pool are *effluent.*"

I covered my mouth with my book to hide my chuckle. "Well, I think the word Trey was looking for was *affluent.* That means well to do."

"You mean rich?"

"Yes, I guess you could say that."

The little boy looked at me with lamenting eyes and asked in all Sammy-seriousness, "Are we rich, Daddy Sam?"

"I wouldn't call us rich, Sammy. I would rather say blessed. God has given us many gifts and lots of love."

Then, with sad puppy-dog eyes, Sammy whispered, "I don't want to be rich, Daddy Sam."

"What's this?" I asked in surprise. "Are you unhappy?"

With downcast eyes, Sammy shrugged his drooping shoulders, signaling that he didn't want to answer.

"Does this have anything to do with Trey thinking we are affluent?"

Sammy replied with another shrug.

I pulled my namesake into my lap and gave him a bear hug. "I'll work on it, Sammy. Don't you worry about it. You just enjoy what God has given us."

The next day, I drove over to Kyle Sims's farm. His property was adjacent to ours but sprawled for forty acres. His fertile, freshly tilled soil produced an abundance of money crops: corn, soybeans, and tobacco. Kyle also grew vegetables for his family, a talent I wanted to learn for mine. When I drove up to his modest red-brick house, Carolyn Sims came out of the kitchen to greet me.

"Kyle is out plowing the field, Sam. He should be coming this-a-way shortly. Can I get you a glass of cold iced tea?"

"Thank you, ma'am. That would be nice." I knocked the dirt off my boots before going into her small but spotless kitchen. "Mmm. Something smells good."

"Peach preserves, and I just took a pan of hot biscuits out of the oven. Would you like to try them?"

"Yes, ma'am. I never turn down homemade peach preserves and hot biscuits."

As I savored Carolyn's preserves, we chatted about our families. She spoke as if she already knew why I was there.

"How is Rachel and the kids, Sam?"

"They are fine and busy as you can expect, Carolyn. I keep thinking Rachel has the parlor just the way she wants it, then she rearranges it again."

Carolyn giggled. "That's what we women do best, Sam. Kyle shakes his head every time I rearrange the living room."

Carolyn paused before asking, "And how is Sammy?"

"Sammy is Sammy. I'm afraid he is going through an emotional growing spurt right now."

"Oh? How do you mean?" Carolyn asked, prodding.

"Peer pressure," I replied.

"I see. Trey also. He watched the whole time your house was

being built and just moped around."

"Do you think their emotional states are connected?" I asked.

"Oh! I didn't think about that. They very well could be."

"I have a plan that might solve both their problems. That's why I've come to speak with Kyle. I'm thinking of putting in a small garden and need to borrow a tractor."

Before I finished sharing my plan with Carolyn, her eyes twinkled, and a light went on. "Good plan. I hear the tractor coming. I'll take your dishes. Would you take these biscuits and peach preserves to Kyle when you go talk to him? He surely needs a snack after plowing all morning. This will give him energy to think up an appropriate strategy."

I walked out to the edge of the field just as Kyle was making a turn. He returned my wave and stopped the tractor.

"Howdy, Sam," Kyle called, jumping down from the tall red International Harvester tractor. "What brings you over this-a-way?"

Kyle greedily grabbed the plate of biscuits and preserves and downed one in two bites.

"Two boys, Kyle."

Kyle chuckled knowingly then asked, "You cookin' up a plan to teach them a lesson?"

"Tryin' to, but I need your help."

Kyle chuckled again and invited me to sit in the shade while he finished his second biscuit. "Trey has sure been mopin' around lately."

"Sammy, too. I think they are comparing their 'wealth'." I laughed.

"If they only knew."

"Exactly. Are you game to help me?"

"Sure. I remember when my daddy taught me a thing or two about comparin'."

"Okay, here's the plan. I was thinking of putting in a small garden, but I don't have a tractor, not to mention the know-how.

If you could take off a couple of hours and help me stake out and plow my field, maybe Trey will see just how rich his daddy is, and how much I need his help."

"Sure. Then, after a hard day's work, we can all relax by the pool, and the boys can play. Then they can find out each other's real value. Sounds like a good plan."

So, Kyle arranged to ride his tractor over to our place with Trey. I played dumb, which was not hard to do, and Kyle displayed his wealth of knowledge of agriculture. Together, along with Sammy and Trey, Kyle and I put in several rows of sweet corn, pole beans, black-eyed peas, and kale. The boys worked hard, and they played hard, pelting each other with clods of freshly turned soil.

When we finished plowing, Kyle instructed me in proper planting, fertilizing, and watering. We played it up good, so that Trey could feel important.

When it was time to play, it was Sammy's turn to feel important. The plan worked. Kyle and I basked in a good day's work, helping neighbors, and 'growing young men.' We enjoyed watching our sons play in the cool water of the pool and solidify a friendship. The rest of the summer, Sammy and Kyle ran back and forth between Kyle's farm and our home, enjoying each other's riches.

"Daddy Sam?"

"Sir?"

"I like Trey. He's fun."

"I'm glad to hear it, Sammy."

"You know what, Daddy Sam? I told Trey how lucky he is to have a farm and a tractor and know all about growing food. It made him feel good."

"I'm proud of you, Sammy-man. God has blessed us all with different kinds of riches."

"Yes, sir."

A knock at the back door interrupted our "manly-man" conversation. It was Trey.

Chapter 17

Her children arise up, and call her blessed; her husband also, and he praiseth her. Proverbs 31:28

nlike the tiny porter's cabin, we had plenty of room. The two-story farmhouse boasted four bedrooms and two baths for a total of nineteen hundred square feet, not common in Florence, Kentucky. Everyone seemed content in our new home. Everyone except me. I still longed for Rachel to marry me and be my wife. I was determined and refused to give up asking her. I knew she loved me, but there was something that held her back.

Thursday morning, the stairs reverberated with laughter and footsteps as the children came down for breakfast. I looked at Rachel and winked. "Ready or not …"

Rachel was ready. Breakfast was hot and on the table.

"Good morning, family," I beamed.

"Good morning, Daddy Sam," the three replied in succession. "Good morning, Mommy."

I picked up my Bible and turned to the passage I had secretly selected. "Family, I want to share God's Word with you before we have this wonderful breakfast. This is taken from the Book of Proverbs, Chapter 31, verses 24-28 and 29-31. This passage extolls mothers."

She makes linen garments and sells them,
and supplies the merchants with sashes.
She is clothed with strength and dignity;

she can laugh at the days to come.
She speaks with wisdom,
    and faithful instruction is on her tongue.
She watches over the affairs of her household
    and does not eat the bread of idleness.
Her children arise and call her blessed;
"Many women do noble things,
    but you surpass them all."
Charm is deceptive, and beauty is fleeting;
    but a woman who fears the Lord is to be praised.
Honor her for all that her hands have done,
    and let her works bring her praise at the city gate.

"Thank you, Rachel, for a wonderful breakfast. Let's pray. Our Father we do thank You for a virtuous mother and friend. Thank you for her constant love and care, and once again, a delicious breakfast. In Jesus's name. Amen."

When I opened my eyes, Rachel was not in her seat. I heard her in the kitchen, busy at something she imagined she forgot. I followed her to the kitchen, and she fell into my arms.

"Rachel. You know there is more to that passage, much more. It not only extolls the virtues of a good mother but of a good wife."

She buried her face in my chest and sobbed.

"Have I said the wrong thing, Rachel, dear?"

She shook her head no but did not look up.

"Rachel?" I asked softly. "Are you ready to give me an answer?"

She shook her head yes and thew her arms around my neck. "Yes, Sam. Yes. Yes, I will marry you."

Chills ran through my entire body, and I embraced Rachel close, so close that we seemed as one.

I heard a soft train's whistle.

Thank You, Lord.

"You're welcome, My son."

Rachel and I returned to six surprised eyes and shared our news with our children. "Children, your mother, has agreed to be my wife."

Dishes and silverware rattled as excited legs and knees kicked and bumped the table.

That summer was magical for everyone, including the angels. The angels flitted back and forth from Joelle's bedroom where she played, out to the pool, and then followed Sammy and Trey on their adventures.

Kayla and Roger spent as much time together as his schedule would allow. The two teenagers spent countless hours around the pool, holding hands and whispering to each other. The angel, Grace, stayed close, watching over Kayla and Roger's secret kisses, while Serenity bathed the teenagers in her watermelon tourmaline to provide peace and deep joy. Serenity was careful to help Kayla avoid the subject of school starting in the fall, for The University of Kentucky had accepted Roger, and he would be leaving for Lexington in September.

Trey and Sammy disappeared for hours on end with their PF Flyer high tops tied together and thrown over their shoulders. The angel, Curiosity, was in her element as she followed the boys in fields and forests. In the afternoons, when the boys returned home wet, dirty, and excited, they talked over each other as they shared their adventure stories. Most often their adventures involved walking through a freshly plowed field. Hot clods of soil delivered a thrilling cool sensation when smashed between bare toes. Then the adventurers' attentions might turn to military maneuvers, hurling clods of dirt at each other, cheering into the air as the clods exploded harmlessly upon landing. An equally exciting adventure for the boys was running into the tall virgin forest that bordered the fields. There, among the native grasses, boulders, streams, and vines, the boys allowed their vivid imaginations to take them into strange places and military maneuvers.

Joelle spent hours in her room trying on dresses, playing with her dolls, and talking to the angels. Occasionally, Rachel treated Joelle to the mother/daughter activity of baking cookies. With the cookies baked and her tummy full, Joelle went to the pool, followed closely by the angel, Harmony. At the pool, Joelle eavesdropped on Kayla and Roger, and Harmony did her best to intercede between the teenagers who felt that Joelle invaded their privacy and the little girl who loved her big sister and wanted to be a part of her life. However, the teenagers were grateful when Rachel called Joelle in for a nap.

On those infrequent times that Rachel and I had any quiet hours, we spent them talking about wedding plans. With the Sears and Roebuck catalog between us, we looked at wedding dresses and veils, bridesmaid dresses, wedding attire for Sammy, tiny pillows trimmed with lace, and flowers … lots of flowers. At first, I suggested a small, simple wedding but quickly learned that I knew nothing about weddings. We did agree on having our wedding at the church with Pastor Johns officiating. To be safe, and to save money, of course, Pastor Johns asked the church secretary to print an announcement in the church bulletin inviting the entire church family to the wedding and reception.

"What about the reception, Sam?" Rachel asked, already glowing like a bride.

"We can have it at the church fellowship hall or …"

"Or we can have it *here* at our new home!" squealed Rachel.

"I think having the reception here would be a splendid idea, dear."

"What do you want to serve at the reception?"

"Cake and punch," I replied in my ignorance.

"Sam?" Rachel squealed, "We have to have tiny finger sandwiches and nuts and mints, and, and, and …"

The "ands" went on and on. Finally, a light went on, and I ventured a suggestion. "Why don't we hire a wedding planner?"

"Oh, Sam, could we?"

Thank You, Lord, I whispered to myself.

"Rachel, will you excuse me? I need to make a run into town?"

With a look of surprise on her face, Rachel graciously consented to relieve me of wedding plans for just this once.

As I drove our baby blue Ford down the dirt road, I heard the distinctive whistle of a train. "Does it show, Lord?"

…

"Yes, I am very happy, happier than I can ever remember."

…

"Of course, Lord. You have given her to me. Of course, I will take care of her."

Just then, I saw Kyle driving his tractor west, back to his house from his cornfield. He waved, but I didn't see him in time.

"I wonder what Kyle thinks of me grinning from ear to ear talking out loud?"

…

"Oh, does he? I'm glad. I thought he was a believer, too. I don't know what I would do if I did not have You to talk to. You have been such a good friend all these years."

…

"I love You, too, Lord."

As I drove up to the jewelry store and parked, the train's whistle gently disappeared in the distance.

"Well, hello, Sam," Mr. Ryan greeted me. "What can I do for you today? Does your watch need to be repaired again?"

"No, Mr. Ryan. Actually, I am shopping."

"Shopping, is it? Cuff links? Tie clasp?"

"A wedding ring," I announced with chills running up my arms.

After buying a suitable wedding ring, I stopped by the bank to ask Ken if he would do me the honor of being my best man.

"Sam! Sam!" Ken came around his desk and excitedly shook my hand and then grasped me in a bear hug. "Of course! I would be delighted. When's the date?"

The date? I shook the silvery cobwebs and wedding bells out of my mind. "Well, Ken, Rachel and I have not discussed a date," I admitted.

Ken laughed. "I know exactly how you feel, Sam. Been looking at wedding dresses and such?"

"How did you know?"

"You have that scared bridegroom look." Ken laughed again.

"Yes. I never knew there was so much to it. To be honest, when Rachel said yes, it took my breath away. I had asked her before, and she wanted to think about it. I never thought of setting a date."

"Have you bought a ring, Sam?"

I reached into my khaki pants and took out the box. When I opened it, Ken whistled his astonishment.

"Well, I guess you did buy a ring. It's a dandy, Sam. I guess you best be going home, then, to give it to your pretty lady," Ken chuckled.

"I guess I'd better. See you later, Ken." I started to leave, then turned. "By the way, Ken, do you have any more property that might make a good investment?"

"I'll keep my eyes open for you, Sam. Right now, you have more important things to think about." Ken chuckled again.

When I got home, Rachel was in the kitchen starting dinner. The stove was laboring with full pots of steaming vegetables, rice, and meat sauce. I tried to compose my thoughts before I called her.

"Rachel?"

"Yes, Sam."

"Just a minute. Let me turn off the stove."

I knew it was silly, but as I waited for Rachel, my legs quaked. "What should I say, Lord? How should I say it?"

To my surprise, the four angels fluttered into the den from the direction of the swimming pool.

"You said it twice, Sam," said Hope.

"Just ask her again," added Courage.

"But this time get down on one knee," giggled Serenity.

"Oh, Serenity, dear, that's a little much, don't you think?"

"Here she comes," cried Courage.

"Yes, Sam?" Rachel said as she entered the den, wiping her hands on her apron.

"Oh," I exhaled.

Oh? Is that all I could say?

"Oh, can you wait a minute, Rachel?"

I went to the back door and called the children. Kayla and Roger were by the pool, Sammy and Trey were trying to wash off the muddy adventures from their feet, and Joelle was, of course, eavesdropping close to Kayla.

"Children, will you come in please? You, too, Roger. You can come, too, Trey."

There, I did it. Step one.

The children came in giggling and slamming the screen door. That was not at all the solemn occasion I was hoping for.

"Rachel, will you sit here please?"

I took Rachel by her shoulders and directed her to the overstuffed chair. Obediently, she sat but stared at me as if I had lost my mind.

"Sammy and Trey, you better sit on the floor. You're still muddy."

As I stood facing Rachel, she still had a puzzled look on her face.

"Rachel," I said, clearing my throat.

"Yes, Sam?"

I could tell Rachel was waiting for my announcement that I bought more property. However, when I knelt in front of her,

Rachel covered her mouth with her hands, and tears gleamed in her eyes. I reached into the pocket of my khakis and held before her a tiny box. Kayla gasped with joy, for she remembered the tiny box Roger gave her for her birthday. That tiny box contained the gold heart-shaped necklace that she wore so faithfully.

"Rachel, I have loved you for a long time and with my whole heart." As I opened the tiny box, a rainbow of brilliant light from a cluster of diamonds gleamed into Rachel's tear-filled eyes. "Rachel, will you do me the honor of being my wife?"

Rachel choked, then nodded, "Yes, Sam, I will. I have loved you for a long time, too. I love you with my whole heart. Yes, Sam. Yes, I will be your wife."

I pulled Rachel to her trembling feet and held her in my equally trembling arms.

"But Daddy Sam," started Joelle, "you already asked Mommy to marry you."

"Yes, baby, but this time, I did it right."

"And I answered right," added Rachel with tears streaming down, making her face shine.

Then, to our surprise, all the children, and even their friends, joined us in our hug with shouts of joy.

"You know what we haven't done, Rachel?" I asked.

"Set the date?" she replied with shining eyes.

"So, my dear, when would you like to be married?"

"Before I leave for college, I hope," added Roger.

"Very well, let's make it September first."

The children danced around Rachel and me as we embraced again, watching our smiling family.

Chapter 18

*I will lift up mine eyes unto the hills, from
whence cometh my help. Psalm 121:1*

The inevitable happened. June turned to July, which turned to August. I couldn't believe how fast my family was growing. Kayla would be a junior in high school; Sammy was chomping at the bit to be a fifth-grader; and Joelle was excited to start first grade.

In the following weeks, Rachel, the children, and I shopped in the Sears catalog for school clothes.

Kayla, of course, wanted the now popular poodle skirt and matching sweaters and straight skirts with crisp Oxford shirts. Oh, and only black and white saddle shoes would do, whatever they were.

Thank goodness, Sammy was still happy with dungarees and t-shirts. However, he didn't want new ones.

"Daddy Sam," Sammy lamented, "I can't play marbles in stiff new dungarees! All the other boys would laugh at me."

So, Rachel promised to wash the new dungarees at least twice before school started.

Joelle, while only six and in the first grade, wanted her full, gathered skirts to almost cover her knees.

"Why do you want your dresses to be so long, baby?" Rachel asked.

"Because, Mommy, if my skirts are too short, my panties show when I sit on top of the monkey bars, and Todd and the other boys poke us girls with sticks and laugh at our panties.

Rachel tried to be sympathetic, but watching out of the corner of my eye, I saw her roll her eyes. "Sweetie, little girl dresses just look better short. How about if you don't sit on top of the monkey bars?"

Joelle wailed with big tears running through the dirt on her face. "What about naptime?"

"What about naptime?" I asked in all innocence and ignorance.

Joelle snuffled her reply, "At naptime, I can't keep my skirt down. My panties show!"

"Sweetie, all the children are supposed to be taking a nap. No one will be looking at your panties," Rachel consoled to no avail. Joelle cried all the harder.

"Rachel, don't the first graders have a mat or rug to nap on?"

"Yes," Rachel replied not knowing where I was going with this.

"Baby, how about if we ask your teacher if you can have a little blanket in addition to your rug? That way you can use the little blanket to cover your panties."

The sniffing and snuffling stopped. "Okay," Joelle whispered.

To my surprise, the compromise was acceptable. Joelle climbed into my lap, snuggled into my scarred face, and rubbed my stubby ears. Another crisis averted.

At the end of August, Rachel and I watched the church bulletin for our wedding invitation. Rachel was giddy with anticipation at the buzz the notice would create.

However, on the anticipated day, there was no glorious wedding invitation. Instead, the entire church family sat in stunned silence when Pastor Johns made a different announcement.

"Dear friends, it is with great sadness that I must announce that the Billings family was involved in an automobile accident while driving their son, Roger, to Lexington. They were taking Roger to look for housing at the University. Betty and Seth are in serious condition in the Boone County Hospital."

A wave of gasps rolled over the congregation.

"Roger, their son, was killed instantly."

A heart-piercing shriek and uncontrollable scream eclipsed the new wave of moans. Rachel held Kayla tight in her arms and let her daughter shake in hysteria and cry in unrestrained sobs.

The angels—Peace, Compassion, and Hope—who had been playing with children sitting with their parents, flew to our teenager's side. Several ladies of the church gathered around the distraught teenager and her mother. I could do nothing but pray.

Why, Lord?

A gentle train whistle sounded in the distance.

Yes, Lord. I trust You. You know I do, but this is just so hard to bear.

...

A different direction for her? She's just beginning her life. She doesn't even have a grasp on the present. What new direction can You have for her?

...

What about Roger, Lord? Doesn't he deserve a choice?

...

Finished? What job did he finish?

...

With You now? I'm sorry, Lord, that's just no consolation at the moment.

...

Forgive me, Lord. Forgive my doubting. Give me Your strength and wisdom to help my daughter understand.

There was not much that Rachel and I could do for Kayla at that desperate moment, so we gathered our stunned family and drove home.

With the joys of poodle skirts, brightly colored sweaters, and saddle shoes forgotten, Kayla refused to leave her room. For nearly a week, Rachel and I could hear her constant sobbing through the locked door.

"Kayla, sweetie, please come out and share dinner with the family," Rachel implored.

"Please leave me alone," Kayla sobbed.

Even Joelle tried to coax Kayla out with their famous tea parties, but Kayla would not even come out for her baby sister. Fearing for Kayla's safety, I called Doc Proctor, and of course, he came right over.

When Doc arrived, I had to unlock Kayla's door and felt like I was violating my daughter's privacy, but I knew it was for her own good. When I opened the door, Doc and I rushed in, followed closely by a panicked Rachel. Kayla lay unconscious on her bed. Her face was sunken as it was when I first saw her, and she moaned in pain. The angels, Peace and Hope, sat on Kayla's bed. Compassion flitted frantically around the room as if she didn't know what to do.

"Kayla!" Rachel cried but could do little more than stand gripped in terror, then leaned into my chest.

When Doc finished taking Kayla's vital signs, he whispered, "You were wise to call me, Sam. It doesn't look good. I'm afraid she has relapsed, and often a relapse can be more serious. I suggest we take her to the hospital."

Rachel gasped and quaked in my arms. I was not much stability for her, for my strength had left me, too.

Doc Proctor admitted Kayla that evening as an emergency case. When Rachel and I walked into Kayla's hospital room, Rachel's body tensed as if rigor mortis had set in. Her rigid limbs refused to move, and her face was ashen. Had I not held her up, she would have collapsed before making it to Kayla's bedside. Was Rachel reliving the nightmare of visiting Randall in the hospital when he was dying? All I could do was reassure her, support her, and pray.

I didn't want to lose her.

Every day for three weeks from the time of her admission, Rachel and I visited Kayla while Sammy and Joelle were in school, and each day, we watched as our beautiful daughter slipped deeper into a coma.

The constant beeping of a heart monitor assaulted our minds with a monstrous, unnerving sound. As our bodies and minds tired, the sound seemed to swell and pulsate, slapping our tormented faculties back to reality. Eventually, however, our minds fought to block it out. When our ears no longer heard that annoyance, the rhythmic whooshing of a breathing machine pummeled us with its stark reminder of the coma that threatened Kayla's life—even all of our lives. As if all that was not enough, tubes protruded from or entered into Kayla's emaciated nose and arm like some kind of otherworldly worms from a horror movie. These tubes seemed to take on an evil life of their own, intent on twining their tenacles around our feet and hands, trying to keep us away from our daughter. Even though orderlies disinfected the room and equipment daily, Kayla's foul breath and the stench of death permeated the room.

"Kayla? Kayla, it's Daddy Sam. We love you, baby girl."

Kayla's blood pressure did not change, and her eyes showed no signs of movement. I willed her beautiful blue eyes to open, but there were no signs of life.

"Kayla, can you squeeze my hand?" I asked, half hoping to feel even a small pressure as her reply, but there was nothing. However, I did not let go of her thin, boney hand. I just prayed.

The angels—Compassion, Hope, Faith, and Courage—fluttered over Kayla, spreading the energies of their God-given gemstones over our daughter. I had seen and felt the gemstones energy before but thought little of them. The gemstones, elements of His own creation, are indeed, beautiful, uplifting, and mysteriously powerful. But now, I saw clearly. I know it was God's power that enabled the gemstones. That it is His light and energy alone, that could heal our daughter.

Despite the nightmarish sounds of life monitoring machines, the angels spread peace and comfort throughout the room. Compassion's opals spread over Kayla's lifeless body, burning through my daughter's wounds, both visible and invisible. The energy from Faith's deep blue tanzanite combined with the fire from Compassion's opals filled the hospital room with added love and empathy.

Curiosity's amber flowed over both Kayla and me to provide a sense of well-being. A yellow glow from Hope's topaz mingled with Curiosity's amber, filling my heart with strength and courage. For a fleeting moment, I was able to imagine Kayla's happiness for a bright future.

Courage sang as she sat on Kayla's shoulder, and her sister angels fluttered over Kayla's withered body.

Abide with me, fast falls the eventide
The darkness deepens Lord, with me abide
When other helpers fail and comforts flee
Help of the helpless, oh, abide with me

"Strengthen my heart, Lord, and let me sing," I prayed.

Courage, always my companion, spread the cool energy of her emeralds over me, giving the sense of emotional strength. "Thank You, Lord."

"You're welcome, My son. Remember, I am always with you."

Little Curiosity joined in the singing. At first, she only hummed the tune.

"Curiosity!" Courage scolded. *"That's a song we sing about the incarnate birth of God the Son."*

"Yes, I know," replied a meek Curiosity, *"but the last half of the song is special for Kayla."* Curiosity sang the words in a whispered voice:

I love You, Lord Jesus
Look down from the sky
And stay by my cradle
'til morning is nigh
Be near me, Lord Jesus
I ask You to stay
Close by me forever
And love me I pray

Bless all the dear children
In Your tender care
And fit us for heaven
To live with You there

As the angels sang, I lifted my tear-filled eyes. I realized at that moment that I had been downcast, sinking in a mire of hopelessness and self-pity. The heavy load on my heart was of my own making, and I felt ashamed.

"Forgive me, Lord. Help me to keep my heart and eyes on You."
With that prayer, I remembered the words to Psalm 121.
I will lift up mine eyes unto the hills, from whence cometh my help.
My help cometh from the Lord, which made heaven and earth.
He will not suffer thy foot to be moved: he that keepeth thee will not slumber.
Behold, he that keepeth Israel shall neither slumber nor sleep.
The Lord is thy keeper: the Lord is thy shade upon thy right hand.
The sun shall not smite thee by day, nor the moon by night.
The Lord shall preserve thee from all evil: he shall preserve thy soul.
The Lord shall preserve thy going out and thy coming in from this time forth, and even for evermore.

After remembering those words, my heart felt lighter and my mind clearer. Then I recalled Pastor Johns's message from 2 Chronicles 20, how the people of Judah and Jerusalem, even in their fear of impending battle, bowed down and sang praises to God for the victory even before the battle began.

Almost immediately, I joined with the angels' song.

To God be the glory
Great things He has done.
So loved He the world that He gave us His Son
Who yielded His life an atonement for sin
And opened the life-gate that all may go in.

Praise the Lord, praise the Lord
Let the earth hear His voice.

Praise the Lord, praise the Lord
Let the people rejoice

Oh, come to the Father
Through Jesus the Son
Give Him the glory
Great things He has done

My heart soared. "Thank You, Lord."

Just then, I heard a familiar sound. But was I in such a euphoria that I was dreaming? No! I heard it. I clearly heard it. I had heard it before, but this time, it was as if I heard it for the first time.

A train whistle, loud and strong, sounded.

"He's coming!" called Hope.

"He's coming!" echoed Faith.
"Sir is coming!" added little Curiosity.

Chapter 19

Florence, Kentucky in Boone County was not a scheduled stop, as witnessed by Sam's arrival home from the war. But today, the train stopped again, and a young man got off.

This man was not a cripple, as Sam was. This young man was strong and handsome and walked with purpose and carried a black bag. This young man's name was Stephen Abbott.

Angels flew over and around Stephen as if they knew God had given him wisdom, skills, and strength of character for a special mission.

Wisdom, dressed in green and purple, showered Stephen with the positive energy of her lovely peridot gemstones.

Red silk organza rustled as Passion moved. Her rhodolite gemstones enhanced Stephen's understanding. The strength God gave him enabled Stephen to use his talents and to share them with others.

Hematite's blue and teal silk organza twinkled as flashes of blue sapphire and brilliant emeralds enhanced Stephen's mental focus, allowing him to stay centered in his heart's wisdom.

Agate, dressed in earthy colors, flashed the healing energies of the lovely rainbow colors of fluorite.

Lastly, Compassion wore pink silk organza embellished with silvery spiderwebs and opals. Compassion's opals carried a spiritual energy that burned through wounds and negative energy.

Recognizing that God created and controlled the energy embedded within their tiny gemstones, the angels took seriously the special mission God the Father had given them. The angels were not there to enhance Stephen's talents, wisdom, and compassion. Their job was just to stay close to Stephen so that the young doctor would remember that it was God's power that healed. Stephen's hands were mere tools to be used to God's glory.

From Kayla's hospital room, Rachel and I heard a hushed commotion and a flurry and squeak of sensible white shoes. I looked out the door. The corridor was alive with hospital personnel walking in hurried steps.

When Becky, Kayla's nurse, entered the room carrying her stethoscope and tray of medicine, I asked, "What's the commotion?"

"A new doctor has arrived," she whispered, trying to contain her excitement.

A new doctor in town was nothing special or unusual, so I turned my attention back to Kayla and Rachel. The angels still flitted about my daughter but now in a hushed rustle of silk organza and whispers.

"Sam," Faith spoke, *"He's here."*

"Yes, I know. A new doctor is in town."

"No, Sam. SIR is here," the angel replied in a reverent voice.

As the nurse left Kayla's room, she turned down the overhead lights so that I had just enough soothing light to read my book. Rachel pulled up a chair next to Kayla's bedside and napped, but Rachel's uneven breathing betrayed her fitful sleep.

All at once, the angels stepped back in deference and were quiet and still. The silence in the room was deafening. Then, a brilliant light shone and pulsed silently, illuminating the space around Kayla.

"Kayla?" a gentle Voice whispered.

When Kayla did not respond, The Voice spoke again, this time with authority. *"Kayla. Open your eyes. Kayla, I say open your eyes."*

Although I had heard The Voice many times before, still, my mouth fell open as I watched and listened. Slowly, Kayla fluttered her reluctant eyes and struggled to focus.

"Daddy Sam?"

"No, Kayla. It is I. You need to sit up and eat," The Voice said in a gentle but commanding manner.

I turned in reverent awe and gently shook Rachel's shoulder.

Painfully, through a dry, raspy throat, Kayla asked, "Daddy Sam, may I have something to eat?"

Now standing, Rachel fell onto Kayla and shook with tears of relief. "Kayla, Kayla. You're back."

"I'm back?" Kayla asked in surprise. "Did I leave?" Then she stopped, as if trying to remember. "I did leave. It was a beautiful place. There were beautiful colors all around, and I was so happy, but I couldn't stay."

When my mind cleared, I recounted the event and mused to myself, *Why was I so surprised?*

"Sam! Kayla is back!" Rachel cried stored up tears onto my shoulder.

"Yes, Rachel, dear. She's back. But why are we so surprised? Didn't we pray, asking the Lord to heal her and send her back to us?"

Rachel was quiet a moment, then shook her head in agreement.

"Thank You, Lord," I breathed my thanksgiving.

After another three long weeks with little sleep, Rachel and I continued to stand vigil at Kayla's bedside. I'm sure we were in the way as hospital personnel tried to do their jobs, but Rachel and I were determined not to leave. Reluctantly, we took turns picking up Sammy and Joelle after school so the other parent could rest and be with our little ones.

My heart broke when Joelle asked, "Daddy Sam, doesn't Mommy want to be with Sammy and me anymore?"

"Of course she does, baby. It's just that this is my turn to be home with you. How about beans and weenies for dinner? Call Sammy." I tried to sound joyful over beans and weenies, but I was afraid I failed.

"Okay." Joelle also pretended exuberance. She missed her mommy, and she missed her big sister, but she wanted us all to be together again, as did I.

As the three of us ate beans and weenies, my attention played out like a tennis match as I listened to Sammy chatter about the fifth grade and Joelle told of her adventures of the first grade.

"We are missing so much, Rachel, dear," my broken heart whispered.

With dinner over and dishes washed, Sammy sat at the dining room table and did math homework.

"Oh, @#$%! I can't get this," Sammy cursed and slammed his pencil on the table.

"Excuse me? Sammy, where did you hear words like that?"

"Oh, sorry, Daddy Sam. All the boys at school curse."

"Well, I know one young man who will not continue to curse, if he knows what's good for him."

Sammy's face fell. He squeezed his eyes shut. When he pushed his chair back from the table, the oak chair fell with an alarming thud, and he ran from the dining room in tears. When I regained my wits, I felt like a fool. My son was having a hard time with all of his emotions, and I was not here to support him.

Numb, I picked my mouth up off the floor and moved up the stairs to Sammy's room, praying as I went. "Help me, Lord. Tell me what to say to my son."

I knocked on Sammy's door and asked for permission to enter.

I could hear the boy sobbing—I thought he was too old to cry. As did he. But I realized that Sammy was feeling the strain of Kayla's illness and hospitalization just as much as Rachel and I were.

"Sammy? Sammy, I'm sorry." I grabbed my weeping son in my arms and held him close, like a valued treasure. "I'm sorry I haven't been here for you, and now that I am, I yelled at you. Can you forgive me?"

Sammy did not answer; he just cried and squeezed my arms that held him.

"Will you and Joelle sleep in my bed tonight?"

I did not hear his answer but felt the nodding of his head.

"Good. I've missed you, Sammy-man."

We sat a long time holding each other. Finally, Sammy sniffed and said, "Daddy Sam, will you help me with my math homework?"

"Oh, Sammy, yes." I squeezed him again, not wanting to let go.

When bedtime came, Joelle ran down the hall and made a flying leap into my bed, then snuggled in the middle.

"Hey. Where am I going to sleep?"

"Sleep next to me Daddy Sam," Sammy whispered.

I did. Gladly.

The next morning, I drove the children to school and smooched their necks. Well, I had to be careful when I smooched Sammy. We hid behind the car door so none of his friends would see. That's not to say that Sammy didn't want to smooch. He just didn't want any of his friends to see.

"Have a good day at school," I called. "Remember, you are mine, and I love you."

Chapter 20

Trust in the LORD with all your heart and lean not on your own understanding; in all your ways submit to him, and he will make your paths straight. Proverbs 3:5-6

I crept into the hospital room, not wanting to wake Rachel. However, to my surprise, both Rachel and Kayla were awake. Rachel's fussing with sheets and blankets spoke louder than her nervous chatter. Dark circles under Rachel's eyes belied the exuberance of a mother whose daughter just returned to the living, while Kayla's own dark circles proclaimed death.

"Well, good morning. How are my two lovely ladies today?" I asked, trying to sound uplifting. Though I was afraid I failed miserably.

"Good morning, Sam," Rachel greeted me with a weak, sleep-deprived voice.

Kayla did not speak.

"Has the doctor been in this morning, Rachel, dear?"

Rachel's eyes moved to Kayla, and the weary mother tried to smile. "No, not yet, but we are expecting him any minute now."

"Rachel, dear, why don't you go home and get some sleep? I'll stay."

"Thank you, Sam, but not until we've seen the doctor."

Machines that crowded around Kayla's bed continued to alternate between their life saving symphony and mind paralyzing roar. Green lines of the oscilloscope traveled across the small round screen, rising and falling in rhythmic beeps. A breathing machine joined in the serious orchestration of providing life-saving oxygen to our daughter. Kayla looked so pitiful restrained in bed by tubes, lines, and beeping machines. When I kissed their captive on her forehead, the heart monitor spiked slightly with a higher *blip* and *beep*.

"That's my girl," I whispered into Kayla's dim but still beautiful blue eyes.

Just then, the door opened and a comical figure of a young man in a white lab coat bounced in. The lab coat he wore looked two sizes too small for his size 42-long body. As he walked, he winced as if the small lab coat pinched his large frame.

At that moment, I thought I heard a distant train whistle.

"Well, top of the mornin' to ya," the young man trilled in a poorly executed Irish brogue and popped a few peanuts into his mouth. If this young man had not looked so ridiculous, he would have been quite handsome. Black wavy hair crowned strong cheek bones, a firm nose supported black horn-rimmed glasses, and a prominent Adam's apple gave the appearance of masculinity. As the young man pretended to study the chart in his hands, chewed peanuts, he winced, and looked up.

"I must be in the wrong room?" he now joked in a mid-western accent. "You can't be Kayla. You look fit as a fiddle." The personable young man winked at Rachel and me. "Let's see what lies my expensive medical equipment will tell me."

With confidence in his eight years of undergraduate and medical school training, the young resident doctor listened to Kayla's heart, then her lungs. Next, he visually examined her belly and thumped her empty gut.

"Well, just as I thought. I'm going home now. You don't need me," he quipped. As he turned to leave, the doctor tilted his head and motioned with his eyes asking Rachel and me to follow.

Once in the corridor, the doctor turned to us. "Good morning, folks. I'm Stephen Abbott, Kayla's doctor."

"Nice to meet you, Dr. Abbott. I'm Sam Burkett, and this is Kayla's mother and my fiancé—Rachel Crews. What can you tell us, Doctor?"

"Well, from what I have read and can see, she is a very sick young lady, but it's nothing we can't take care of," the almost cocky doctor replied in his immodest demeanor. Funny though, his arrogance did not offend Rachel nor me.

"Forgive me, Doctor, but what is your specialty?" I asked in my ignorance.

"Oh, this and that," the doctor continued to quip. "Right now, it's mostly this. Why don't you folks go home and get some rest. Kayla and I are going to be busy."

Reluctantly, but with great relief, Rachel and I left the hospital and drove home in our … that is … Kayla's baby blue Ford.

When we walked into our new home, a rich fragrance of cedar and cypress paneling wafted over us, and the mantle clock chimed twelve-thirty. Except for that greeting, the house was quiet. There was none of the customary squealing, running, and slamming of doors that brightened our home. However, the house was cool and inviting, and we had almost three hours before we needed to pick up the children from school.

"Shall we take a nap on the couch?" I asked in a hopeful tone.

"I would like that, Sam. I need you to hold me."

With a stubby yet tender hand, I led Rachel to the over-stuffed sofa in the living room. I sat against the back and arm of the sofa and invited her to snuggle in my arms. The sofa held back nothing. The thick blue floral cushions cradled two exhausted parents, allowing us to melt into the soft folds of its fabric.

Before I drifted off into deep, healing sleep, I breathed, "Thank You, Lord. I love you, Rachel."

My darling was already asleep. I embraced her warm body closer to my chest, and we both slept.

At 2:00, Dr. Abbott entered Kayla's room with his signature bounce and a mouthful of peanuts.

"Well, Miss Kayla, I see you're having lunch," the doctor said with a wink and his head tilting toward the I.V. "I bet it's yummy."

When he went around to the "business side" of her bed, Dr. Abbott checked the buttons, valves, and pressure cuff. Almost immediately, his demeanor changed from cocky to caring. "Ah ha! Your pulse and heartbeat are much better than this morning. I wonder why that is? Could it be my winning personality?"

"I don't think Daddy Sam liked the way you joked about me," Kayla croaked through parched lips.

"Oh, that," Dr. Abbott said with a wave. "That's just my act. I have to be charming. Otherwise, the parents will never leave."

Kayla's lips turned up in a tiny smile.

"Now, Miss Kayla. Let's you and me get down to business," Dr. Abbott said as he examined Kayla's emaciated body. "How old are you? Oh, sorry. I'm not supposed to ask a lady her age. What grade are you in? Oops, that's the same thing. Okay. How about if you ask me some questions?"

"How old are you?" Kayla asked in a weak giggle.

"Hey! No fair," the doctor teased. "Let's just say I am over twenty-one. Next question?"

"Where are you from?"

"Down the hall. I was just in room 332 before I came here." Kayla giggled a bit stronger.

"Okay, my turn. When did you first stop eating, Kayla?"

Kayla hesitated. She did not want to answer. Answering meant admitting there was a problem. Finally, unable to endure Dr. Abbott's silence, Kayla replied, "When I was seven."

"There. That wasn't so bad, was it? Okay. Here is a tough one. What triggered your anorexia?"

Anorexia? Kayla thought to herself. *What a horrible sounding word.*

"My parents fought a lot, and I felt like it was my fault," Kayla's raspy voice cracked, and she choked before she could finish her story.

"You know now, don't you, that it is not fair to allow a child to assume guilt and responsibility for her parents?" the compassionate doctor asked.

"Yes, sir."

"Oh, no you don't! Don't be calling me *sir.* That's Mr. Abbot's, my father's, name. You can call me Stephen. Now, when did you come to live with Sam and Rachel?"

"I was fourteen," was all her voice would yield.

"I see. How did that turn out?"

"They were both so kind to me."

"I see, so now you are about thirty-one?"

Kayla giggled again, the best she could. "Sixteen."

"Ah. Sweet sixteen and never been kissed."

"Not exactly," Kayla whispered, then diverted her eyes.

"So … you have secrets?"

"Not anymore," Kayla said as her eyes filled with hot tears.

"Sorry. When did you lose your secret, Kayla, dear?"

"Just before school started."

"What year?"

"What?"

"It's a test." Dr. Abbott winked. "So, you went into depression and refused to eat?"

"Yes, sir … I mean, Stephen."

"I see. Humm. Well, this is going to be a difficult case. I think I best go to my office and read a book."

"Really?" Kayla asked in a startled voice.

"No. Not really. This will be very easy … as long as you help me."

"How can I help you?"

"Oh. Hold on a minute," Dr. Abbot said, pulling a note pad out of his lab coat. "Here it is," he said as if reading. "Patient must cooperate with physician. Patient must cooperate with psychologist. Patient must cooperate with nutritionist. A healthy diet may consist of Cheerios …"

Kayla held her empty stomach and laughed. Dr. Abbott winked.

"So, Miss Kayla, are you ready to follow orders?"

"Yes, sir," Kayla saluted the best she could with a hand less restricted by tubes and needles.

"Very well. I will make my report. I will see you tomorrow. Carry on." Dr. Abbott returned the salute. "Are you up to eating a tiny bit of soup?"

"May I have two Cheerios and a toy teacup of apple juice with a pink straw?" Kayla asked in a weak giggle.

"Of course, you may. I will alert the kitchen. Is there anything more I can do for you, Kayla? Do you need anything to help you sleep?"

Kayla's eyes twinkled ever so slightly when she replied, "No thank you, Stephen."

Refreshed after a much-needed nap, a family dinner with chattering younger children near us, and a good night's sleep, Rachel and I traveled back to the hospital.

When we entered Kayla's room, Rachel's body stiffened. Shock waves rushed over us then between us and back again as wild sparks of an electric current might. Her bed was empty and freshly made. The life-monitoring machines were gone. Fear consumed our minds, and we stood like zombies, motionless and dead-eyed, imagining the worst. Then, we heard a commotion down the corridor.

"Are you ready for this?"

"Yes! Yes! Yes!"

"Okay, hold on to your britches."

Then Rachel heard the sound of wheels speeding down the hallway, metal pans rattling as orderlies jumped out of the way and nurses scolding, some giggling.

"Again?"

"Yes!"

Just then, Rachel and I stepped out of the hospital room, and the jubilation stopped.

We stared.

"Top of the mornin' to ya," greeted Dr. Abbott, wearing roller skates. This time, his lab coat fit much too big, so he shortened it up with a black bull clip.

Kayla, seated in a wheelchair, still showed signs of blackened and sunken eyes. But at this moment, she also wore a giant-sized, toothy smile.

"Sam? Rachel?" she gasped as if caught doing something naughty.

"We were just going through exercise therapy," wheezed Dr. Abbott, out of breath and with the same guilty expression.

"It looks like wonderful therapy," Rachel replied, not yet recovered from the shock of an empty hospital bed.

"Oh, Rachel, Stephen … I mean, Dr. Abbott is just wonderful," Kayla gushed. "We've been outside eating ice cream cones and feeding the birds and squirrels."

"Good morning, folks." Dr. Abbott changed into his professional demeanor. "This therapy is designed to associate eating with pleasure."

"Rachel, I saw the sky. I really saw the sky. It was so blue and clear. The squirrels were just adorable," Kayla prattled on.

"My thesis is that if patients associate eating with happiness, healing will quickly follow," explained Dr. Abbott.

"Tomorrow, we're going to eat pizza in the conference room and have a dance!" thrilled Kayla. Then she gasped and her sunken eyes almost popped. "Rachel, can you bring me a party dress?"

"Of course, sweetie," Rachel answered somewhat overcome

with surprise.

At that moment, an announcement over the intercom interrupted the discussion of therapy. "Dr. Abbott, Dr. Abbott, you're wanted in room 345."

"Oops. Got to go. Excuse me, folks." Dr. Abbott performed a sassy two-foot spin on his roller skates before speeding down the hall. "Tally ho!"

Rachel and I still stood like statues with mouths on the floor. "Let's get you back to bed," Rachel said, scurrying around like a mother hen with her feathers fluffed up.

"Oh, Rachel, do I have to go back to bed?"

A nurse came in with her usual stainless-steel tray of medical equipment and a glass of apple juice.

"Well, it's about time." The nurse winked. "You've had a busy morning, haven't you, Kayla? Let's see just how busy."

Rachel and I unconsciously moved closer to the wall to be out of the way.

The nurse put on her stethoscope and listened for a heartbeat then a pulse. "Wow! Busy, busy, busy! How do you feel, Kayla?"

"I feel wonderful!" exhaled Kayla with rapt emotion.

"Feel like drinking a little juice?"

"Thank you," Kayla replied, taking the tiny glass of juice and drinking with gusto.

"Dr. Abbott will be very pleased," the nurse said, taking the empty glass and tucking Kayla into bed. "What do you have on tap for tomorrow?"

"Pizza and a dance!" Kayla almost squealed.

"Well then, you need to rest up. Sounds like a big day."

Rachel and I glanced at each other, then giggled.

"Well, it appears we are not needed here," I winked and kissed Kayla on the forehead.

"Oh, don't go," she begged, then yawned.

"We'll stay for just a while," whispered Rachel.

"All of your classmates send their get-well greetings, Kayla. They want you to get well and hurry back to …"

Kayla didn't hear the end of my sentence. She was asleep. "Sweet dreams, baby girl."

"We love you, Kayla," Rachel whispered, touching Kayla's face and arm, as if needing to memorize each part of her daughter.

When we reached the elevator, Dr. Abbot met us. "May I ride down with you?" he said, absent-mindedly pushing the button several times.

"Certainly," I replied, hoping to continue our discussion on his unique personality, medical theories, and practices.

The elevator whirled to a stop, and the doors opened. We stepped in, and I pressed the first-floor button. Dr. Abbot stepped in behind us and pressed the button … again several.

"I know you must think I am moving too fast, but in my experience, I have found that the sooner the patient's depression is treated, the sooner the rest of the body will also heal. Please, don't misunderstand. I am not saying that her life with you was unhappy. On the contrary. She shared with me that you and the kids have been so kind and supportive. I also read Dr. Proctor's notes, and you have done all the right things. However, it's that earlier trauma that is still holding her mind captive. Here, she is getting psychological therapy without knowing it as such. She is receiving nutritious meals along with a few fun foods. However, introducing foods is a trial-and-error treatment. The I.V. has given her system time to adjust from starvation and dehydration to a healthier balance, but when her delicate system cannot tolerate one food, we eliminate it and move to another. We are also moving closer to Kayla having a happier outlook on life. She told me about Roger. That's why we're having the dance tomorrow. There are many children and teenagers here in the hospital, as well as adults, suffering from anorexia and bulimia for a variety of reasons. My thesis is that they can help each other heal. I think you will agree that peer pressure plays a significant role in a teenager's happiness."

"Thank you, Dr. Abbott. We hope you are right," Rachel said with more than a little skepticism.

"Try not to worry, folks. Anorexia is quite different from, say, cancer or heart disease, in that the underlying causes are abstract. However, if we can erase those initial stimuli, the whole psyche will take over."

"And humor also plays a part in healing, Doctor?" I asked, trying not to sound sarcastic.

"Most definitely," replied Dr. Abbot with certainty. "Especially when applied by a role of authority."

"When can we bring the children to see her?"

"Any time. However, due to hospital regulations, you must visit in the waiting room or outside. I would prescribe outside. There is a lovely pond on the hospital grounds, and the kitchen will supply all the stale bread you want to feed the ducks."

Rachel's body finally relaxed, and she exhaled a cleansing breath. "Thank you, Dr. Abbott."

The quirky doctor gently took Rachel's hand, admiring her engagement ring of clustered diamonds and said, "You are welcome, Mrs. Crews. Oh, by the way, Kayla said there is a wedding in the cards. When will it be, Mr. and Mrs. Burkett?"

"It was scheduled for this past September, but then the accident and Kayla's illness put the plans on hold … again," I replied.

"Well, brighter days are ahead." The elevator bell sounded, and Dr. Abbott held the door so Rachel and I could exit. "Bye, folks."

"Goodbye, Dr. Abbott. God bless you," I whispered.

"He surely does. Every day," replied the wise doctor.

When Rachel and I returned to the hospital, an uncustomary

and unabated excitement permeated through the third floor of the hospital. Chatter, positive energy, and angels tumbled out of hospital rooms into the corridors and almost bounced off the walls. Today was pizza and dance day. Nurses and orderlies with flushed, shining faces and propelled by the collective energy of the excitement rushed about performing their duties.

When Rachel walked into Kayla's room, the giddy teenager with sunken eyes squealed and hopped from the bed.

In happy excitement, Kayla grabbed the poodle skirt and sweater Rachel carried. Then she gasped again when she saw her saddle shoes in my hand.

"What time is the dance, sweetie?" Rachel asked.

"It starts at 12:30. Oh, I can't wait!" Kayla exclaimed in an excited wiggle.

"Do you need help dressing? Remember how I helped you dress for the prom?"

"Oh." Kayla's face fell for the first time since Dr. Abbott started treating her.

"I'm sorry, Kayla," Rachel gasped in disbelief. "Can we pretend that this is your first dance?"

Shaking her head as if shaking out cobwebs, Kayla raised her head and replied with a victorious, "Yes. Let's do."

In her excitement, Kayla unintentionally tied a knot in the hospital gown, slowing down the changing of clothes.

Kayla donned the skirt in excited teenage chatter, then abruptly stopped and stared at Rachel with pleading eyes, and her joy imploded. Kayla had lost so much weight and body mass that the skirt was now much too large.

"It's okay. It's okay. We can fix this," Rachel promised, reaching for her purse. "I always have safety pins with me," she mumbled into the leather handbag, more to hide threatening tears than to search for illusive safety pins. "Here. See?"

Rachel hummed nervously as she busied her hands pinning up

the much too-big-skirt. "There. No one will ever know once you put on your sweater."

But the sweater was another issue, for it swallowed Kayla's boney shoulders.

As if saving the moment, Dr. Abbott walked in. "Well, now. That is much better than a hospital gown," he said, twirling Kayla around in her bare feet. "But …"

"But what?" Kayla squeaked in distressed anticipation.

"Don't you want to wear shoes?"

Forgetting about the pinned-up skirt and the beautiful sweater with the delicate lacy collar that hung from her shoulders, Kayla laughed.

"Sit down, so I can fit this glass slipper on your princess feet," Dr. Abbott teased.

With lace trimmed white socks and black and white saddle shoes, Kayla popped up from the chair and beamed.

"The touch of the master's hand." Rachel winked at Dr. Abbott and held out a bottle of the newest fragrance from Prince Matchabelli, 'Beloved.' "Just a little," Rachel cautioned.

After Kayla dabbed the fragrance behind her ears, Dr. Abbot inhaled from a safe distance and rolled his eyes to the ceiling and crooned a dreamy, "Perfecto."

At 12:30, the noise of excited chatter that had rolled from the third floor moved in waves into the elevator, then tumbled out to the first-floor conference room. Six children ages seven to twelve, fifteen teenagers, and four adults, some dressed in gay party attire and others still sporting hospital gowns pinned closed for modesty's sake, crowded into the conference room. A rotund orderly, usually seen dressed in white shirt and trousers, now sported a wildly colored sport shirt and equally loud shorts, manned the phonograph. Hospital kitchen staff faithfully kept plates filled with bite-sized pizza and chips. The conference room rocked as the music rolled and punch flowed.

Parents, grandparents, and special friends stood around the perimeter of the room just listening and watching in quiet joy.

At first, there was just chatter, as patients sat eating pizza and chips and listening to soft songs like "Mona Lisa," "Oh My Papa," or "Secret Love." But like magic, when "April Love" finished playing, the orderly replaced the soothing love song with a boisterous new record, "Rock Around the Clock," and every inch of empty floor space soon filled with whirling, twirling, and happy gyrations.

Sadly, a nurse escorted a few patients back to their rooms, but Kayla was determined to stay and dance, albeit in self-disciplined restraint.

The party broke up at 2:00. Although party-goers moved with less energy now, the excitement lingered. Rachel and I escorted Kayla back to her room to help her undress and tuck her in bed. This time, there was no moaning or grumbling but deep exhales of satisfied delight.

"Wasn't it a wonderful party, Rachel?"

"Yes, sweetie, it was, and you looked so beautiful."

"I had such a glorious time," Kayla chirped. "Did you see Adam? Wasn't he adorable? We call him our little man."

"Yes, he was, baby girl," I agreed.

Kayla sighed as she drifted off to sleep, entertaining happy dreams.

"Sleep tight, baby girl," I said, kissing our exhausted teenager on her forehead.

I looked at Rachel, and she nodded in agreement. We tiptoed out and got to the school just in time to pick up the children.

"When can we see Kayla?" Joelle begged.

"Tomorrow," Rachel replied.

Chapter 21

A merry heart does good, like medicine, But a broken spirit dries the bones. Proverbs 17:22

On Saturday morning, even before the sun was up, Joelle knocked on my door. "Daddy Sam," she whispered. "Daddy Sam?"

My eyes rebelled at such an early wake up call, but then I remembered it was the 'baby' calling, and I rolled out of my warm bed.

"Just a minute, baby."

As I walked out of my cozy room, tying my robe around me, she hit me with it, "Daddy Sam, can I have fifty cents?"

I am sure this is a female tactic: hit them when they are most vulnerable.

Strike one.

I blinked my eyes, trying to encourage them to focus. "What do you want with fifty cents?"

"Cheerios."

"Baby, we have plenty of cereal for breakfast."

"Daddy Sam, can I have fifty cents?"

Another female tactic: pound them until they submit.

Strike two.

"Look on my dresser."

"Thank you, Daddy Sam," Joelle trilled her love and admiration.

Still a third female tactic: sweet talk them so they won't know what hit them.

Strike three. You're out.

As I exited the bathroom, I heard her little bare feet padding the floor as she ran back to her room. I still didn't know why Joelle wanted fifty cents, but right now, I needed coffee. Since I was awake, and it was too early for the rest of the family to be up, I took a cup of coffee and my Bible to the back porch.

"Good morning, Lord. Another beautiful day. Thank You, Lord."

…

"No, there's nothing particular on my mind. I just wanted to say good morning and thank you for today. Oh, and thank you for a wonderful party for Kayla yesterday. That new doctor really seems to know what he is doing."

…

"You did?"

…

"I'm sorry, Lord. Once again, You amaze and surprise me."

Just then, the screen door opened and softly closed. It couldn't be Sammy. Sammy does not know how to close screen doors softly.

"Good morning, Sam."

I felt a welcomed peck on my cheek and a soft nuzzle on what remained of my ear.

"Good morning, Rachel, dear."

She pulled up an Adirondack chair beside me. The scraping sound of the chair on the wooden deck seemed to awaken the birds, and the air filled with happy chirps. Rachel exhaled as she sat in the cushioned seat. "What a beautiful morning."

"Yes. I was just thanking the Lord for His morning and all His blessings."

"We are so blessed, aren't we, Sam?"

"Yes. We are very blessed."

We sat quietly, watching the glow of the sun spread its soft apricot light over the horizon.

"Oh, by the way, speaking of blessings. Joelle came to my room this morning before I was up and asked for fifty cents. In my sleep induced stupor, I gave it to her. What does she want with fifty cents?"

"She wants to go see Kayla today, remember? I think she wants to take Kayla a box of Cheerios. It's a sentimental thing between the girls."

"Must be," I admitted. "It's very sweet."

"We have sweet children, Sam."

"That we do, Rachel. That's because their mother is so sweet." I said, lifting her left hand and kissing the finger that wore the cluster of diamonds.

"Daddy Sam!!"

"Oh, well," I said, winking at Rachel, "it was nice while it lasted. That must be Sammy."

"Remember, you just said they are sweet." Rachel chuckled. "Out here, Sammy."

"Daddy Sam, are we going to see Kayla today?"

"Yes, sir, I thought that we would."

"What time are we going?"

"I guess after breakfast. How does 10:00 sound?"

"That'll be great. I'll have plenty of time," Sammy chirped before running out to the field that surrounded the house.

"What was that?" I asked in my usual ignorance.

"Another sweet child," Rachel crooned. She kissed my cheek before going in to start breakfast.

"Wildflowers? You picked wildflowers?" cried Joelle, feeling out-done by her brother.

"They are for Kayla," Sammy said, gazing at the gaily colored but soon-to-be-wilted flowers.

"Mommy, can we stop at the grocery store?" Joelle begged.

"Ask Daddy Sam. He's the one driving."

"Daddy Sam, can we stop at the grocery store, p-l-eee-a-s-e?"

I know when I'm licked, so we stopped at the grocery store for Cheerios.

As I expected, when we arrived at the hospital, Kayla was outside at the pond with some of her new friends. As always, Dr. Abbott was close by.

"Good morning, Dr. Abbott," I said. "Those fish are going to get fat," I joked. "Is stale bread a healthy diet for fish?"

"Good morning, Mr. Burkett. Mrs. Crews." The doctor nodded to Rachel. "Whom do we have here?" Dr. Abbott, kneeling down to speak to Joelle and Sammy.

"I'm Sammy. My real name is just Sam, but Mommy calls me Sammy. This is Joelle. She's my little sister."

"Two sisters. How did a man get to be so lucky?"

"Good morning, Dr. Abbott," Rachel said, beaming at the compliment the doctor gave to her children.

"As you can see," continued Dr. Abbott, "my charges are enjoying the morning even after a wild party yesterday."

"What wild party?" asked an envious Sammy.

"Oh, it was an exhibition. Your sister was dancing on the tabletops. She was the belle of the ball."

"No, she wasn't, Sammy. Don't let the doctor trick you," I winked.

"But she did have fun, Sammy. She even ate pizza and potato chips," clarified Rachel.

"Who's that?" Joelle pointed and asked just a little too loud. The young man Joelle pointed toward turned, smiled, and waved. "He's cute!"

"Oh, he's not the only one, Joelle. We have two or three cute boys, and some are just your age," Dr. Abbott teased.

"Please. Don't give her any ideas, Doctor. I don't want any more competition just yet," I pleaded with a wink.

Joelle and Sammy forgot about the Cheerios and wildflowers and ran down the grassy embankment to join the other children at the pond.

Taking advantage of the quiet opportunity, Dr. Abbot gave Rachel and me an update on Kayla's condition. "She is doing remarkably well. I couldn't be happier. I suspect, though, it is not my medical talents, but the strong foundation you laid for Kayla when she first came to live with you. You did an excellent job," Dr. Abbott praised.

"Thank you, Doctor. I'm afraid, however, that we cannot take the credit. We honestly believe that the Lord did it."

"Well said, Mr. Burkett. I like to think of myself as God's hands. He has the power. I lend Him my hands, and follow His lead," Dr. Abbot shared in deep humility.

Rachel, the doctor, and I shared a quiet moment in agreement.

Interrupting our peaceful communion, "The Boogie Woogie Bugle Boy of Company B" blared over the loudspeaker. At that invitation, a crowd of young people ran up the embankment, talking, giggling, and some carrying little ones.

One smaller patient struggled to propel his wheelchair up the embankment. I wondered why one of the bigger boys did not help this little one. After a few second of watching his determined struggle, an older patient did help push the wheelchair up the embankment. This freed up the small boy's hands, and he cheered and laughed, begging his pusher to go faster.

As soon as the noisy swarm reached the patio, they stopped, turned, grabbed a partner, and danced. I was very much impressed that the young girl pushing the wheelchair swung the chair around, grabbed the grinning occupant's hands, and swayed around the wheelchair. Even Sammy and Joelle joined in. When the music ended, happy cheers went up, and the revelers proceeded in appropriate hospital fashion to the dining room.

"Won't you have lunch with us?" Dr. Abbott invited.

"Yes! Say yes, Daddy Sam!" two little excited voices begged.

"Well, I guess we will," I chuckled.

In the dining room, I was surprised to see most of the children and teenagers eagerly eating small portions of soup, fruit, and vegetables. For many of the patients, there was still the gagging reflex associated with anorexia, but for those patients on the way to recovery, those symptoms, for the most part, had disappeared. However, my heart broke as I watched some of the newest and youngest patients struggle with even the smallest portions of food.

I was so proud when I watched Kayla sitting with these children. She spoke gently with them and encouraged them to think happy thoughts and taste an apple or pudding. She could share with those anorexia sufferers because she had journeyed down that road.

As I watched my beautiful daughter caring for younger patients, a young man caught my attention. It was quite evident that he had caught Kayla's attention as well. He moved over to her side and took a seat close to her. Then he turned his attention to another young patient and spoke encouraging words to him. It was a tender moment—a victorious moment.

I have heard it said, if you can teach someone, you can feel certain you know the subject. In Kayla's case, she can teach these young ones, because she knows her subject personally, all too well.

Thank You, Lord, for healing my daughter and for giving her a heart of love and sympathy to help others.

"You are welcome, My son."

Dr. Abbott moved over to where Rachel and I stood. "She's remarkable, isn't she?"

"Yes," I beamed. "We think so. Who is that young man

with her?"

"That is Gregory. He came in a little ahead of Kayla, and they have been great healing partners," Dr. Abbott added.

"Then who is Adam?" Rachel asked.

"Adam?"

"Yes, when the children were returning from the pizza dance, Kayla asked me if I saw Adam. She commented on how cute he was."

"Oh, yes, Adam." Dr. Abbott said with sparkling eyes. "Well, Adam is kind of my secret medicine." The doctor paused to let that declaration sink in. "I like to say Adam has a powerful healing presence. Adam was born with spina bifida and hydrocephalus, but has more spunk than a rowdy teenager."

"Exactly what is spina bifida, Doctor?" I asked.

"Occasionally, as a baby develops in the mother's womb, the boney spinal column may not form and close properly. If the spinal column remains open, the spinal cord can bulge out from the damaged area. This can be either internal or external spina bifida.

"In the most severe form of this birth defect, tissue fails to form over the spine, leaving an open hole. Then, as the nerves begin to form and grow, they protrude through this opening. In these instances, a thin, fluid-filled sac forms to protect the exposed nerves. Unfortunately, if the sac ruptures during delivery, the baby will require immediate surgery to push the exposed spinal cord back into the spinal column and close the opening.

"That is what happened to Adam. When he was born, the sac ruptured, and our team had to perform emergency surgery. He suffered a mild form of hydrocephalus, or fluid build-up on or around the brain. The team placed a shunt to drain the fluid and … Well, you saw him at the pond and then dancing. He needs assistance with his wheelchair, but don't tell him that. He thinks himself as strong and tough as anyone out there.

"That is his secret healing power. The patients with anorexia look at Adam and consider themselves to be very blessed. This is the beginning of their healing."

"How does Adam maneuver his wheelchair at the pond? Isn't the ground soft?" a caring Rachel asked.

"Our team is quite accomplished in writing grant requests. It was through their successful grant to the Spina Bifida Foundation that the hospital could build a concrete path around the pond and in other areas of the recreation grounds. Contributions to this foundation have benefited spina bifida patients in countless ways and has been to us, shall we say, a God-send."

All of the sudden, a commotion interrupted our conversation. Nurses and orderlies, rushed to a young patient in distress. "Well, no rest for the weary," said Dr. Abbott and excused himself.

"May we go, Stephen?" begged Kayla and Gregory.

"Perhaps not just yet. Let's let Timmy get comfortable first. Yes?"

"Yes, sir. Come on, Kayla, let's go back. There are plenty of others to help," Gregory said.

"What a remarkable young man," Rachel noticed.

The door to Kayla's hospital room swung open and her nurse bounced in, chirping, "Good morning, Miss Kayla." The cardinal's song from the tree outside the window could not compete with nurse Becky's happy singing.

"Good morning, Becky," Kayla replied, pushing back her now empty oatmeal bowl.

"Good girl," the nurse praised.

Kayla wiped her sweetheart-shaped lips and asked, "What's up for today?"

"I think you have an appointment with Dr. Abbott in his office. Aren't you the lucky one? Only the most successful patients in the program receive an invitation to the doctor's office."

"Will Gregory be there?"

"No, sweetie, this is a private doctor-patient conference. Besides,

Gregory has already been discharged."

"Discharged? Gregory discharged?" Kayla asked. "He didn't even say goodbye."

"I think he was too exuberant and busy packing his things, sweetie."

"Oh."

"Speaking of belongings, I think it would be a good idea to pack yours and take it with you to Dr. Abbott's office."

With drooping shoulders and dragging feet, as if walking through thick slime, Kayla made her way to Dr. Abbott's office and tapped on the door. Dr. Abbott was sitting at his desk, wearing a tall gold party hat. His infamous skates and too-short lab coat hung on the wall.

"Come in. Good morning, Kayla. Please have a seat." Dr. Abbott did not seem concerned about Kayla's downcast expression.

"Hi, Doctor."

"Well, let's see," Dr. Abbott said opening Kayla's file. "It appears that over the last twelve weeks, you have made remarkable progress. How do you feel about that?"

"Okay, I guess."

"Well, I feel better than okay. I feel terrific, as should you."

"Yeah."

"So, let's get down to business," said Dr. Abbot, peering over the file at Kayla. He pretended to read. "Week one: When patient first came to us, she had just had a traumatic event and was comatose. Patient received I.V. fluids and constant monitoring of vital signs.

"Weeks two and three: Patient suffered from depression and refused to eat.

"Weeks four and five: Chart indicates small improvement.

"Week six: Patient showed signs of a smile. Patient agreed to assist physician with her own healing.

"Week seven: Patient received personalized eating therapy and group therapy. Patient attended a pizza dance and met new friends.

"Weeks eight thru twelve: Patient progressed to assisting others in their healing process and became somewhat of a mother figure to younger patients."

Dr. Abbott peered over his half glasses but registered no emotion.

"In conclusion," he said, "I, Stephen Abbott, MD, PhD, PsyD, declare patient's anorexia nervosa in remission. Is that an accurate assessment, Kayla?"

"Yes, I suppose so," Kayla replied with neither eye contact nor enthusiasm.

"Okay. Very good. Now, do you think you have learned to control your depression and not let your depression control you?"

Kayla answered with a shrug.

"Do you think you have learned to associate eating with happiness?"

Another disconnected shrug.

"Very well then, I think I am going to sign your discharge papers and let you resume your life, a life of joy and happiness, I might insist."

After signing the discharge papers, Dr. Abbott stood, extended his left hand, pushing his silly party hat back from his eyes with the other. It was as if the doctor was pushing Kayla out of his office.

"Have a good life, Kayla. Oh, I have notified your mother of your discharge. She should be here soon to pick you up."

With reluctant resignation, Kayla whispered, "Goodbye, Dr. Abbott, I mean Stephen," and left the doctor's office with breaths of heavy despondency.

As Kayla trudged from Dr. Abbott's office, her heavy feet wanted to run back to the refuge of her hospital room. However, the angels that had been her constant companions, pushed and encouraged Kayla to follow Dr. Abbott's instructions to "have a life of joy and happiness."

Finally, her labored steps traversed the dark and foreboding twenty feet to the elevator. As she extended her finger to push the button, that button that would open doors of the mysterious and frightening unknown to her, she heard a familiar voice.

"Hey, Kayla, wait up."

Kayla whirled around and, without restraint, threw herself into Gregory's arms and wept.

"Hey, girl, why are you crying? This is the best day of our lives … so far."

When she finally controlled her tears, Kayla asked, "What do you mean the best day of our lives? You're leaving me."

"Didn't Stephen tell you?"

"He just pushed me out of his office and said to have a good life."

As if on signal, Stephen Abbott walked out of his office and met the teenagers at the elevator.

"No, Kayla, I can't believe he did that! He didn't tell you?" Gregory stammered.

"No, Gregory, I wanted you to tell her," he said. "It would mean more coming from you. You see, Kayla was under the impression that you had left without saying goodbye." Dr. Abbott paused then continued in a joking manner. "I'm going to have to have a talk with that nurse Becky." He chuckled. "Go on. Tell her, Gregory."

"Tell me what?" Kayla begged.

"The Board of Directors here at the hospital has awarded us, you and me, four-year scholarships for our undergraduate degrees."

"And," Dr. Abbott cut in, "between terms, starting now, you will be returning to the hospital to be my assistants to help encourage my patients. You already have experience."

Dr. Abbott grinned.

"Oh, Gregory! That is the best news … the best day of our lives." Then she turned and, with misty eyes and a timid smile, said, "Thank you, Stephen."

The elevator bell sounded, and the doors glided open. "Off with you then," encouraged Dr. Abbott. "Remember, meet me in my office the very first day of your school breaks, including Christmas vacation next year. You will have lots of challenges."

The two glowing teenagers entered the elevator hand-in-hand, their feet seeming to float above the floor. When the doors glided closed, ensuring their privacy, Gregory turned to face Kayla, and the teenagers embraced, laughing.

Gregory was the first to speak as the doors opened. "Come on, Kayla. We have some catching up to do. Let's ask your mom if she will take us to the school."

"Do you think we can catch up on three months, Gregory?"

"Sure, we can. Remember what Stephen said. 'With God's help we can do anything.'"

Chapter 22

Truly my soul finds rest in God; my salvation
comes from him. Psalm 62:1

Just as Dr. Abbott said, Rachel was at the hospital to pick up Kayla. But it was not only Rachel; the whole family came. It was not unlike a family reunion. The hugs started with Rachel, of course. Rachel hugged Kayla with happy laughter, then she turned to Gregory and gave him a big mamma bear hug, again, complete with giggles. As Rachel hugged Gregory, I grabbed Kayla in my arms and smothered her with warm teary kisses.

"Thank you, Lord. You are so good to us," I whispered into Kayla's neck.

The kissing line proceeded. It was Gregory's turn to receive a papa bear hug. I must have startled the young man, because I had forgotten about my stubby hand and face. With unabated emotion, I clasped Gregory's hand, then pulled the surprised young man to my chest and gave him several welcome pats on the back.

It was evident to me that Gregory had not experienced such a show of affection. The young man seemed startled and confused and even reluctant to return the hugs. But, given our family's pension for hugging, he soon learned and hugged and kissed with glee.

Sammy and Joelle waited impatiently for their turns. Joelle danced on tippy-toes the whole time. Even before Joelle finished hugging Gregory, Rachel started the second round of hugs. The hospital staff who escorted the teenagers out watched the happy family, and overcome with emotion, they even started hugging each other. It was a sweet spirit.

"Let's go home, you two," Rachel shouted.

"Rachel," Kayla began, "Gregory was wondering if you could take us to the school so we can meet with our teachers."

"Sweetie, school is out for Christmas vacation. Can we do that later? I'm sure your teachers won't mind."

Kayla looked at Gregory with disappointed eyes, but her healing partner encouraged her. "We've had a busy morning, Kayla. I, for one, need to rest."

With beaming eyes, Kayla agreed. She had great confidence in Gregory and thought him to be so wise.

"Gregory," Sam interrupted, "we would love for you to go home with us. Don't you need to notify your parents first?"

"No, sir. I'm eighteen and have been on my own for three years. My parents keep track of me, but they don't invade my space. Don't get me wrong, I love my parents. It's just that we have never seen eye-to-eye."

"Where do your parents live, Gregory?"

"North Dakota, ma'am. If you don't mind, I'd rather not talk about it."

"Let's go, then!" Sammy shouted, saving the day. "We will all be home for Christmas!"

When the family walked into the new house, the scent of cypress and cedar paneling wafted in the air. Now, however, now the scent of balsam fir added to the welcoming ambiance. Sammy ran to plug in the Christmas tree lights, and immediately, a blaze of colored lights dazzled the room. Kayla's eyes popped, as did Gregory's, and she clutched Gregory's arm and sighed. "I've never seen anything so beautiful."

"Me neither."

Sam sauntered over to the fireplace and lit starter kindling. Soon, an inviting fire filled the room with warmth. However, the warmth from the fire was small compared to the warmth of the family's love.

Traveling back in time, Sam remembered the porter's cabin and how he first lit a fire in the tiny cabin. He was cold, depressed, and alone. What a difference these past few years has brought.

"Gregory, would you like to go to your room and freshen up or take a nap?" Rachel asked.

"My room?"

"Well, the guest room."

"Yes, ma'am. That would be nice. Just point the way."

"I'll show you!" Sammy yelled, bouncing up the stairs with excited glee. "Your room will be right next to mine."

Gregory placed his small duffle on the bed. The room was a corner room with two windows: one faced east and the other faced south. It was at the frosty south window that Gregory stood and took in the beauty of the Kentucky countryside. He admired the tree line at the far end of the property where Sam had planted blooming trees whose leaves twinkled in the sunlight. The split rail fence and gaily-colored flowers completed the inviting scene. As Gregory surveyed the property, he promised himself, *One day, I'm going to own a piece of property like that.*

He opened the window and let in the cold December air and breathed in, filling his lungs with sweet Kentucky air. It felt good. It had been a long time since he felt that sense of peace, and he wanted more. Right now, however, he would settle for a nap.

"Kayla, dear, don't you want to take a nap?" asked the ever-attentive Rachel.

"Oh, Rachel, I just couldn't nap. I have so many things to share with you." However, a deep yawn gave her away.

"I think I can wait to hear your stories, dear. I'm just glad you are home."

Kayla kissed Rachel and turned to go upstairs.

"Kayla," Rachel called, "I redecorated your room. I hope you like it."

When Kayla opened the door to her room, a full-size bed covered with a crisp bedspread of large pink and white cabbage roses accented with blue and green greeted her. Then, her eyes moved to the windows and feasted on curtains hanging crisp and white with layers of ruffles. On the oakwood floor, a throw rug echoed the bedspread's accent colors of Heavenly blue and spring green. For a moment, Kayla was speechless. She just wanted to breathe in the symphony of colors, wood paneling, and sunshine. Then she turned and ran back downstairs.

"Oh, Rachel, it's beautiful. Thank you. Thank you."

"I'm so glad you like it, dear. I wanted you to come home to a lovely new room."

"Oh, I do love it."

Rachel returned to making dinner, and Kayla ran back to her room to bask in the serene beauty of her bedroom. Standing at the foot of the bed, Kayla fell back, letting the new bedding engulf her and swaddle her in the cool fabric and soft padding. Even though she said she couldn't take a nap, it didn't take long before Kayla drifted off in a deep, peaceful sleep.

When she awoke, the light outside her north window was now soft and shadowy. Kayla stretched, yawned, and rubbed her eyes. She was home, and she smelled Rachel's stew. "Thank you, Jesus."

"You are welcome, My child."

Kayla's eyes glowed as if she just heard a beautiful secret and smiled a peaceful, knowing smile.

Chapter 23

With another date for our wedding set, Rachel and I made an appointment to speak with Pastor Johns. I knew it sounded silly, but we were both nervous and trembling.

"Good afternoon, Sam. Hello, Rachel. Come in. Have a seat," Pastor Johns greeted us. "Well, are we finally going to do this?"

"We do hope so," replied Rachel.

"Shall we open with a word of prayer? Our Father, who art in Heaven, hallowed be Thy name. We thank You and praise You for bringing us here today and ask Your blessings on Sam and Rachel. Lord, remove all obstacles from their paths, and protect their family from further harm. Grant them a beautiful wedding ceremony, Father, to the glory of Your name. Amen."

For a serene moment, a pause settled over us until Pastor Johns said in a joyous voice, "Now, let's do this. Just for the record, when is the date?"

"We were thinking of a Sunday service on February 12, if that is agreeable with you, Pastor Johns," I stated.

"I think we can do that. I can't think of anyone in our congregation who would oppose it. Everyone has looked forward to this wedding as long as you have and wants to celebrate it with you."

"That is very kind," whispered Rachel, already getting teary eyed.

"Just one thing, however. Since I am the pastor here, there are certain things you must agree to," Pastor Johns said in all seriousness.

"Anything," we both said at the same time.

"Good. Now, tell me, what do you have in mind?"

With child-like excitement, Rachel and I shared with Pastor Johns our plans and wishes. Rachel was apprehensive about whether or not Pastor Johns would approve of some elements we had planned. Yet, to our surprise, the pastor agreed and even admired our thoughtfulness.

"So far, so good. Sounds like a fairly traditional wedding," commented Pastor Johns.

But that was just the beginning of the service. Then, we sprung on him our favorite part of the ceremony.

"Yes. Can we do that?" asked Rachel with bated breath.

"This is your wedding, and you can do it any way you want to. I think it is a splendid idea, and very touching," said Pastor Johns in a low voice. "Do you mind if I add my own touches?"

We were so relieved that we would have agreed to almost anything.

"Not at all. We know you will make it tasteful and reverent," I replied.

"Well … I'll try," winked Pastor Johns. "What about a reception?"

"Sam and I were thinking of having an outside reception at our new house, but in February, it's going to be cold …"

"So, we agreed to have a simple reception in the fellowship hall with cake and punch," I added.

"Very wise decision."

"We can have a big party later in the spring," Rachel added.

On Sunday, January 22nd, our wedding announcement was in the order of worship. For weeks, the topic of conversation at the church and around town was the wedding, house colors, sizes, etc. I acted clueless, which I must admit, was not difficult.

The next question people asked was, where would we spend our honeymoon? Many well-meaning people gave me advice, most saying that the popular honeymoon spot was Niagara Falls. People were almost giddy as they spoke of honeymoon destinations. I didn't have the heart to tell them that Rachel and I agreed that we wanted to stay at home.

Then, there was the traditional question, what color is your kitchen? Your bathroom? When we answered that we really did not need anything, our friends were downcast, then insistent. We hated to disappoint our friends, so we just thanked them and said, "Whatever you want to give us is fine with us."

Finally, the big day came without accidents or health issues. For that, Rachel and I were indeed grateful, and the entire congregation was in anticipation and ready for a wedding. As were we.

The Sunday service went on as normal until morning prayer. Then, Rachel, the children, and I slipped out. With the closing prayer and the last amen, and before he exited, Pastor Johns asked the congregation to stand and sing Hymn 132. The organist played the introduction, and our friends lifted their voices in glorious praise to our God.

Praise to the Lord, the Almighty, the King of creation! O my soul, praise Him, for He is thy health and salvation! All ye who hear, now to His temple draw near; Praise Him in glad adoration.

Praise to the Lord, who o'er all things so wondrously reigned,
Shelters thee under His wings, yea, so gently sustaineth!
Hast thou not seen how thy desires e'er have been granted in what He ordaineth?

Praise to the Lord, who doth prosper thy work and defend thee;

Surely His goodness and mercy here daily attend thee; Ponder anew what the Almighty can do, If with His love He befriend thee.

Praise to the Lord, oh, let all that is in me adore Him! All that hath life and breath, come now with praises before Him; Let the Amen sound from His people again, Gladly for aye we adore Him.

Rachel and the girls waited in the back of the church, while Pastor Johns, Sammy, Ken, and I waited to enter at the front.

That's when it happened! Pastor Johns leaned to whisper into my stubby ear, "Remember, I am the pastor, and you agreed to anything I wanted to do."

That sounded ominous, and my legs quaked all the more. However, it was too late to change my mind. All I could do was nod in blind assent.

The congregation sang the last line, the lyrics and melody faded, and everyone continued to stand, waiting for further instructions. There was a pause, but there was no traditional organ interlude, no singing. Nothing! Then, from their positions unobserved, three men dressed in formal attire stood behind the choir and simultaneously snapped their shining brass horns to their lips in regal form and echoed each other in several musical bars of a glorious fanfare.

When I caught Rachel's eye at the back of the church, she looked as stunned and mystified as I was. Neither of us had any idea that this was going to happen. After the surprise fanfare, then the organist played the hymn we chose with great gusto but plenty of reverence, pomp, and circumstance. Pastor Johns winked at me and asked, "Shall we?" and led the way to our positions where we waited for my bride.

Joelle entered first. Like a pro, she marched in half step. A cool but gentle breath of air filled the sanctuary. She sought my eyes for approval, which I gave without hesitation. The multilayers of her pale pink silk organza dress fluttered with every step. Joelle looked at me again, and this time, she lifted her nosegay of pink and white roses sprinkled with baby's breath to smell them with gratitude. The nosegay was my surprise to her. I winked, and she blushed.

Close behind Joelle marched beautiful Kayla. Her royal blue gown also swirled in the breeze and glinted off her blue eyes, now alive with joy and love. The seamstress did a wonderful job of taking the dress in so that it fit Kayla perfectly and enhanced her figure, which was now filling out with a healthy glow. Her nosegay was of a deeper pink accented with sparkling royal blue ribbons, also my gift to her.

My girls were beautiful. But the most beautiful of all was my Rachel. She looked so happy, she glowed. Her dress was of the same multilayered ruffled pattern as Kayla's and Joelle's, but Rachel's was an off-white trimmed in lace. She argued that traditionally, it would not be appropriate for her to wear white, since she had already been married before. However, I won that argument by insisting that it was *my* first wedding, and I wanted my bride to wear white. I think secretly, Rachel was pleased. She did look radiant. Lights danced in her golden hair, playing with stray curls once held by roses, and the veil of candle glow tulle played in the breeze. The bouquet she carried, also a gift from me, tried to glow, but could not equal the glow in Rachel's eyes.

Joelle and Kayla stood to Rachel's left, and Ken and Sammy stood to my right. I must admit, we men did present ourselves well, even if we did wear only blue suits. Our blue suits complimented Kayla's royal blue dress and the blue flowers in the bouquets.

When Rachel got halfway down the aisle, I left my position and went up the aisle to join her. Then, I escorted her to the altar where Pastor Johns waited.

Pastor Johns followed our requests perfectly. My heart fluttered as I said my vows to my bride.

"Sam, repeat after me: I, Sam, take you, Rachel, to be my

lawfully wedded wife, to have and to hold from this day forward, for better, for worse, for richer, for poorer, in sickness and in health, to love and to cherish, for as long as we both shall live."

I looked deep into Rachel's eyes and, with shaking hands, gave her my vow. Then in return, Rachel said her vows to me. I could feel her quiver.

When we exchanged rings, Rachel gasped as I placed an engraved gold band on her finger next to the cluster of diamonds. I felt the same quiver of joy when she placed a plain gold band, very masculine, on my left hand. Pastor Johns invited me to kiss my bride, which I did with great joy. Pastor ended with a prayer of dedication.

Usually, that was the end of a traditional Protestant wedding, but this wedding was not completely traditional, as evidenced by our wedding march and Pastor's gift of the horn fanfare.

To the surprise of the congregation, Pastor Johns directed Rachel and me to take two steps to the right, then he continued, "Joelle, will you step forward, please."

Joelle, too, was surprised and shaken, but Pastor Johns's kind voice calmed her, and she followed instructions.

"Sam, please join Joelle and take her hand. God's Word tells us in Proverbs that, '*Children are indeed a heritage from the Lord,*' and further, '*Blessed is the man whose quiver is full of them.*' Sam, I know you have prayed a long time for a family. I believe the Lord has answered your prayer. Therefore, Sam, do you take Joelle, to be your beloved daughter, to have and to hold from this day forward, for better, for worse, for richer, for poorer, in sickness and in health, to love and to cherish, for as long as you both shall live?"

I stumbled a bit when I lost my composure but then looked at a now weeping Joelle and said, "I do."

Pastor Johns turned to Joelle. "Joelle, do you take this man to be your beloved Daddy Sam, a gift from God?"

Joelle composed herself long enough to look into my eyes and whisper, "I do."

"Please join your mother."

Pastor Johns paused, then called Sammy.

Sammy was just as surprised as Joelle, for neither of the children knew of this part of our wedding ceremony.

When Sammy stepped forward and to my left, Pastor Johns asked me and the trembling young man the same questions.

With an audible gulp, Sammy answered, "I do."

"Please take your place with your mother and Joelle.

Pastor deviated. "Rachel, will you join your husband here in front?"

With joy, Rachel stood at my right side and leaned into my shoulder.

When Pastor Johns turned to Kayla, our beautiful teenager lost her composure and melted into a puddle of tears even before Pastor Johns asked her to join Rachel and me. It was Gregory who rushed to Kayla's side and guided her to stand beside Rachel. But to my surprise, Gregory did not return to his seat but stood with us.

"Rachel, Sam, do you take Kayla to be your beloved daughter, to have and to hold from this day forward, for better, for worse, for richer, for poorer, in sickness and in health, to love and to cherish, for as long as you shall live?"

"We do."

"And Kayla ..."

Pastor Johns did not get to finish asking the question. Kayla beamed through her tears and shouted, "Yes. Yes, I do. I do."

When Pastor Johns asked Joelle and Sammy to join us, we turned and faced the congregation.

"My dearly beloved," Pastor Johns said to the congregation, "it is my great pleasure to present to you Mr. and Mrs. Samuel

Burkett *and family.* "

The congregation broke into a spontaneous and joyous applause. When the applause died down, the three horns again played an echoed fanfare and the whole congregation sang in great jubilation, *"Praise to the Lord, the Almighty, the King of creation!"*

As we walked down the aisle together, I whispered my joy, "My family and I," then looked at my bride and repeated, "My family and I, Mr. and Mrs. Sam Burkett *and family.*"

When we exited the church, I heard a train whistle in the distance.

I squeezed Rachel's hand and whispered, "Thank you, Lord."

"You are welcome, My son."

Chapter 24

Give instruction to a wise man, and he will be yet wiser: teach a just man, and he will increase in learning. Proverbs 9:9

The children could not stop talking about *their* beautiful wedding, and *our family* honeymoon was perfect.

Earlier in the week, we had stopped at Mr. and Mrs. Cooper's grocery store and stocked up on food. Rachel insisted that we get good, wholesome food, but I lobbied for junk food. As it turned out, we had plenty of both … for everyone.

As usual, Trey was a constant visitor, and we all enjoyed a glorious two weeks of spring break together before school started back in March.

I was proud of the children and their friends, for they respected Rachel's and my quiet time together. Joelle even busied herself in the kitchen with paper and crayons, then surprised us with a sign, "Do Not Disturb" with plenty of hearts. I promptly hung it on the master bedroom door—the bedroom where Rachel and I now slept together. My heart still thrills when I think of this. For so long it was the bedroom where I slept, often with Sammy. Now, it was my bedroom where I slept with Rachel, my wife. Sometimes we even slept, other times, we snuggled and whispered our love to each other, or sometimes, we snuggled and made plans.

Gregory never left after Christmas but decided he wanted to stay and be a part of our family. That was fine with Rachel and me. We had plenty of room, and Gregory had no place to go. Even though he insisted he had been on his own for several years, he was still only eighteen and needed a family. So, when the townspeople discovered that Gregory would be living with us, there were no sideways glances. They knew Rachel and I would see that our home was a place for God and family, just as the porter's cabin had been. Besides, since school was on spring break, Kayla and Gregory spent most of their time at the hospital with Dr. Abbott. Just as he said, there were plenty of challenges for teenagers. New patients—some young, some not so young—needed encouragement and often someone to talk to, someone who understood.

"Sam."

I knew by her tone that she wanted to talk about serious issues. On our honeymoon? "Yes, dear."

"Sam, Kayla and Gregory have one more year in high school," she began.

"So, they do. What's on your mind?"

"What do you think they will want to do after graduation?"

"I imagine they will use the scholarship the hospital gave them and go to college."

"Will they get married?"

I could see where this was going … to the bank. "Well, dear, they seem to be responsible young people. I think we should pray about it and leave it up to the Lord."

"You are right, of course, Sam. I was just thinking."

"Could your thinking have anything to do with my parent's little house?"

"Well …"

"It may be possible that it's too early to be thinking along those lines, dear. But I like the way you think. I would love to have them close by, too."

"Thank you, Sam."

For a moment, we were quiet. I was fulfilled just to hold Rachel in my arms and say nothing, but I waited.

"Sam?"

"Yes, dear?"

"What would you think about building them a little house on this property?"

"That is very generous of you, sweetie, but I think that needs to be their decision. If Gregory asks me, I will, of course, be happy to help him. But let's not start planning a nursery just yet."

"Oh. You." Rachel giggled and punched my ribs. "But, will you think about it, Sam?"

"Yes, dear. I will go talk to Ken next week. There are some other issues I need to talk with him about anyway But right now, I think I see a spot I have not kissed yet," I said, pulling her into my arms.

When spring break ended, the children reluctantly went back to school. I had to remind them that there was a mere three months of school left, and they should continue to do their best. So, it was off to school for them.

Florence public school was a small K-12 community school. I liked the idea of the children all being at the same school. I don't know why; it just made me feel good. I also liked the idea that Gregory drove them to school.

It was the funniest thing that when Gregory and Kayla were at the hospital during spring break, I hardly thought about the car. I was content to stay home with my new wife and my family. Even though we did the same chores, reading, and playing together that we did before, the realization that I was a married man with a family made everything new and wonderful. But I still needed to have a talk with Gregory about school transportation. However, while the children were at school, I planned to enjoy my wife until she chased me out of the house with a kiss and a pop on my behind to do my gardening. I didn't mind. Being outside gave me time to talk to the Lord and think, and when I came inside, she was glad to see me. I never knew being married could be so good … so simple and good. *Thank you, Lord.*

After the children came home, I asked Gregory to walk out back with me. Sam and Joelle knew what that meant and turned white. When we two men came back inside, Gregory went to his room, and Rachel told me later that while we were outside, there was much speculation about what Gregory did to get into trouble.

I chuckled. We just had "manly man" things to discuss. In fact, he and I needed to make a trip into town and talk with Ken. I kissed my wife deeply as if I were going on an extended business trip, and to my delight, she returned my kiss.

"We will be home soon. It's already 3:30, and the bank will be closing soon. I love you, Rachel."

"I love you, Sam. Be safe and hurry home."

When Gregory came out of his room, Sam and Joelle stood with questions dancing in their eyes, but they said nothing. They knew how embarrassing it was to go out back with Daddy Sam.

On the trip into town, Gregory drove, and I gratefully sat in the passenger's seat, enjoying having someone else do the driving.

"Did you give any thought into what we talked about?" I asked.

"Yes, sir, I did, but I'm going to need your advice."

"Ken will help us with that."

When we walked into the bank, Ken was patrolling the lobby and greeting customers. His eyes lit up when he saw Gregory and me, and he made his way over to greet us. "Hi, Sam. What can I help you with today?"

"Do you have a little time, Ken? We men need some advice. You remember Gregory?"

"Sure, nice to see you again, Gregory. I didn't get to speak to you much at the wedding. Are you settling in with Sam and at school?"

"Yes, sir. It's all good. However, I feel like now I'm about to get a different kind of lesson."

Ken chuckled. "I will try to make it easy for you." Ken turned to me and asked, "What kind of lesson does Gregory need, Sam?"

"You know. The usual lessons every eighteen-year-old boy needs … decision making, finance, mortgage, property management, the usual."

I looked at Gregory from the corner of my eye and saw the young man's eyes bugging. "We didn't discuss any of that, Sam."

Again, Ken chuckled. "So, Sam, where would you like to start?"

"How about property management and finance?"

I heard Gregory gulp.

Ken knew me well enough to know how to play a game and still get business done.

"That's a lot for this poor man to chew on, Sam. First, I think he is going to need an income."

Ken was enjoying watching Gregory squirm just as much as I was.

"Well, Ken, let's talk about income first," I said.

"That seems a logical place to start. Gregory, how much income do you have?"

Gulp. "Well, I … I …"

"Just as I thought. You have no income?"

Gregory squirmed again.

"So, I propose we generate a little income." Ken picked up a file and pretended to read. "Gregory, do you have any experience in property management?"

Gulp. "No, sir," Gregory said, wiping beads of sweat from his upper lip.

"Too bad." Ken closed the file with an audible and definitive snap. "Sam, what do you propose?"

I looked at Gregory for several seconds, first with a face of serious contemplation, then with a chuckle. "I think we need to let the poor boy off the hook. Ken, are all my properties occupied?"

"Yes, I believe they are."

"Which one is doing the best?"

"That would be the Creek Road property."

"What is the income from that one?"

"Rent is seventy dollars a month with a two-year rental agreement. The renters are responsible renters and good neighbors."

"That will do fine. I would like for Gregory to take over the management of that property, with your help of course. That will give him a little experience and a bit of income as well. From that income, let's agree that he will pay his insurance and maintenance on a car."

"Done. Miss Riley, will you come in please? I promise this won't take long."

"Does this sound acceptable to you, Gregory?"

"Yes, sir, Sam," replied the wide-eyed boy. "I was expecting something awful. But what about when I graduate and go to college?"

"Responsible young man, Sam. Better hang on to him."

"Believe me, Rachel is trying. I won't tell you what she was talking about a week ago. It might frighten Gregory off for sure."

We all shared a laugh and went outside to the repo auto lot before Gregory had time to contemplate my last statement.

I had already discussed with Gregory the issue of the car, and his next lesson involved decision making, namely keeping the baby blue Ford or choosing a different car. According to our previous agreement while walking out back, if he wanted to keep the baby blue Ford, then I would get a different family car. When he surveyed the inventory of the repo lot, he made the wise decision of keeping the Ford. Then, the ball was in my court. I had to choose a family car that everyone, especially my new wife, would like.

I was looking over the repo inventory when Ken reminded me that I had not taken advantage of my VA disability auto allowance. That's when he led me over to a black 1950 Oldsmobile Rocket

88 coupe and handed me the keys. Ken said my auto allowance would cover the cost of the new Oldsmobile. I told him I would be back in the morning to sign the papers.

I knew Gregory wanted to ask me how I could afford to buy a car without a down payment and tons of paperwork. He didn't need to know that right now, maybe at a later date, but eventually, he would need to know the secrets of wise and prudent investing.

After finishing our business at the bank, we drove home in tandem. Gregory drove the Ford up to the back of the house, and I followed far enough behind so as to create plenty of questions and heightened excitement. I was not disappointed.

Kayla was first to come out and welcome Gregory but didn't notice anything out of the ordinary. Then Sammy and Joelle came running out. Sammy was the first, of course, to notice there was the baby blue Ford and Gregory, but where was Daddy Sam?

"Mommy, Gregory is home. Daddy Sam is not with him."

The timing could not have been more perfect, for when Rachel came outside, I was just driving up in the black, shiny, Oldsmobile Rocket 88.

"And just where did you get that?" Rachel asked with a grin.

"Oh, I found it alongside the road, and she followed me home."

"You did, huh? And have you named her?"

"No, I thought you would like to do that."

Rachel rushed into my arms and covered my deformed face and ears with her warm kisses. "Can we talk about it after, you know, dinner?"

"Certainly. I think that is an excellent idea," I replied with a wink.

Chapter 25

It is of the Lord's mercies that we are not consumed,
because His compassions fail not. They are new every
morning: great is Thy faithfulness. Lamentations 3:22-23

I knew Ken was managing my bank account and properties, so I didn't worry about them. However, with all the expenses we had this year, I thought I had better pay him a visit. Besides, since we shared the same sense of humor, we always had fun together.

This visit to the bank was not out of the ordinary. I sat with Ken, and we looked over available properties. I thought it a good time to make another investment purchase and found a likely opportunity that was within my means. This property was a five-acre parcel abutting mine on the south. I really didn't have plans for that property, but I knew Rachel had dreams.

When I came home from the war in 1945, Ken was amazed at the accumulation of my military pay that had been deposited into his bank. With those funds and my parents' house, I was able to start purchasing income property. Over five years, I had five more properties around Florence and Boone County. With property income, my annual VA disability compensation, and other VA benefits, the Lord provided a comfortable living. With these funds, and my good friend, Ken, my blessings continued to grow. Now, I could count a real family among my blessings, and the Lord keeps adding blessings.

In May of 1950, Gregory graduated from high school, and he and Kayla drove the baby blue Ford back and forth to the hospital to fulfil their summer internship requirements.

June was even more lively with its customary joys, including giggles and squabbles between Sammy and Joelle, Trey's frequent visits, imaginary military maneuvers in the woods, dress-up for Joelle, and pool parties. The pool was always a popular party place, which meant our house and yard were full of activity, laughter, and snacks for teens and children from school and church. I was busy with reading, property management, and outside chores.

Unfortunately, Rachel spent a good deal of time between the bed and sofa in the family room. At first, I thought she was just exhausted from providing snacks and meals, doing laundry, and gardening, but after about three weeks, I was becoming more and more concerned with her health, so I called Doc Proctor.

Although I encouraged her to go faster, the Oldsmobile would not go any faster than was safe. When I finally reached the town limits, the speed limit forced me to slow down. However, I still made it to the bank in record time.

The panting car pulled up into the bank parking lot with squealing tires and a cloud of dust. She barely had come to a stop before I jumped out and dashed into the bank, disheveled and out of breath.

Upon hearing the commotion downstairs, Ken came out of his office to find me standing in the middle of the bank causing a scene. I took the stairs as quickly as my prosthetic foot would allow.

With concern etched in his face, Ken held me by my shoulders until I finally caught my breath, then we sat together.

"Ken, I need to take out a loan."

With wide eyes and silent concern, Ken looked at me in disbelief, then finally found his voice. "A loan? This is unlike you, Sam."

"Yes, I know. I am not myself," I paused for effect then

continued. "I am a daddy. I am a real daddy! Rachel is pregnant!"

After Ken and I finished giggling like two teenagers, we completed the paperwork to add a nursery to the new house.

In February 1951, Rachel, my love, presented me with a beautiful baby boy. He weighed seven pounds, six ounces and measured nineteen and a half inches long.

When the nurse came in with the birth certificate, she asked Rachel the baby's name. With no hesitation, my wife gave me another blessing, "His name is George Samuel Burkett."

With tear-filled eyes, I kissed my wife. "You have given me much joy over these five years, my love, but this one is the best. I never thought I would have a son of my own. Now I have an entire family. Thank you, Rachel. Thank you, Lord."

"You are welcome, My son."

Praise God, from whom all blessings flow;
Praise Him, all creatures here below;
Praise Him above, ye heav'nly host;
Praise Father, Son, and Holy Ghost!
Amen.

The End

About the Author

Joyce Crawford

Born in Gainesville, Florida, in 1949, Joyce started her writing career after her retirement. Her first book was a children's chapter book, *The First Adventures of Thelma Thistle and Her Friends,* which quickly became a series of seven books.

As one reviewer shared, "The shift from children's books to *The Warehouse* is a strategic move for author Joyce Crawford, showing her versatility which highlights her ability to go deep and address a different audience. Still possessing the same playfulness and creative imagination, Crawford weaves a novel emphasizing a God who respects humanity and never dictates but has generously given free will—and even a storehouse for His gifts and blessings. Crawford's primary strength is in her ability to turn something simple into a metamorphosis of its most extraordinary potential by revealing its cryptic meaning. This has been apparent in her previous literary masterpieces but especially so in her latest accomplishment. The story, itself, is beset with excitement, discovery, and magical moments. Crawford's picturesque style of writing can take readers deep into the story and into greater heights."

When asked if she would continue writing, Mrs. Crawford replied, "As long as there are children to learn, there will be books to write."

In her first novel, *The Warehouse*, a young adult novel that adults can enjoy, Mrs. Crawford packs historical facts to educate young minds, or in some cases, to remind us, a more mature audience, of these facts. This book, *The Train*, contains the same style of historical facts and descriptions meant to not only entertain but also to educate.

Above all, Mrs. Crawford wants to share God's love and care with all her readers.

If you enjoyed this book, please leave your comments on Amazon.

https://www.amazon.com/
Train-God-Cares-His-Children/dp/1733897755

More books by Joyce Crawford

<u>The Warehouse: Crawford, Joyce:
9781733897723: Amazon.com: Books</u>
Print ISBN 978-1-7338977-2-3

The Royal Order of the Last Coin
ISBN 978-1-7338977-9-2
A work in progress

The Royal Order of the Last Coin The New World, Jamestown
ISBN 978-1-7369857-0-0
A work in progress

And Of Course

The Adventures of Thelma Thistle and Her Friends
A seven-book series of children's chapter books